ASUNDER

The Tale of the
Renaissance Killer

Steve Stranghoener

Dedication:

Saul of Tarsus (AD 5 – AD 34)[1]

Apostle Paul (AD 34 – AD 67)[1]

Romans 7:14-25

1 Approximation ... actual dates are uncertain.

INDEX

Part 1: Deadly Encounter

Part 2: Final Parting

Part 3: Reunion

Part 1 - Deadly Encounter

1 Eden's Doorstep

My life was as close to paradise as one can get in this world. No, we weren't filthy rich and didn't live in a sprawling mansion, belong to an exclusive country club, drive fancy cars or maintain a vacation home replete with a cleverly named yacht. But we possessed priceless treasures nonetheless: youth, good health, friendship, gainful employment, true love, a happy home, hope and the boundless optimism of a bright future. That is, until the day that Charles Darwin Cane darkened our doorway. He took everything from me that can be taken from a man; my marriage, family, career, aspirations, joys and peace and even fractured my most fundamental beliefs. That this man would vex my soul for the rest of my life seemed quite ironic given that we had never met before 1987 when I turned thirty. Our lives could not have been more removed from one another with nary an intersection except that we happened to attend the same university for one year. Although it was unbeknownst to me, there was one touch point that would prove to be pivotal; Cane crossed paths, ever so briefly, with my wife to be, Sylvia, when we were seniors and he was an inconsequential freshman.

To ponder how such an insignificant and fleeting stitch in time could come into play in such a life-altering way some nine years later is bone chilling. Syl did not even remember Cane's name which is rather forgettable. It's much easier to recall the moniker he later gave to the authorities, the Renaissance Killer.

Cane's childhood and mine could not have been more disparate even though we were both raised in the St. Louis metropolitan area. I was born to working class parents, Bud and Lilly Newman, who instilled in me their Protestant work ethic and drummed an appreciation for higher education into my head. They were proud patriots of a simpler, nobler generation of Americans. The notion of self-esteem, at least as it is conceived today, was foreign to them. Respect was something you earned through the sweat of your brow; determination and perseverance. Like so many people of their generation who were bright but never had the opportunity to get a good education, they valued higher learning immensely and wanted nothing more for their children. My dad fancied me as a great author someday, a man who would use his head instead of his hands, and thus saddled me with the name of our home state icon, Twain. Mark would have suited me fine. My mother, more a fan of the dramatic arts, was relegated to second place in this contest of wills and thus my middle name became Rennie in honor of her favorite screen actor, Michael Rennie. Later for a time in high school, I went by TR to avoid the confusion and stigma of the name Twain if not the ongoing pressure of my father's vicarious dreams of literary fame. It would be much later that I would attach something other than literary significance to my first name; there came a time when I wondered if it was providence that marked me as a man divided in two.

There was no confusion between right and wrong in the Newman household. There were no shades of gray when it came to Bud's Commandments. You followed them or your bottom was introduced to the calloused palm of his hand. My mom was complicit in the discipline that was meted out to us. You didn't mess with her or you'd get a good tongue lashing along with a dose of corporal punishment, as needed. Later on when we outgrew her ability to inflict pain with her bare hands, she would employ a thick leather belt to get her point across. They weren't mean in the least but they believed firmly in the notion, spare the rod and spoil the child. I never received any punishment that I didn't deserve and it made it that much more meaningful to receive their praise when it was truly warranted. As I said, they weren't into self-esteem and instead constantly encouraged us to look out for others; to consider their feelings and needs and extend a helping hand whenever possible. They practiced what they preached with others and us kids and, thus, we always felt loved in spite of or, perhaps better said, because of their judicious but uncomplicated disciplinary ways. I had a simple childhood. We were taught to love God, country, family and our fellow man ... and work hard and aim high. We often heard the refrain, "Something worth doing is worth doing right." But, although we had solid guidelines to follow, our lives were largely unstructured. We were left alone to make our way independently for the most part. My parents were busy working and never saw much value in organized activities like little league baseball, Cub Scouts and the like. We were expected to go to school, pitch in on chores and complete our homework without a lot of prodding. Free time was ours to do with as we pleased, as long as we stayed out of trouble. Summers were particularly free-wheeling. Our parents might see us in the morning for breakfast and evening at supper time. In between, we'd hang out with the neighborhood kids playing sandlot baseball, building a treetop fortress in the woods, exploring the creek for snakes, frogs and crawdads or collecting old soda bottles to raise some spending money. Life was good. We didn't have a lot but we had more than we needed. We learned to make friends and get along. We learned to fend for ourselves. It seemed easy to succeed in school because it was expected of us.

I always did well in school, right up into my high school years. Although I was a good student, I had difficulty shouldering the burden my father placed on me. Oh, I didn't have a problem in pulling straight A's in English, American Literature, Composition or Creative Writing and didn't mind being nudged into the Lit Club or serving on the yearbook staff. But my heart wasn't completely in it. I had a good deal of interest in literature and enjoyed it to a point but just didn't have the same extreme level of enthusiasm as my dad. My interests were more varied. I liked other things too; sports, cars, hanging out with the guys … and pretty girls. Some girls liked the literary, egg head types but most preferred macho jocks. As for the guys, it was no contest; you flirted with trouble by being too artsy fartsy. So, I walked a fine line and tried to balance my desire to please my dad and satisfy my own interests in the arts while juggling more manly pursuits too. I also discovered that I had a practical side and a good head for figures and sprinkled in as many math and business-related courses as time and credit requirements would allow.

My dad, while well intentioned, was a little too bent on steering the boat when it came to my life and ambitions. Unlike the other dads, he was less than thrilled when I made the varsity football team. He saw it as a dead end pursuit, distraction and waste of time. It also drew me into a crowd that didn't meet with his approval. Dumb jocks, as he called them, were not his cup of tea. Thankfully, my mom was much more open minded and willing to give me free rein. She didn't really like football or understand it for that matter but was willing to go along because, bless her heart, she just wanted me to be happy. I'll never forget the first time she came out to a game looking like a fish out of water. A week earlier in practice I had bruised my arm pretty bad and was given a forearm pad to protect it during the game. Dear old mom made a scene and embarrassed me badly by accosting the coach demanding to know why her baby was playing football with his arm in a cast. I wanted to crawl in a hole and could have done so easily since I felt about two inches tall. The only thing that kept my mom from starting an anti-football crusade is that she enjoyed the fact it made me more popular with the girls. She got a real kick out of meeting them and took a particular shine to Sylvia Adams.

Syl was different from any of the other girls I knew. She was very bright and possessed a maturity beyond her years. Syl was soft spoken, polite and respectful but didn't shy away from engaging my parents in conversation like most of the giddy, giggly teenage girls we knew. The first time Lilly trapped her for a kitchen table summit, she was able to hold her own in an intelligent but charming and down-to-earth manner. Syl was a natural. She was even able to win over old Bud who normally didn't waste time on idle chit chat with my friends. He really liked the fact that, while she discovered me through football, she eventually took a genuine interest in me for more cerebral reasons. When he found out that Syl appreciated the arts and hoped to teach English someday, he was sold. As for me, I liked everything about her. Unlike most popular girls, she wasn't hung up on herself. Her interests were varied, like mine, ranging from sports and the outdoors to academics. She was spirited, lively and enthusiastic but never loud or obnoxious. Syl could be serious and studious but wasn't bookish. Her personality was elastic; she could be the life of the party or just as much at home watching a movie together or strolling through a quiet park. I didn't have to play the part of a jock, party animal or scholar around her; with Syl I could just be myself.

My interest in Syl was not purely platonic. To be quite honest, at first, the attraction was purely physical. She was a dark-haired cutie with sparkling eyes. However, if you weren't paying attention, you could easily overlook her even though she was a knockout. She dressed modestly in a toned down fashion that didn't reveal much. But a sharp eye like mine was able to gather that, underneath all that fabric, she had a body that wouldn't quit. There was something much more intriguing about a girl that had it but didn't flaunt it. However, there was no fabric that could hide that certain bounce and wiggle she possessed once my radar locked onto her. My predatory instincts were confirmed when I caught a glimpse of her in a bikini as I was thumbing through one of her family's photo albums that included shots from their last beach vacation. Yes, I am guilty as charged ... it was not love but lust at first sight that drew me to Syl. My raging teenage hormones provided the footing for our relationship but the foundation was formed from a more lasting substance. Syl's interests went hand in glove with mine and ... now this is going to sound ridiculously corny ... I was sincerely able to respect her. She was honest, trustworthy, patient, kind, thoughtful, self-sacrificing, courageous and humble and possessed a quiet faith that proved to be much more steadfast than my own.

There was nothing forced when it came to Syl and me. Our relationship just fell into place naturally and followed a course that seemed predestined. There was no pressure whatsoever but I stopped knocking around with the guys so much and spent more time with Syl. We just enjoyed being together. This made Bud happy. Things fell into place as we finished high school. We both wanted to go to our home state university, Mizzou, and were interested in similar courses of study: education, English and literature. We had no problem getting accepted and money was not an issue. We were able to win some scholarship support and both of our parents made up the difference. Syl's mom and dad came from a similar station in life so it wasn't easy for them but, like Bud and Lilly, they placed a premium on a good education. As you might expect, Bud put his money where his mouth was and had scrimped and saved to make sure his future literary giant could afford to go to a good college. Syl's parents were just as willing and eager to make similar sacrifices for her.

The transition to college life was actually very smooth. A lot of kids bomb their first semester due to being homesick, a lack of discipline in their studies or by partying their brains out. Since Syl and I had each other to help cope with these challenges, we had it easy. My biggest concern was managing the lingering pressure of Bud's expectations. But even that seemed less foreboding with Syl at my side. We quickly settled in at Mizzou and enjoyed some of the best times of our lives. I was just about to say, looking back I wouldn't have changed a thing. However, back then, we had no idea an only child would be joining us at Mizzou in three years; a snot-nosed, silver spooned, maniac-in-the-making that would change our lives in a way we could not imagine. At that point, Charles Darwin Cane had not yet graduated to human subjects. He was still content to satisfy his disturbing desires and hone his aberrant skills on the sufferings of insects and small animals. If I could go back in time, knowing what I know now, would I take Syl and attend a different college? Would it be better to skip college altogether and avoid that single contact Cane had with Syl? Would I go so far as to break up with Syl to spare her? Perhaps none of these things would have helped change our fate. I will never know. And that's one of the demons that still haunt me.

I wish that I could block out the tragedy and limit my memories to all the good times. The years passed and we continued on our merry way, meandering together through our studies and daily duties while lost magically in love. We didn't really talk about it much but Syl and I knew, deep inside, that we were meant for each other and would someday be married. Now, as you will recall, my hormones had a way of affecting my judgment back then and my faith, while solid, was not as reliable as Syl's. Thus, it only made sense to me that we should consummate our inevitable relationship. Time was wasting. Here we had a parting of the ways. Syl saw things differently. All of those qualities I admired in her were now coming back to bite me. She made some convincing arguments about why it would be so much better to wait. I could not agree but had no choice but to acquiesce. She was not a prude but she would only go so far. She blocked my amorous ambitions so many times that I wondered if I was destined to be like Moses and gaze upon but never enter the Promised Land. In retrospect, she was right and it proved to be a benefit in the long run but it sure seemed unreasonable to me at the time.

We had so much in common but sometimes our very natures seemed like polar opposites. How was it that Syl was able to fight off temptation? I still marvel at her inherent goodness. Now, I realize of course that no one is perfect, including Syl, but it just seemed like she always made the right choices even when I was ready to steer off in the wrong direction. And she was so at ease; never appearing conflicted or caught up in a flight of fancy like I could be. What was the difference? We were both baptized as infants, attended church regularly, went to Sunday school and survived the rigors of confirmation. Our families were very similar and shared most of the same values including a clear sense of right and wrong backed up by strict discipline. And yet, although I wasn't some kind of holy terror, I committed all sorts of youthful indiscretions in high school while Syl always took the straight and narrow path. She was comfortable with herself and was content to march to the beat of her own drum rather than caving into peer pressure. However, she wasn't preachy or holier than thou about it. Syl's maturity displayed itself by the way she was able to accept my wild spurts as something I just naturally needed to get out of my system. Her judgment was so much better than mine too in that she knew where to draw the line between harmless fun and something more dangerous that could put me in real jeopardy. The thing I remember most fondly about her and always brings a smile to my lips was her ability to forgive and forget. I used to tease her about how she was able to stay so fit without a hint of strenuous exercise while I had to work out like a fiend to stay in shape. One time, she leaned into me with a twinkle in her eye and whispered into my ear, "I'll tell you my secret for maintaining my weight. I never consume heavy things that can weigh you down … like bitterness, anger or grudges. Oh, especially not those grudges because they weigh a ton."

I was so drawn to Syl's kind and gentle nature that it drove me to the biggest decision of my life very early on. Perhaps it was the certainty of it all. That we would share wedded bliss seemed like a fait accompli. Thus, I made up my mind to take a big leap at the tender age of twenty one. Many would claim it was foolish to make such a critical decision so young, at the start of our senior year in college. But in my mind, I thought it only made sense to get on with the inevitable. And maybe, at least subconsciously, I was being swept along by impatience and my delightful visions of crossing over the River Jordan on our honeymoon. In any case, when Parents' Day arrived, I put my secret plan into action as Syl's dad, George, and I snuck off at half-time of the football game to find a cold beer. Being a traditionalist, I thought it was only fitting that I properly obtain George's blessing before popping the question to Syl. I expected a long lecture about how we were too young and should take the time to make sure our relationship was on solid ground before rushing into something that we might regret later. I was all prepared to counter that we had already been dating steady for four years, including our senior year in high school; a longer test run than most engagements. To my surprise, George didn't throw up any opposition other than to say, "Have you given this plenty of thought? Are you sure this is what you want to do?" After I assured him this was not some rash decision he gave me one of those serious father-of-the-bride looks and said, "I'm pretty sure after watching you and Syl over the past few years that I already know the answer but I have to ask you, do you love my daughter?" "More than anything in the world," I volunteered without hesitation. That was good enough for George, "I can tell you that Syl's mom feels the same way and will be delighted." I asked him, with a big grin as I floated on air, to keep a lid on it so I could surprise Syl.

The next step in the process was to bring Bud and Lilly into the loop. Again, I encountered very little opposition, that is, except when Bud grilled me, "When are you planning on getting married? You're not going to do anything stupid like dropping out of school, are you?" Once I cleared that hurdle and assured him that we would not be getting married until after graduation, I got the green light. It was easy pickings really since Bud was totally taken by Syl and my mom had adored her from day one. It's funny how practical matters don't come into play when the heart takes over. I gave no thought to the financial burden this would place on Syl's parents and George never mentioned it. They would find a way to absorb this blow on top of all her college expenses. I hadn't given any thought to a ring either but would empty my meager savings and borrow whatever I needed to get the best stone possible, however modest it might be. Knowing full well that Syl wouldn't make her decision on the basis of dollar signs, I focused my attention on the proposal itself. I wanted to surprise her and make the biggest splash I could, so I decided to wait until homecoming and drop to one knee during the football game. I went so far as to ask the PA announcer to help me hatch my scheme publicly, halfway through the third quarter. This might seem like overconfidence boarding on arrogance or foolishness or insensitivity about putting the prospective bride on the spot but, in my case, it was nothing of the sort. It was simply a sincere and innocent outcome of being struck by Cupid's arrow.

I tried to contain myself during the build up to the homecoming game so as to not tip off Sylvia but I think she could sense that my mind was preoccupied. However, she could not imagine that I would pull such a hair brained stunt and luckily her radar was scrambled by all of the festivities taking place. This was our last homecoming celebration as students at Mizzou so we took it all in; the parades, pageantry, camaraderie and, of course, tail gating. We knew how to do it right at Mizzou, given that MU started the whole college homecoming tradition way back in 1911. It was a beautiful, crisp fall day warmed by generous sunlight. I consumed my share of beer; just enough to calm my nerves and control my excitement but was careful not to cross the line to where I might botch the big finale. Memorial Stadium was packed; Faurot Field was bathed in black and gold and the mood was euphoric as Mizzou held a commanding lead. I put my hand in my pocket to clutch the ring as we neared the midpoint of the third quarter and the PA announcer took advantage of a lull due to a TV timeout, "I would like to address your attention to the East side of the stadium, near the twenty five yard line in section FF about halfway up in row thirty seven, seats twelve and thirteen." He had everyone's attention including Sylvia's but she didn't really put two and two together even as the crowd's focus zeroed in on us. I guess it never registered that he had called out our seat numbers until, right on cue, I took the jewelry box out, opened it to expose the ring and dropped to one knee as he declared, "Sylvia, Twain would like to know if you would accept his hand in marriage." When I said, "Will you marry me?" it was barely audible due to the collective gasp of the crowd who then fell silent in anticipation. Syl was amazing. She wasn't flustered or perturbed over being put on the spot this way. While I caught her completely off guard, she was prepared by the same sense of certainty I possessed. As if she had rehearsed this moment, Syl said yes and then nodded emphatically so everyone could see before we embraced in a long, passionate kiss that brought a rumbling roar to the electric crowd who then went into their emphatic, signature chant. M-I-Z ... Z-O-U! Then they added the icing on the cake when the band kicked in with Hey Baby (Will You Be My Girl?) and the entire crowd sang along.

In all the excitement of homecoming and our engagement, Syl forgot to tell me about something that happened that morning. I guess it didn't really seem worth mentioning at the time. A gangly freshman seemed to materialize out of nowhere as Syl left her dorm to meet me and awkwardly asked her if she had a date for the dance that evening. She thought it was cute how he approached her so nervously and tried to let him down easily by mentioning she was leaving to meet her boyfriend but appreciated his kind offer. He looked so crestfallen that she offered to introduce him to one of the freshman girls in her dorm but he assured her that it wouldn't be necessary and quickly departed to hide the deep red embarrassment flooding his face. She had to think hard to recall his name, Charles Cane, from their brief encounter in his introductory elementary education course that she had been tasked to monitor for two weeks as part of her assignment in her senior seminar in advanced elementary education techniques. He had been quite taken by Syl and she occupied a prominent place in his imagination. Syl never heard from him again while we were at Mizzou and soon forgot all about his seemingly innocent entreaty. But, although he never forgot about her, he was careful to only admire her from afar.

Later that evening, I thought just maybe I could translate the mood into a romantic grand slam but was once again denied. You have to give me credit for persistence. Instead of getting caught up in the moment, she gathered more resolve from the fact that it was now only a matter of time. This led us into a discussion of when to marry and we both agreed that the shorter the engagement the better and settled on a June wedding right after graduation. The rest of 1978 and the first half of 1979 went by at the speed of light. In addition to completing our course work, preparing for graduation and starting the job hunting process, we were all wrapped up in wedding plans. Well, at least Syl did some heavy lifting on the latter. I tried to limit my involvement to picking out the groomsmen, tuxedos and boutonnieres while avoiding as much of the other arrangements as humanly possible. Maybe it was because of all of the other priorities we were juggling but somehow Syl took planning the wedding in stride with her natural aplomb. Things continued to slide right into place in our charmed lives and fate seemed to always be on our side. We graduated without a hitch and I landed a job at a local high school back in St. Louis teaching English and Syl was hired as a kindergarten teacher at our church back home in the Christian day school. The wedding was a completely joyous occasion and our families got along famously. There has never been a more beautiful bride than Syl was that day. Yes, life was good and about to get even better.

The next day, we planned to drive to Florida for our honeymoon but our first night together was spent in the little, one bedroom apartment that would serve as our new home. I carried Syl over the threshold and she immediately took control in an uncharacteristic and enticing fashion. She instructed me to unwind in the living room while she retired to the bedroom and shut the door. She displayed a side I had never seen before as she teasingly gave me periodic updates as she made her preparations from the privacy of our room. Between her playfully stern directives, suggestive hints, the buzz from the beer and champagne we had consumed with gusto and my long, pent up desires, I had never experienced such intense anticipation. Then she opened the door a crack and silently beckoned me with the wave of a finger. Before I could enter the bedroom, she scurried into the bathroom and shut the door. Then in a throaty voice that sent a tingle down my spine she instructed, "Shut and lock the door and turn out the light." Needless to say, I did as I was told while kicking off my shoes and tossing my shirt aside. I almost flipped my lid when she posed an insanely unnecessary question in the most randy tone, "Are you ready for me, big boy?" I thought, "Who is this girl?"

Syl then demonstrated her dramatic flair in a sultry, titillating fashion. She slowly, painstakingly pulled the door open with the bright light from the vanity silhouetting her alluring form. I would have done a double take but I didn't want to take my eyes off of the siren inching her way toward me in the short, silky, lacey negligee that looked like something you'd find in a store where Syl would never shop. She was in complete command as she helped me doff what remained of my monkey suit. Just as I was about to take charge, she extended her arm, pushed me back onto the bed and stepped back outside of my reach. Then as if a fine gallery was unveiling a priceless artwork, she pulled the spaghetti strap from each of her shoulders and let the negligee ooze down her body and slither to the ground. For someone so modest and genteel, it surprised me that she revealed no hint of self-consciousness. I felt as if I was dreaming as my eyes luxuriated in this stunning creature with her gorgeous curves and perfect proportions. Then, to finally feel the soft warmth of her body radiating against mine made the long years of denial and waiting all worthwhile.

I can still remember how lucky I felt that day; being married to someone like Syl. And while I miss her dearly and feel so terribly empty when I think of how she was torn away from me, I still feel like the luckiest man in the world having enjoyed eight years of marriage together. Over time, I came to learn that Syl's extroversion in the bedroom with me was not out of character with her normally modest, humble and well-grounded persona. What we enjoyed together in private was ours alone. There was something about the complete trust and faith we shared that allowed her to give herself to me completely in an uninhibited way that still remained true to her wholesome nature. We enjoyed the freedom and thrill of the kind of love and intimacy that only comes from the total assurance that neither one of us would ever violate the sacred trust between us. It was rock solid and, by the grace of God, would remain so throughout all our years together. That is, until the day that Charles Darwin Cane returned to tear our world apart at the seams.

It was such an idyllic world. The only thing missing was a white picket fence. As educators, we never expected to get rich but had no trouble living within our means. There's something to be said for job satisfaction and it's impossible to put a monetary value on the kind of contentment we enjoyed at home and at work. As a teacher, I took advantage of my schedule, especially that first summer off, to pursue my literary ambitions. Much to Bud's delight, I found out that I was not only good at the craft but really enjoyed it. There was such a wonderful sense of accomplishment in finishing a piece of work and sharing it with family and friends. I was very disciplined and cranked out my first novel by the end of summer. It seemed like a monumental achievement and I was so elated I nearly busted my buttons. Then reality set in. When you get to where the rubber meets the road, literature is still a business and it comes down to making money. Publishers don't want to see manuscripts from new, unproven authors and leave it to independent literary agents to do their screening for them. Agents also look at wannabe authors as plague carriers. It takes an act of congress to get them to review a manuscript from a new author. This frustrating process quickly sapped my enthusiasm for the writing game but it taught me some valuable lessons.

It wasn't long before I needed to apply some of those lessons. That's because Syl became pregnant and we could see the hand writing on the wall. I wanted to give Syl and our unborn child the best of everything but knew that would be next to impossible on a single income, especially a teacher's salary. My practical side kicked in and I took stock of my inventory of skills and interests. I was strong in language arts, enjoyed literature; had an eye for talent, good head for numbers and a knack for business. Put this all together and it told me I might be happy and much more successful operating on the business side of the literary equation. With that, I pounded the pavement until I landed a job with a local publishing house. Although I started out fairly low on the totem pole, I was able to increase my salary by forty percent over my pay as a teacher. Go figure. I missed being in the classroom but found the challenges of my new career rewarding in more than just the monetary sense. Even though I had to shelve my own literary aspirations for the foreseeable future, there was a great deal of satisfaction in bringing other authors' stories to life. Of course, Bud was greatly disappointed but I tried to assuage him with the thought that being an insider might someday help me in my quest to break into print.

Syl was a great mom from day one. She handled pregnancy like everything else, as natural as falling off a log. Even though she worked right up until her due date, she never seemed stressed and remained as cheerful as ever. That's one of the things I miss most about her. Without Syl as my anchor, my temperament is much more erratic. With her around, it was easy to maintain an even keel. She wasn't prone to mood swings, seemed impervious to stress and maintained an endless supply of infectious smiles that could light up any room. They talk about pregnant women having a certain glow and it was definitely true with Syl. As her tummy ballooned, she became even cuter, if that's possible. Our strong bond was galvanized with each passing day of excited anticipation. I'll never forget when Devon finally arrived. His birth occupies the penthouse in our pantheon of memories, right up there with our wedding day. The first time I stared into his bright eyes and he beamed at me with his rosy little face, I saw myself and Syl in a miraculous amalgam that only God could create.

We really lucked out with Devon. Having a baby will really rock your world and it can be difficult to adjust. But he was easy as infants go. He was a good eater and, thankfully, inherited his mother's disposition. If his stomach was full and diaper empty, everything was copacetic with Devon. He'd coo and laugh, stare at the TV and smile or snuggle quietly in your arms. He started sleeping through the night within a matter of weeks. We tracked his progress with glee as he traversed all the critical milestones … turning over, eating solids, holding his own bottle, crawling, walking, talking and, hallelujah of hallelujahs, potty training. There were so many fond memories and joyous recollections stored away as the pages of the calendar turned in a blur. Before we knew it, we were sending Devon off to kindergarten. Even Syl's composure took a hit as we watched our little man take his first step toward making his way in the world. I don't like to admit it but I had to wipe a little moisture from the corner of my eyes too. As he stepped up onto the school bus, he might has well have been scaling Mount Everest as far as Syl and I were concerned.

2 The Renaissance Killer

If we were dwelling in paradise, we were only on Eden's doorstep. No matter how ideal things seemed within the cozy confines of our happy home, there's no escaping the world at large which is often times a filthy, corrupt and very dangerous place. We may have been living in our own little Eden in 1987 but there was a sinister serpent lurking about. It's tough to sense danger when everything is coming up roses and daffodils. Old Bud liked to tease us in his folksy but somewhat coarse way by saying we had the world by the ass with a downhill pull. I had to admit good fortune seemed to have found a permanent parking spot in our driveway. I had risen through the ranks at Spirit Publishing to become a VP of Development, Sales & Marketing. Over the course of six plus years, I had applied my skills and work ethic well and became adept enough at generating new revenue that I decided to strike out on my own and set up a private literary agency. I'd like to claim great foresight but more accurately, through some good fortune and dumb luck, I hit pay dirt with one of my first clients. Money was not in short supply; we had a nice, quaint home and didn't have to stretch too much to make ends meet when Syl became a stay at home mom. In time, Syl elected to do some substitute teaching once Devon entered school. It helped her to stay connected to her profession and maintain a good balance in her life and interests.

Devon was something else; mom's little man and the apple of his daddy's eye. It was an exhilarating time for me because, without my prodding which was incredibly difficult to resist, Devon decided he wanted to play JFL football. It was such a blast to see him out there in his little pads and helmet learning the game I loved. And he was an aggressive little booger too; not afraid to stick his nose in there at full speed. He also made Syl proud by being such an active participant in Sunday school. Of course, that pleased me too but Syl was still the rock of faith in our family and helped to keep us all on the right path. If I forgot, she would always give me a daily reminder to get the Bible out and lead us in a family devotion. Devon was precocious and possessed the same type of advanced maturity his mother had demonstrated. He asked great questions and demonstrated a surprisingly deep understanding of our Bible lessons; he was quite the little theologian. Although I hadn't played organized sports prior to high school due to Bud's laissez faire attitude and desire to spawn independence in us, I was happy to see Devon in the JFL. It got him out of our protective cocoon and exposed him to a whole different mix of kids.

It's a hard call to determine where to draw the line with kids. You want them to be able to operate effectively in this world but not pick up a lot of its bad habits or be exposed to some of the very real dangers. Although the simpler times of my childhood were long gone, things were still much easier in 1987 than today. Now days, you can't turn on the TV without being *entertained* by the disgusting deeds of some vicious killer. We seem to be obsessed with perversion and the gorier the better. There are absolutely no boundaries of decency. The ones that I abhor the most are the weekly news magazines that present actual murder cases as television mysteries to be enjoyed with popcorn and soda as if penned from the imagination of Alfred Hitchcock, Rod Serling, Agatha Christie or Edgar Allen Poe. Why waste time and money commissioning writers to craft tales of intrigue, mystery, suspense and mayhem when you can go every day and pick things up for free off the police blotter that are much stranger than any fiction?

Even back in 1987, you'd be thrown in jail if you let your kids roam the neighborhoods and parks unattended all day long like we did when I was a boy. But way back then we weren't aware of most of the threats that plague us today. Stories of Jack the Ripper or Truman Capote's famous chronicle of the brutal murder of the poor Clutter family in Kansas seemed too surreal and far, far away to really hit home. The concept of a serial killer was not in our stream of consciousness in the early Sixties. I'm sure they existed in one form or another long before then but the first time I really paid attention to anything like this was in July 1966 when mass murderer, Richard Speck, raped and slaughtered eight student nurses in a Chicago dormitory. For me, that was a turning point that robbed me of my innocence and removed my rose colored glasses for good. Oh, that didn't keep me from bounding through the rest of my childhood on a lark like most kids do but it gave me a little more sense of wariness after that. I'll never forget the creepy and vulnerable feeling I got whenever I thought about Corazon Amurao, the sole survivor who lived to tell the shocking story by suffocating the urge to scream while silently hiding under a bed where she had to witness the whole horrid process as Speck methodically tortured and killed her eight cohorts.

The pace of madness really seemed to pick up after that and changed forever with Charles Manson and the rampage his bizarre *family* went on in 1969. To this day, I still think that the media frenzy that made a circus of his trial and turned him into some kind of demented rock star got the ball rolling and started the avalanche that has engulfed us today. Serial killers are not unique to the United States but we definitely have cornered the market when it comes to sheer volume. Much of the credit must go to Hollywood and the media who delight in turning these poor, twisted freaks into celebrities. They not only dominate the news but are hoisted up on made for TV movies and even the silver screen. David Berkowitz, the Son of Sam, held sway in New York City and across the nation in 1976-1977. Ted Bundy and John Wayne Gacy were in the spotlight from 1972 through 1978. There were a host of others like Richard Ramirez, the Night Stalker, who terrorized LA in 1984 and 1985.

There's something perverse about assigning clever, spooky nicknames to notorious murderers to stimulate the baser instincts of the public. But I guess that's to be expected if it sells newspapers. Give them what they want, right? Most often, the media assigns these names and sometimes it may be the police but it's very unusual for the killer to do so. However, that's exactly what happened with the Renaissance Killer and I guess it made sense in that nothing else about him seemed to fit the mold of a serial killer. First, he started at the tender age of nineteen while still in college. His first victim was a beautiful senior at Stephen's, a college for mostly affluent girls in the heart of Columbia near Mizzou's campus. Her bare body was found at the old quarry which was home to many late night beer fests called keggers. She had been raped and stabbed multiple times. Of course it caused quite a stir on campus and resulted in heightened security for a while but, as time wore on, everything returned to normal. The only thing out of the ordinary was the meticulous manner in which the killer had made sure to leave no clues. The crime was never solved and eventually was chalked up to perhaps being the work of some drifter that had likely moved on. While this pleased RK to a degree, it didn't satisfy his huge ego and this slowly ate him up.

He killed five more times before graduating in 1982 but each time the victims fell into the annals of unsolved murders and they were all considered separate events. One occurred in Jefferson City and another back home in St. Louis. There was absolutely no pattern to link the crimes together and they were spaced far enough apart so as to not set off a panic that would result in unwanted vigilance. RK was highly intelligent but it wasn't just his IQ that allowed him to ply his devilish trade in anonymity. It came down to motive which was pure evil rather than some unconscious urge. There was nothing in his motivation to drive any sort of pattern. He killed for one simple reason, for pleasure alone and had the unique ability to control his behavior rather than being a slave to it. RK decided when to kill, how to kill and who to kill on the basis of cold, lucid calculations designed to baffle the authorities while serving his prurient interests. Serial killers are normally driven by particular demons that sooner or later cause them to reveal their identity through some type of trend that betrays them. It might be linked to the calendar or the method of death. Sometimes it may be geography. Often times it is manifested by the type of victims selected. But none of this mattered to RK. He wasn't seeking vengeance for a childhood trauma; exorcising demons from some terrible physical, mental or sexual abuse. He knew exactly what he wanted and it could come in any variety of forms without adhering to some damning pattern; he derived pleasure from the pain of others. To RK, variety was the spice of death.

He only had one weak spot, his ego. RK was able to satisfy this for a long while, through his graduation from college, by internally boosting his inflated self-esteem with the rush he got by stumping the authorities. He knew he was much more intelligent than most and it stroked his sense of pride to easily outwit law enforcement with their vast resources. It pleased him to no end that no one ever linked his crimes together and tickled him that he so easily fooled his classmates and professors. He was able to appear quite normal without revealing the evil that lurked inside him. He was adept at compartmentalizing. The most frightening thing about RK was that he was quite sane. Even at those times when he unleashed the inner beast on his hapless victims, he remained a most rational maniac, thinking through every move with clarity and purpose. Pride finally got the better of him though when he moved back to St. Louis. Inflicting terror and seeking sexual gratification were no longer enough. He wanted to elevate his sense of self-worth to even higher, monolithic proportions. As a cold blooded serial killer, he aimed to be the best, the best ever. With that, he decided to mimic the masters but then take it to a whole other level to demonstrate the vast superiority of his mind and imagination.

His self-confidence reached megalomaniacal heights to where he no longer feared the police enough to cloak his deeds. He didn't share any insights into past murders since even the thick skulled authorities might put two and two together if they identified multiple locations in Columbia, Jefferson City and St. Louis. But going forward, he not only took credit for his work but supplied them with an appropriate moniker. For his first *work of art* after relocating back home, he chose a hooker in the red light district on Washington Avenue. Her body was found in a nearby abandoned warehouse along with a lengthy, type written note from the killer. RK explained that her disembowelment and genital mutilation were performed with surgical precision so as to intentionally mimic Jack the Ripper's classic work. Then he went on to demonstrate how he, as the master, trumped the Ripper by adding elements of psychological terror on top of the physical torture, pain and death. RK went into disgusting, lurid and extensive detail about how he dressed the part and adopted an English accent to educate the poor, uninformed street walker about the history of Jack the Ripper and his rampage through Whitechapel. He described with clinical accuracy how she reacted, down to her facial expressions and pitiful pleadings, as he forewarned her about the exact procedures he was about to perform on her. RK had struck gold. He found a treasure trove of sick pleasure in the cerebral interaction with his victim. In exercising his mental prowess and thoroughly dominating the mind of his victim, he experienced a thrill well beyond anything to be gained from the physical acts of cruelty. He loved the sense of total control, the manipulative power and the feeling of complete superiority as he, the puppet master, pulled the strings that wrenched utter horror. A true monster was unleashed that day.

The local police thought they had seen everything but were not prepared for what they read in RK's letter. They would have liked nothing better than to write it off as a sick prank or demented hoax but they could not ignore the accuracy of the details provided. RK explained how he posed as a John, the specific drug he used to tranquilize the prostitute while taking her to the warehouse and binding her on the makeshift cot and where he placed each internal organ he had removed. It shocked and sickened the authorities to think of just how premeditated this crime had been. The letter had been typed in advance so every aspect of the abduction, torture and murder was carefully planned and followed to a T. As hardened veterans, these cops had seen just about every bad thing you could imagine but a cold chill shivered down their spines as they read how RK had employed psychological terror. They winced as they thought about what that poor girl must have gone through as he paraded in front of her in garish costume and make-up while affecting an English accent. She had never heard of Jack the Ripper until RK provided a thorough education that must have gripped her in crippling fear. The crime scene was every bit as disturbing as the letter. To cap off the blood and gore, RK had printed out a copy of Di Vinci's Mona Lisa and affixed it to the victim's neck with the murder weapon, an untraceable razor sharp scalpel. Just before doing so, he had cut the corners of her mouth to horrifically mimic the famous smile. In a fitting conclusion to the galling letter, RK signed "Renaissance Killer" in the victim's blood and added a foreboding P. S. He pronounced himself the true master of murder and promised to provide more proof that he could take the art of killing to new heights beyond anything seen before.

Fear gripped the police. They had every reason to believe the maniac would follow through on his warnings. Somehow they had to nip this in the bud and stop RK before the rampage could gain steam. They launched an all-out investigation in frenzied determination but were quickly stymied by a complete lack of evidence. RK was a meticulous planner and left no witnesses or forensic evidence that could be traced back to him. It seemed uncanny that there were no fingerprints, blood, hair, skin or semen from the perpetrator. He left no record of purchasing the costume, make-up or scalpel. No one saw him prepare the abandoned warehouse or solicit the prostitute. How could he be so lucky? They would find out that luck had nothing to do with it. Soon enough they would learn that they were dealing with a remarkably intelligent, knowledgeable, strategic and tactical mind and, unfortunately, a uniquely deviant one. They hesitated on calling in the Feds. There was no doubt they could use their resources and expertise but they didn't want to draw attention to the situation and cause a panic. Thus, they refused to let the cat out of the bag and didn't alert the media about their investigation or the letter. However, RK's hungry ego would not stand for such secrecy and he blew the lid off their plans by sending a copy of the letter to the Post-Dispatch along with a picture of the victim he had snapped at the crime scene. Pandemonium ensued and RK delighted as he watched the police chief stepping and fetching in front of the media.

Like everyone else, I was gripped by the breaking news. This kind of thing just didn't happen every day in sleepy St. Louis; in fact, it never happened. I found myself getting caught up in the story, not to the point of panic but certainly caution. We took extra care in vigilance and safety matters, especially when it came to Devon. But we found some assurance in the notion, promoted by the media, that the killer was probably some sicko who had it in for prostitutes. This caused quite a stir on Washington Street and other red light districts and put somewhat of a damper on their business. RK followed all of this closely and found it hilarious that the police were spending time protecting rather than busting call girls. As for the *oldest profession*, their loss was our gain. While they fretted the rest of St. Louis fell into a false sense of security. And over time, everything settled down a bit. RK was not a rampage killer; he controlled his urges and not vice versa. He knew it was to his advantage to let some time pass. No one suspected Charles Darwin Cane. He was as normal as cherry pie; no more threatening than a perfectly rounded scoop of vanilla ice cream. For heaven's sake, he was a fresh faced substitute teacher who spent most days watching over unsuspecting, little, elementary school kids ... just like Syl would do in a few short years.

RK took his time and planned out his next few masterpieces with trademark precision. He continued to be amused at the way the police plotted their strategy on the basis of a non-existing pattern, continuing to obsess over prostitutes in whom he had absolutely no interest. He chortled at the prospect of the FBI trying to develop his profile and purposely took as divergent a path as possible to drive them crazy in their efforts to home in on his identity. RK was an equal opportunity murderer who showed no partiality on the basis of sex, race, age, religion or political affiliation. Sometimes he sought sexual gratification and other times not. He was not biased toward any given weapon; gun, knife or rope, although he did like to improvise in peculiar ways. Sometimes he struck quickly within a couple of months and other times he was willing and able to hold off for many months; anything to throw the police off the trail and keep them guessing. He was not partial to any particular geography within the area and even ventured further into Southern Illinois once just for a change. The only consistency was in his careful planning, stealth, ability to leave a dearth of evidence and, of course, the grotesque creativity he employed in satisfying his lust to inflict pain and maximum torment on others. Oh, and one other thing ... he always satisfied his gargantuan ego by notifying the media of his latest accomplishment. With each killing there was a new letter signed by the "Renaissance Killer" and a copy of some classic artwork was left at the crime scene: Renoir, Monet, Degas, Picasso, Gauguin, Rubens or Rembrandt.

As each new killing splashed across the news in tabloid fashion, a new level of panic set in throughout the area. It was clear that no one was safe and the police were pathetically clueless. Even though I, like almost everyone else, was too busy with day-to-day cares and responsibilities to be completely fixated with the Renaissance Killings, it began to dominate my thoughts more and more as the bloodshed mounted. On the one hand, there was some solace in the simple odds since there were only a handful of victims out of a local population of roughly three million. But still, there was something eerily disturbing about just knowing that such a deranged individual was lurking somewhere in our community. It got to the point where it really began affecting our lives in tangible ways. There was a palpable wariness and uneasy caution that hung in the air like a stench hovering over a sour landfill. Try as one might, it was impossible not to harbor irrational suspicions about neighbors and strangers alike. But then, RK would remain dormant for long stretches. And when he did strike, there was no apparent rhyme or reason. There were no practical warnings the police could issue, no specific dangers to avoid; only vague, general cautions. It was maddening. RK loved it. He felt as if the entire population was under his control.

Over three years had passed since the one man siege on St. Louis began and it was hard to sustain a constant vigil. RK felt just as challenged to maintain his warped standard of excellence. But his ego seemed to supply endless energy and a maniacal urge to exceed his last feat, reach even greater heights of depravity and add to the great edifice of his legacy and legend. With that as his motivation, RK plotted something over the top, even for him, as we entered the summer of 1985. He had been focused on the classics and had every intention of maintaining an eye for history but began to feel jealous of the attention given to some of his contemporaries, in particular at that time, LA's Night Stalker, Richard Ramirez. Then an idea, an evil inspiration came to him one morning as he was enjoying breakfast at a local Denny's Restaurant. As he savored the famous Denny's Combo, it struck him in a dastardly, gleeful flash that he didn't have to choose between eras ... he should straddle the expanse of history and come up with his own RK's Combo.

From the more distant past, he chose Albert De Salvo, the famed Boston Strangler who had a penchant for raping elderly women. That was something new to which RK had no particular aversion. Anything goes, was his motto. If he put his thinking cap on, he was sure he could combine the Strangler's signature approach with that of his current day rival, the Night Stalker, in a friendly little game of one-upmanship. For his inspirational artist, he thought it would only be fitting to enlist the talented madman, Vincent Van Gogh. Only an evil virtuoso could combine such disparate elements into a classic concerto but RK was confident that he, as the Beethoven of bedlam, was well up to the task. He studied the press clippings of one of the Night Stalker's recent attacks just over two months before. Ramirez had invaded the home of Vincent and Maxine Zazzara in the middle of the night, shot Vincent dead through the temple and then turned on Mrs. Zazzara who had retrieved a shotgun from under the bed only to discover, unfortunately, that it was unloaded. Ramirez shot and killed her, stripped her down and tied her to the bed. He then proceeded to try to cut out her heart as a trophy but was so clumsy he couldn't get past her rib cage. This so enraged him that he unleashed a fit of fury and gouged out her eyes instead and then mutilated her body with multiple stab wounds.

Although Maxine was only forty four years old, 20 years younger than Vincent, RK selected an older woman out of deference to Albert. Claudette and Wilber Perlmutter were sixty six and sixty eight respectively and lived in a non-working farmhouse surrounded by ten acres of land in New Melle, past the outskirts of St. Louis County. The site was perfect in that it was very remote and secluded mostly by woods. Careful casing of the joint revealed that visitors were rare and ensured RK that he would not be surprised by neighbors, police patrols or relatives.   He would need some undisturbed time to create his greatest masterpiece to date. He made short work of their old hound and the Perlmutters were easy prey in the middle of the night. He bound the old man to a chair, very much reminiscent of the great painter's At Eternity's Gate. Then he forced Claudette to disrobe and raped her in full display of her husband. Wilber's high pitched wailing and pleading only added to RK's excitement and incited him to more frenetic brutality. When it was over, RK flashed a copy of Van Gogh's self-portrait of 1889 with the bandaged ear and proceeded to give them both an unsolicited history lesson. Once finished, he calmly pulled out a gleaming buck knife and proceeded to lop off Wilber's ear. A new wave of horror swept over Mrs. Perlmutter and then utter disbelief when RK demanded that she consume the bloody appendage right there on the spot. In shock, she fainted only to be revived by the relentless killer who put her to the test by holding a gun to Wilber's head. Somehow, under the unfathomable pressure of knowing that this madman would surely snuff out her husband's life if she resisted, Claudette held back the bile rising in her throat and choked down the disgusting morsel while trying to imagine it was just a piece of gristle from a cheap steak. As she finished this super-human feat in order to spare her beloved husband's life, the monster pulled the trigger. Claudette vomited before losing consciousness. RK employed the smelling salts once again. She was nearly catatonic as he read the press clipping from the Zazzara murders and matter-of-factly informed her that he would succeed where the Night Stalker had failed in removing her heart.

When the police found the bodies, Mr. Perlmutter's regurgitated ear was carefully placed on the copy of Van Gogh's self-portrait where the bandage covered his missing ear lobe. Then there was the matter of Claudette's mutilated body with the heart and eyes removed and multiple, carefully arranged stab wounds. Rather than leaving the scene quickly, RK had taken the time to paint the remains with black, blues and splashes of light gray and white in a macabre but somewhat recognizable rendition of Starry Night. He had been as meticulous as ever and provided all the unwanted details, as usual, in his signature letter but this time there was something different. He actually notified the police anonymously to ensure that the bodies were discovered before decay might set in and destroy his precious artwork. The authorities remained baffled and their frustration mounted as the community became more impatient and unhinged. Once again, there was no evidence leading to the perpetrator, only more divergent facts to confuse matters; now an old woman, a new locale, cannibalism and the murder of a couple rather than a single victim. There was one thing the profilers seized upon that they thought might work to their advantage. RK loathed competition and wanted the spotlight all to himself.

RK went back into his shell, leaving the police to grasp at straws for who knows how long. As for the public at large, we couldn't understand how this could go on for nearly four years. Outrage began to set in. I'm not a joiner or an activist by any stretch of the imagination but I actually participated in a civil protest at one of the police press conferences. Like a lot of people, I just wanted to vent at someone. Of course, it didn't help matters. The police were doing everything humanly possible but they were up against a chameleon, an evil genius who was extremely careful and self-controlled … that is, if a self-absorbed, deviant, sadistic, mass murderer can be properly labeled as under control. If the police could have shared some hint of a possible break in the case, it might have helped alleviate the tremendous stress and offer some glimmer of hope but they had not even been able to develop a credible suspect or person of interest. The only crumb they could toss to us was the assurance that sooner or later the perpetrator would trip up and make a mistake like they always do. They weren't very convincing since they had their own doubts about the killer's fallibility. As for me, I continued to take every precaution possible without upsetting Devon. Nothing rattled Syl. For her, life went on uninterrupted and she calmly offered prayers to God, putting her faith completely in him.

Roughly four months passed without incident and anxiety grew as it seemed only a matter of time before RK claimed his next victim. The police were restless too and wanted to do something, anything to get ahead of the curve and smoke out RK. They decided to take the one arrow they had in their quiver and give it their best shot. The only reliable insight into RK's character was his inflated ego and his obsession to be number one. During RK's hiatus, the Night Stalker had been quite busy killing eleven people since May 29th and raping three others while subjecting four *lucky* victims to only robbery, brutal but non-fatal beatings and a failed rape attempt. The authorities knew it was extremely dangerous to try to incite a killer like RK, perhaps inadvertently putting the unwitting public in the unenviable position of becoming some type of bait trap or guinea pig in a failed experiment. But they couldn't sit on their hands waiting for the next murder and decided to take a chance to coax him out of his comfort zone and trick him into making a mistake. With the cooperation of the local media, they released a piece of the worst kind of tabloid journalism under the headline of Night Stalker Puts Renaissance Killer to Shame. It may have been gallows humor aimed at expressing the public's outrage but wound up pitting one murderer against the other, as if it were a competition, and chronicled how the prolific Night Stalker had left RK in his dust. Several quotes attributed to the police hit a note of sarcasm and more or less taunted St. Louis' *minor leaguer*. It was no consolation for local folks to know that at least St. Louis' troubles were not as monumental as LA's. This struck me and the rest of the Post's readers as something way beyond inappropriate, causing another uproar against the police. But it had the desired effect on RK. He was livid.

While RK was intent on picking up the gauntlet and showing up the police as rapidly as possible, he refused to get sloppy. He picked up the pace but didn't cut corners on his planning. If anything, being called out by the police in such a brash, public manner drove him to new heights, or should I say depths of depravity. This time he would do something so outrageous that no one would ever dare to compare him to a boorish, low life amateur of the Night Stalker's ilk. To add crowning glory to his already prodigious body of work, he needed something iconic, a paragon of popularity. Although Thanksgiving was still two weeks away, his inspiration came easy during a trip to the local mall. The trimmings were hung in the halls with such care, a fine hint of pine seemed to float in the air; green and red filled the aisles like fresh boughs of holly, a man laughed through his beard making everyone jolly. Who didn't love jolly old St. Nick, especially this particular Santa? Peter Kosulis was a fixture at the mall. He was the real deal ... he was old but tall and robust and filled out his red suit well with a little added padding to create a round tummy. He had ruddy, red cheeks, twinkling eyes and his long, flowing, white beard was completely authentic. He was so into this cherished role that he even carried business cards for Kris Kringle, North Pole. Most importantly, he loved what he did and the joy emanated from his rosy countenance whenever he was able to bring cheer to the kids and the young at heart.

We loved old Kris Kringle. My heart still aches at the mere thought of what he endured at the hands of the Renaissance Killer. To think that this type of deliberate and profound inhumanity sprang from a person's warped mind and resulted in so much devilish pleasure and satisfaction at such a terrible cost to a fellow human being is impossible to comprehend. In this case, it was somehow even worse because RK was seeking more than self-gratification; he wanted to send a message at poor Kris' expense. It was more than just an admonishment to the police for their terrible slight. It went beyond another vain expression of his perceived intelligence and superiority. This crime was meant to be a repudiation of everything good; RK intended to thumb his evil nose at God himself. One other thing changed. RK would not be satisfied by leaving a detailed letter at the scene. For this masterpiece, he planned to go high tech with a video recording of the whole sordid, despicable, gut wrenching nightmare.

When the police arrived at the abandoned cathedral on the city's north side, it was hard not to notice the stark differences between the majestic spires, ornate stonework and glorious stained glass remnants that stood in contrast to the boarded windows and deteriorating edifice with its general lack of maintenance and care. It was inspiring yet creepy but the latter gave no indication of what they would find inside. Old Kris Kringle, still in his Santa garb, had been hoisted onto a sturdy wooden pike that had been honed to a sharp point for his impalement. The agony of his excruciating, slow death was still etched upon his contorted visage. To make matters worse, his arms ended in dark stumps that had been crudely cauterized so as to stem the flow of blood and extend his suffering. His severed hands were tacked to the ceiling a la the Sistine Chapel to simulate Michelangelo's Creation of Adam with each one posed just right to depict

God's outstretched finger extending to bring life to the first man. This time, instead of a letter there was a movie marquee fashioned by RK announcing, Now Showing: Christmas in Transylvania starring Kris Kringle and Vlad Draculea, directed by R. K. DeMille. The CD was nearby with a mock coupon for a free popcorn and soda with a reminder to please visit our concession stand.

It was difficult to find volunteers from the force to watch the video. Everyone had seen enough of RK's crime scenes to shudder at the thought of witnessing the act in progress but two of the senior officers reluctantly accepted the task along with three FBI agents strictly out of their steadfast sense of duty. They paid a dear price. Their psyches were rent forevermore and they would suffer through many sleepless nights. One of the officers, a combat veteran, involuntarily heaved the contents of his heretofore cast iron stomach. What transpired is simply too morbid and ghastly to recount here. If there was any redeeming value to be taken from the ordeal, it was the faith and courage shown by Peter Kosulis. At one point, RK or rather Dracula, took a page out of the Night Stalker's book and demanded that Kris "swear your love for Satan, Santa and I will spare you". RK was so pleased with his clever little play on words by moving the n in Satan two spaces. The humor was lost on Kosulis who would have liked nothing better than to bring his pain and suffering to an end but he was a devout Christian and elected to suffer martyrdom before denying his Savior. He exclaimed in as loud a voice as he could muster, "Praise Jesus Christ!" Then he almost inaudibly recited the 23rd Psalm from memory. RK replied, "As you wish Santa." Then speaking to the audience rather than Kosulis, "Take heed Night Stalker fans and remember, quality is more important than quantity."

Impalement is a most fiendish and infamous method of torture that typically involves a veritable eternity of suffering prior to death.   If there was any relief for the unfortunate viewers of RK's movie debut, it was that Kosulis' prayers were answered and he thankfully slipped unexpectedly early into death shortly afterward much to the dismay of RK. As unpleasant as it was to suffer through the video, the investigators at least had some hope that close analysis might reveal meaningful clues to RK's identity for the first time. They went over it time and again with a fine tooth comb only to be flummoxed once more. In addition to the long cape, wig and thick Dracula make-up, RK made sure every inch of his body was covered so as to not reveal any distinguishing marks or even his skin color or age. He revealed an amazing talent to change his voice, adopting a near perfect impersonation of Bela Lugosi. The tone and timber shed no light on his age and his articulate speech was conducted in classic English of a bygone era that was devoid of any contemporary slang that might provide a demographic hint. RK also adroitly used the camera angles to enhance his camouflage. It was next to impossible to gauge his height, build or weight. Any hopes of tripping up RK were completely dashed. Of course, the police had no intention of releasing the video and even though the media received a copy from the killer, they drew the line on such sensationalism deeming it much too barbarous for public consumption in any form, edited or not. However, RK breached this gap by mailing copies to a few unscrupulous bloggers. Soon after posting, it was quickly shut down by the sites' owners but the genie was out of the bottle.

The diabolical murder of our beloved mall Santa by the outlandishly evil Renaissance Killer resulted in a virulent, knee-jerk reaction from the public. The general sentiment was enough is enough but it was expressed in an irrational way that only added to the exploding sense of panic. RK had released a torrent of pent up emotion that had the visceral feel of a lynch mob. But without a clear object of our ire on which to focus our attention, we lashed out in every direction with pointless threats and accusations. However, there was no satisfaction in flogging our favorite whipping boy, the police, again so our burst of energy eventually found a constructive outlet and cooler heads prevailed. Steps were taken to form neighborhood watch groups across the area and everyday citizens volunteered in droves to help the police with the task of tracking down RK. Cane was caught off guard by the public's reaction. On the one hand, in his sick mind, he took it as flattery that so much time and attention was being devoted to him. It fed his gigantic ego and made him feel imperial; so far above the foolish masses that he was able to manipulate and elude so effortlessly. At the same time, as his deviant self-control defensive reflex kicked in, he realized he must take new precautions to protect his secret identity. He had that unique ability to contain the insatiable bloodlust that eventually did in other serial killers. The Renaissance Killer took a long sabbatical that stretched more than a year. By the time 1987 rolled around, we had all settled into a normal routine; speculating, hoping and praying that RK had moved on, was somehow rendered forever dormant or, most preferably, had met his demise.

No one ever suspected Charles Darwin Cane. How could they with his youthful good looks, affable demeanor and dedicated service to elementary school children? He was a master of disguise. There were no cracks in his mild-mannered, urbane façade to reveal the monstrous evil residing within. He relished killing but didn't need to kill for gratification at the expense of blowing his cover. Unlike most serial killers, RK was able to bide his time safely in *hibernation* while continuing to reap pleasure from his ability to elude capture and demonstrate his innate superiority. He had his triumphant memories to keep him warm. While Cane was able to appear congenial and even charming and interacted comfortably with others in any situation, he rarely socialized outside of work related environments. He had no close friends and largely kept his relatives at arm's length. Much like Bundy, he was a likeable, sociable loner who didn't draw attention to what was largely a rather strange, solitary lifestyle. As serial killers go, Charles Darwin Cane was a very odd duck. He was so self-possessed that if it came down to choosing between his personal freedom and acting out on his evil desires, he was easily able to bottle up the latter in deference to the former. Cane was not wont to be a team player, in any capacity. His god was self and the thought of being incarcerated, subject to some authority besides his own; reduced to a number within a crowded penal system, was his worst nightmare. He would never let that happen, or so he thought.

There was one irrational, insatiable urge buried so deep within Cane that he didn't realize the potential disaster lurking somewhere in the dark recesses of his reptilian brain. To anyone else, the fleeting memory would seem so inconsequential ... but to Cane it was monumental, a defining moment. It's so ironic and, to me, infinitely regrettable that something so happenstance would break the fetters containing Cane's one, uncontrollable craving. I have pondered a thousand times since then whether it was fate or just a ghastly coincidence that Devon's second grade teacher suffered an accident that laid her up for over a month and, worst yet, she was replaced by a substitute on extended assignment named Charles Darwin Cane. We trusted the school's judgment in such matters and had long since forgotten the chance encounter between Cane and Syl during our last college homecoming back in 1978. Devon talked about his substitute teacher in glowing terms and all seemed well. Then, by some cruel quirk, Cane gave the class an assignment which was a variation on show-and-tell with career day combined. He asked the kids to each make a presentation on their mommies and/or daddies and talk about their background and jobs. It was aimed at developing their public speaking skills while giving them insights into various career choices. As a side benefit, it was supposed to encourage kids to involve their parents in a homework assignment and help the students take pride in their families.

In spite of the strained relationship he maintained with his own family, Cane kept up his wholesome façade and appeared captivated even though he was bored to tears by their mundane musings. He asked probing follow up questions to feign genuine interest and smiled as they provided him with useless details. However, this changed radically during Devon's turn in the barrel; the last of the day at the end of the week. Cane was plodding through the assignment dutifully; barely listening with his mind drifting toward the weekend. Devon had talked about me and then proudly announced that his mom, Syl, was a teacher just like Mr. Cane. As Cane fulfilled his mandatory obligation to seem enthralled with such ennui, he asked, "And where did your mommy go to school to learn to be a teacher?" Devon said, "She's a Tiger … she went to the University of Missouri!" This piqued Cane's interest as he exclaimed, "Well, isn't that something? I'm a Tiger too." Cane's curiosity prompted him further, "I wonder if we attended Mizzou at the same time. How old is your mommy?" Devon beamed, "Oh, I remember from her last birthday; she's thirty." Cane was intrigued enough to ask a somewhat intrusive question that would have stumped most seven year old boys, "What was her name in college?" Devon's unusual maturity and intellect had always been a source of pride but, oh, how I regret that he couldn't have been clueless about such things like his little peers. He volunteered cheerfully, "Her name was Adams back then but now it's Newman just like me."

Everything changed at that very moment. A latch was turned somewhere inside and Cane's worst obsession was unleashed. It was all he could do to contain himself for the few remaining minutes of the school week. Any slight chance of him regaining his composure vanished when he staked out our house and saw Syl returning home from work. It took just one glimpse of her to set his terrible plot in motion. He took to stalking her whenever possible and when he was alone her image consumed his thoughts. Cane was terribly conflicted; must he serve his infatuation and lust or satisfy his ravenous appetite for vengeance over the painful rejection she had mercilessly inflicted upon him? Was she his one, true love destined to receive his endless devotion or a traitorous tramp deserving to be consumed by his just wrath? In his tortured mind, there was only one way to know for sure. He would have to put her to the test personally.

Cane, the master of self-control and deception, was rendered a runaway freight train by the prospect of resolving his long suppressed discord. It was nothing short of utter lunacy but, in his fractured mind, Syl's long ago, polite declination of his fanciful, freshman entreaty had been an unforgiveable affront that ruined his life. It was truly absurd to project such feelings onto a perfect stranger but, in Cane's mind, he had been spurned by his one, true love. That one thought dominated every waking moment and fundamentally changed his approach to everything. He was no longer the puppet master who planned meticulously. His safety and independence were no longer paramount. Every ounce of his being was committed to one thing and one thing only: she would repent and make proper amends by devoting herself to him forever or he would exact his vengeance in a way befitting the malevolent genius of the Renaissance Killer. Driven as uncontrollably as he was, he threw every caution to the wind and his plan consisted of nothing more than waiting until I was out of town on business to strike. Cane came late at night under the cover of darkness. They were easy prey and he had no difficulty in surprising, restraining and immobilizing them. Syl, like any normal person, was unable to comprehend Cane's macabre and ludicrous logic; his hallucinatory world was too completely foreign, and, thus, she could only hopelessly invite his wrath. Once the conflict was resolved in his mind, Cane was strangely able to regain enough composure to calmly carry out his vengeance in a calculating fashion worthy of RK's worst crimes. Nevertheless, he was operating on the fly rather than following one of his carefully scripted plans and left many clues that would lead to his apprehension. The entire city was overjoyed and relieved by the capture of the Renaissance Killer, that is, except for one, miserable, shattered, solitary soul. The Renaissance Killer was history, never to plague us again. But I would remain haunted for the rest of my life by one question: "Why, why did his last two victims have to be my precious darlings, my loves; beautiful, sweet, faithful Syl and the apple-of-my-eye, my dearest, little Devon?

3 Shattered

Isn't it something how tragedy can rearrange all of our priorities within a single stitch in time? I guess it was normal at first that I was so detached; floating in some kind of ethereal, nether world. Everything around me was devoid of any real meaning. It was as if I was a spirit living in an abstract dimension where sights and sounds didn't fully register in my mind. I would say it was dream-like but in dreams there is a sense of caring where normal emotions can exist. My life had been torn asunder by Cane. Losing an arm and a leg would have been infinitely more tolerable than being rent apart from Syl and Devon. Suddenly, I was able to relate to the shock and disorientation of losing a limb in battle; staring at a shredded, bloody stump, gazing in horror at a dismembered arm and feeling only hollowness and a terrible sense of loss. Now I understood some wartime accounts I'd read where numbness replaced the pain but phantom feelings remained as frayed nerve endings tried desperately to signal commands to the severed appendage. My feelings were similar but, in a way, much worse. It was as if my heart had been ripped out of my chest yet somehow I remained conscious and alive to suffer through the worst kind of tortured, isolated existence.

The main thing that kept me from dissolving into a catatonic puddle of goo was the normalcy of going through the motions: the funeral, media inquisition and trial. The funeral was the toughest duty of all. Such ceremonies are meant to bring closure and peace of mind. They draw upon faith to mend broken hearts but, in my case, it only deepened my wounds. Perhaps it was simply the image of the twin coffins which represented my entire life being buried. Or maybe it was my emotional state that rendered the soothing words meaningless in my fractured mind. Instead of stirring my faith, the well intentioned words of family, friends and our pastor only raised questions that echoed in my head, over and over. So often in the past I had been able to reconcile bad things happening to *good people* … when it was someone else's loved one. But now, it was my family, my cherished loved ones … my darlings. Yes, I had been rightly taught that God didn't wish tragedy upon his children but we suffered nonetheless because of the sin, original sin that corrupted God's good world. But without Syl there to prop me up with her rock solid foundation, my faith crumbled into dry dust. My own reason, a most unreliable, foolish and undependable shepherd, took over and led me astray. Syl **was** good! There was no one on earth less deserving of such a fate. And Devon, poor, little Devon was innocent. He was pure as the driven snow and did not deserve to die. The height of futility is to feel anger toward our loving God who sacrificed everything to redeem us and bless us with eternal life. But I fell prey to my worst instincts and gave myself over to anger against everything I had been taught and believed. Whenever faith tried to rescue me, I slammed the door in his face with one single-minded question, "Why God, why?"

No one at the funeral could have guessed that I was gripped by such terrible, internal turmoil. I maintained a stoic façade that must have appeared as normal grief. It was ironic that I was surrounded by so many sincere, caring people who wanted to somehow share my pain and help shoulder the burden but I felt so all alone. I suppose it was not surprising that I was able to shut them all out since I had already cut off God who was the only one really able to provide true comfort and peace. I was like a pitiful, hopeless drug addict refusing the one thing he needed more than anything, an intervention from those that loved him most. By the time Syl and Devon's caskets were lowered into the ground, I was completely out of reach. The worst time for me was when they began to cover the coffins with dirt. With each shovel of earth, I felt a heavy, iron door shutting; closing me inside a claustrophobic mausoleum pitted in utter darkness and hopelessness. I felt the cold, smooth stone but it was not in the walls of that mausoleum; it was my lifeless heart.

The best thing for me would have been to seek a lifeline from someone like our pastor. But instead of seeking his private counsel during the weeks that followed, I avoided him altogether. My church attendance dropped to the minimum acceptable while still avoiding a personal visit from the pastor or an elder. I provided clever excuses for my absences and went through the proper motions when I attended so as to not raise any eyebrows. It's funny but out of shyness or respect, people tend to leave you alone under such circumstances. I guess they're just not sure what to say so it seems better to say nothing and leave well enough alone. Time heals all wounds, right? Yeah, right … I found out the hard way that this is a crock. My wounds just festered. Oh, I appeared so calm and peaceful and followed the liturgy and church protocols religiously. No one had any idea of the troubled thoughts that occupied my mind, that is, no one but God who alone can read the heart. He could see clearly that his little lamb was a lost sheep headed for trouble and danger.

Like a lot of people who've gone through a terrible tragedy, I threw myself into my work as a defense mechanism. I worked feverishly and spent long hours laboring at my job. But, make no mistake; it was just that, a job and not my business or career any longer. It certainly was not dedication since I was only trying to occupy my time which seemed so plentiful now without Syl and Devon in my life. I couldn't have cared less about the business. Building something, getting ahead, amassing wealth and unearthing literary treasures for the betterment of mankind seemed so trite. What was the purpose? I had no one to share my achievements with anymore. The former value I placed upon such things evaporated like a drop of dew in the Saharan sunrise. The workplace was worse than church in terms of the isolation. As long as I appeared busy, everything but the direst warning signals would be ignored. Being the victim of a tragedy was almost like having a handicap. People turned a blind eye to my problems as if acknowledging them would be a terrible affront. Everyone was happy to pretend that everything was peachy even though I was uncharacteristically sullen. And when I passed over a manuscript that was dripping with potential, no one bothered to question why I was so far off my game. Let sleeping dogs lie, even if they might be a touch rabid.

It was crazy really. I was doing my best to avoid the thing I needed most; human contact and meaningful dialogue. And the people that cared for me the most were more than willing to accommodate me out of misguided concern and well intentioned respect for my privacy. Ironically, the people with selfish interests and absolutely no compassion for my feelings inadvertently threw me a life preserver that kept me from being totally stranded. First, media types rudely intruded upon the sanctity of my mourning without a second thought for my personal feelings. I was the closest, direct link to the sensational story of the most infamous serial killer that had ever stalked our fair city and they were duty bound to hound me for every lurid detail they could squeeze out of me. In the name of journalism they trampled my fragile sensibilities like a herd of mad buffaloes. In spite of their unforgivably boorish behavior and my certainty that their first duty was to fatten their own wallets, I rather welcomed their improprieties and intrusions. It was one of the few connections I had to reality and forced me to dwell on something other than self-pity. As emotions go, anger at their offensiveness was a welcome change of pace from constant melancholy.

With my broken faith and the rebelliousness I felt at that time, it was impossible for me to reconcile my spiritual turmoil and turn back to our gracious God. But there was an advantage to being the center of the media's attention regardless of their questionable methods. It gave me unusual access to a wealth of information about Cane and his string of murders. I was not in a position to apprehend spiritual peace but the thought began to creep into my head that perhaps I could at least gain some peace of mind by figuring out Cane. If I couldn't find out why God allowed this to happen, I could find some solace in seeking a secular explanation for what caused Cane to snap; what started him on the rampage of terror that finally engulfed Syl and Devon?   Finding the answer to this question became my cause célèbre. It gave me a reason for being and rescued me from the pit of despair. Unlocking this mystery consumed my time and attention. It was a blessing and a curse; it freed me from my gloomy prison but everything else suffered including my job and any frayed relationships that remained.

My quest was aided by the jury trial that commenced thereafter. Between the media exchanges, trial preparation and courtroom proceedings, I was flooded with useful information. I kept careful notes that later would form the basis for a book but I didn't really entertain such a possibility then. It was just my habit. Although I considered them to be untrustworthy mercenaries, some of the best insights about Cane came from the defense's position. I loathed Cane's attorneys as somehow being part of the opposition and in league with Cane if not exactly complicit in the murders. But oddly enough, I was still able to consider their arguments and evidence objectively because I craved answers as much as I did justice. Nothing they said evoked even a hint of sympathy in me but I did start to feel like I understood him better. There were times when I almost gained a modicum of satisfaction in knowing there might be some logical cause behind Cane's tragic crimes ... a horribly flawed chemical deficiency or hormonal imbalance, a tragically crossed wire in his demented brain, a life-altering atrocity resulting in his misshapen character ... something ... something so terrible, so wrong that it might explain if not justify his inexplicably evil deeds. I soaked In every bit of information I could and feverishly analyzed it to draw my own conclusions. Whenever I got close to something that might make sense, my mind would reject the notion like an unwanted organ transplant. In addition to my life being ripped apart at the seams, I was torn asunder inside. As much as I wanted peace of mind, I rejected every prospect, not on the basis of logic but uncontrollable rage. Every time I saw the light of day peeking into the mausoleum, the vision of Syl and Devon would rise up and I would be convulsed in a fury that slammed the door shut tighter.

There was no question about Cane's guilt, at least not when it came to the murders of Syl and Devon. It was harder to pin the other murders on him but, with Syl and Devon, his uncharacteristic loss of control resulted in a plethora of incontrovertible forensic evidence that nailed him. The defense team didn't mount an attack on the evidence, instead laying claim to their only hope through a spirited insanity plea. It was pretty hard to argue that Cane didn't have some major screws loose but, in the end, the jury was not prepared to absolve him from accountability for his actions. Although the other murders were not officially considered in this trial, the details were public knowledge and surely weighed on the minds of the jurors. Thus, the toughest hurdle came from RK's own pen where he laid out his cruel plans in his letters to the police in such a blatantly premeditated fashion. It also didn't help that he taunted the police and took such obvious pride in laying claim to his deeds. They may not have been able to try and convict Cane for the other murders but his reputation as the Renaissance Killer stuck to him like tar, linking him to the whole blood trail. In the case of Syl and Devon, the guilty verdicts were swift and easy.

The tougher assignment came when the jury was tasked with the punishment phase. As far back as 1987, many churches had abandoned the basics and were being swamped by political correctness even though that term didn't really come into its more current, pejorative form until the 1990s. The notion was well entrenched nonetheless and many churches didn't espouse the traditional view of capital punishment. If the topic, which was verboten, came up, most reformed churches began to take the theologically impossible and completely contradictory view that God somehow prohibited capital punishment through the Fifth Commandment. This position, while popular and pragmatic, was highly hypocritical on the part of such churches since they otherwise typically avoided any mention of the Commandments in favor of a distorted social gospel. I on the other hand had been instructed correctly from childhood on up and was well aware of the proper biblical position. However, I did not weigh in on the basis of theology. When I received my chance to sway the jury as a surviving family member, I made an impassioned plea that touched all the right buttons. I was ever so careful to play the part of an innocent victim reluctantly seeking justice and not vengeance. When I spoke through tear filled eyes, it was my chance to repay Cane with my own virtuoso performance. Faithfulness to God's clear commands did not enter my mind and I certainly did not entertain any Christian notion of forgiveness and compassion. Although it never showed, my only motivation was white hot anger. I wanted Cane dead in the worst way and wished the torments of hell upon his soul.

I was successful in my appeal to the jury's sense of justice. Cane was condemned to death row. And yet, I didn't find peace as I glowered into his eyes as his sentence was announced. The pitiful excuses offered up by the defense didn't assuage me one bit. Syl and Devon's senseless deaths were completely irrational and unexplainable. What did Cane have to gain through his diabolical mayhem? He wasn't motivated by greed. The only thievery was the robbery of my peace and purpose, commodities that can't be transferred from one person to another like so much silver and gold. We hadn't done any harm to Cane; we didn't even know the man! Was it displaced anger? Was there anything that could have been done to Cane to justify such cruel retribution from anyone? The defense had certainly not made that case. As much as I tried to sooth my pain with delicious daydreams of Cane being strapped down like a helpless animal and launched into hell with a lethal injection, it didn't take away the crippling emptiness deep inside my bowels. I had gained a better understanding through the trial, was able to confront the killer and received justice, at least such as could be measured by the court system; temporal rather than metaphysical. However, none of that really mattered because I was still alone, still suffering much worse torment than Cane would ever experience. Worst of all, I knew and my shattered conscience reminded me every minute of every day that none of these things, nothing in the world could bring back Syl and Devon to me. I was torn asunder in a way that no doctor could heal. I had not lost an arm or a leg. It was my heart and soul that was missing and there was no prosthetic replacement to make me whole again.

4 Poison Seeds

The media coverage and trial had exposed me to the losses of so many others at the hands of the Renaissance Killer. Yet, I had no real compassion for them. What happened to me? Bud and Lilly had always taught me to think about the other guy and walk around in his shoes before dwelling on myself. They set a good example in that regard and always pointed to the perfect example of compassion and grace, the sinless Lamb of God who paid the price for all our transgressions. However, in spite of everything I had been taught to the contrary, I was completely self-centered. As Bud would say, "doe ray me and the heck with everyone else". I couldn't help myself. I was like a scarecrow whose very fabric had unraveled at the seams with my insides strewn about like so much straw; church and family, faith and tradition had deserted me. My life remained in disarray and I displayed about as much purpose as one of those mindless zombies in a cheap horror flick. Work was nothing more than a necessary burden that put food on the table and a roof over my head. My foolish anger against Almighty God was still kindled to the point where meaningful church involvement was out of the question. I had cut myself off from everyone and was such a surly sad sack that no one dared to attempt to breach the walls I had constructed. Headed toward rock bottom, I turned my attention to the one thing that had provided a pinch of hope before. I set my mind on solving the mystery of Charles Darwin Cane.

What a strange hobby; instead of trying to forget him and put my tragedy behind me, I made Cane the centerpiece of my world. The time and effort I devoted to Cane-ology should have earned me a PhD. It truly was a fascinating topic that captured the interest of many legitimate scholars. But for me it was an odd pursuit that entailed dangers I failed to see. It was such a long and gradual process that I didn't recognize the personal toll it was taking. I was like the proverbial amphibian in a pot of water that was heated so gradually I didn't realize I was destined to become some hungry diner's frog legs. I was the moth and the Renaissance Killer was the enticing flame. Cane's grip on me was so distant and invisible that it belied the type of control he still had over me. Little did I know that, instead of the release and freedom I sought, my voyeuristic journey into his world of weirdness would trap me in a tangled web of unwanted transformation.

As time passed, more and more information came to light. What is it about serial killers that warrant such interest and attention? We devote more time to their study than we do to Washington or Lincoln these days, or so it seems. Is it something as noble as seeking to uncover the root causes so as to prevent future suffering at the hands of these monsters? I seriously doubt it. That may be an element that motivates some of the more altruistic scholars and researchers but it can't explain the voluminous mounds of print and video ascribed to Cane's chroniclers. I'm convinced that the primary motivation is exploitive; aimed at creating wealth and fame from the bloody entrails of RK's victims. But there is something deeper and more disturbing at work. As crazy as it sounds, I think there is an element of vicarious satisfaction in all of us. While we would, heaven forbid, never perform such acts ourselves, reading about the animalistic exploits of someone else who crossed that chasm tweaks an unholy curiosity that sparks an unspoken, perverse pleasure. It's the same pleasure that drives people into movie theaters to derive entertainment from the dramatized but horribly authentic torture, dismemberment and mutilation of innocent victims. True life occurrences are even more powerful. They speak to the fascinating, dirty little truth that we all know but none would ever admit: we realize that, deep down, we're all capable of becoming, Manson, Gacy, Bundy or Cane. In any case, my personal theories aside, one thing was sure; there was enough information churned out over time by the media and experts in the fields of medicine, psychology, criminology and elsewhere to fill a small library. My task was to gather, glean and make sense of it. The following brief, synopsis paints a pretty accurate picture of the making of RK, if I do say so myself.

Three years after Syl and I came into the world, Charles was born to Gerald and Daphne Cane in 1960, the year they graduated from college together. Both were raised by parents of Bud and Lilly's generation, his blue collar and hers well to do, in strict households with very traditional values they would later deem puritanical. In college, Gerald and Daphne appeared to be the perfect match. Both gravitated toward the social sciences, embraced the ethos of the Beat Generation as it morphed into the 60s counter-culture and adopted activist causes that allowed them to thumb their noses at the bourgeois norms of their parents. In their anti-establishment fervor, they were determined to break from the past in raising little Charles according to the new zeitgeist. Even his name was chosen as a stamp of secularism to free him from the religious convictions of his grandparents. Rationalism replaced God. The only nod grudgingly granted to conventional wisdom was their marriage shortly after graduation and months prior to Charles' birth. But this was done for practical reasons in a civil ceremony rather than in deference to any sincere religious or moral obligation.

Charles was raised in a protective bubble by his overbearing parents to shield him from the dangers of, in their view, a decadent society rife with corruption, imperialism, racism and sexism, built on a military-industrial complex propped up by religious superstitions aimed at oppressing the masses at home and abroad. In such a world, there was very little room for anything associated with their repressive past, including grandparents. Daphne's parents died very young in an unfortunate accident but Gerald's folks were alive and kicking and lived much too close for comfort. During the infrequent visits when Charles was allowed to spend time with them, Gerald and Daphne provided close supervision to make sure Grandma and Grandpa didn't impart any of their anachronistic views or values to Charles. He was the very center of attention in this sheltered, little, new age world and Gerald and Daphne worked tirelessly to see that Charles' self-esteem was constantly cultivated.

Eventually, cracks and fissures began to threaten their utopia. Gerald went on to earn his PhD in sociology and was consumed by self-aggrandizement in academia. In spite of the feminist ideals they both trumpeted, when push came to shove, Daphne's academic aspirations were sacrificed at the altar of motherhood. She had to be the primary care giver to Charles and, out of economic necessity, go to work to help support Gerald's scholarly pursuits. This failure to walk-the-walk caused her much disillusionment, bitterness and frustration. But this was not what caused their split. Their union did not dissolve as a result of their paths drifting apart, not even when Gerald began his dalliances with young co-eds. No, what really destroyed their family was a philosophical divide that widened with each passing day. They were living in two separate worlds; Gerald in a cozy abstract while Daphne ran the rat race. A funny thing happened as Daphne faced harsh reality and her maternal instincts kicked in; she began to see some of the wisdom of her bygone parents and their world view. To Gerald, the committed ideologue, that was the last straw, the unforgivable sin.

From Charles' perspective, his life was shattered and he was subjected to the worst kind of consequences; not only the tortuous rigors of joint custody but a venomous bitterness between his parents where he was constantly exposed to one downgrading the other in the cruelest terms. The greatest harm inflicted upon him was that each of his parents, perhaps out of guilt, redoubled their efforts to build up his self-esteem to compensate for the stigma of coming from a broken home. It was anything goes for precious Charles, a life devoid of any parental discipline and a shocking propensity for them to overlook any of his transgressions. They were unwittingly creating a megalomaniac. The only saving grace for Charles was that scheduling conflicts between the parents allowed more exposure to his surviving grandparents. Unfortunately, their lifestyles were so very incongruent to what he had known for so long that it didn't register with Charles. It only caused confusion, angst and deep resentment … against whom he was not sure; his parents, his grandparents or the world in general. In any case, it drove him further into his own little world. As he moved into his teen years and gained some independence, he avoided his grandparents and used his growing mobility and freedom to take advantage of his parents' busy schedules and growing lack of attentiveness. He had plenty of reason to avoid them anyway. Each of them remarried and he was troubled by the notion of them sharing a bed with a different partner. He couldn't stand the thought of his parents sharing such intimacy with someone that seemed so distant to him, so detached. It was not really the case since the step parents went overboard in trying to make him feel loved and wanted but, in his mind; they didn't come close to sharing the bond of a biological parent. For Charles it was all about him and these step parents were not up to the task. He was used to his parents revolving around him, caught in his inescapable gravitational pull. And, horror of horrors, these pretend parents brought other kids into the family; a most unwanted invasion of his inviolate territory.

Charles became a loner. He also became a master liar so skilled at concocting plausible reasons for his absences that neither of his two families suspected that anything was amiss. But it was; it certainly was. Charles had so much time on his hands and nothing fruitful to occupy the hours. With nothing constructive or productive to keep him busy he developed some very strange habits and interests to fill the void. In his world, he had absolute power and was the center of his universe. He was an angry potentate who needed an outlet for his wrath. Charles was never taught any empathy for others and never given the chance to develop a clear sense of right and wrong. His greatest commandment, planted deep in his psyche and cultivated ever so carefully, was to satisfy self. He discovered through some ghastly trial and error, first on tiny bugs and later on small animals, that he was gratified most when he inflicted pain and torture on other beings. It somehow allowed him to transfer his own pain and leave him with a euphoric sensation; one that was almost like a sexual release; one that later he would find could be heightened to ecstatic proportions when combined with actual sexual gratification. As he honed these skills, he experimented with some of the subtler talents he had gleaned from his father. He found that employing the use of psychological terror was, in some ways, more satisfying than inflicting physical pain. He delighted in cat and mouse techniques which became an entertaining outlet for his very creative and active imagination.

I'm no psychologist but I think Charles' sexual hang ups are understandable. His life was devoid of any formal religious training in the traditional sense. Make no mistake, he received religious instruction but it was a very different type of religion, centered in man rather than God. It denied the true God and gave man the capacity of a god. The golden rule was, to thine own self be true. It had to be very confusing for a young boy. His parents' words contained a false piety that encouraged doing the right thing while their beliefs and actions espoused an anything goes attitude … if it feels good, do it. While he was shielded from his grandparents and their out of touch views, Charles was smart enough to recognize that a keen difference existed. He couldn't quite grasp how his parents and grandparents could be so diametrically opposed but it was clear that something important was at stake and he was intrigued by his grandparents' taboo beliefs, however ill-defined they might be due to his parents' attempted speech and thought control. He wondered what his grandparents had done to produce such a violent rejection of their core values. Of course, he succumbed to his parents' will but always had an innate sense; call it conscience if you like; that there was something to be said for an old fashioned, monogamous relationship between a man and a woman. Over time, he received periodic reinforcement for this foreign notion. Most importantly, his grandparents seemed to practice what they preached and offered a good, loving example to follow while his parents drifted apart.

All of their preaching and protestations to the contrary could not cover up the plain and simple truth. Gerald and Daphne's marriage was crumbling in front of his eyes. Their arguments became more heated and their words harsher. As the battle lines were drawn and hardened, they demonstrated less and less interest in trying to keep their differences from Charles. Near the end, it became so bad that they actually preferred having him as an audience as if they were presenting closing arguments to the jury and Charles was the presiding judge. Gerald, the highly educated professor, presented the more cogent intellectual treatises that seemed consistent with the philosophies both parents had so enthusiastically inculcated into little Charles. Daphne seemed inconsistent now that she had abandoned much of the flawed ideology that didn't cut it in the real world. But mom's views seemed more genuine if odd in the context of Charles' upbringing while Gerald's cerebrally solid declarations seemed kind of hollow. This tug of war took its toll on Charles and finally resulted in irreparable damage when Gerald's unfaithfulness to Daphne came to light. Sure, it was very consistent with their anything goes philosophy but it just didn't seem right to Charles. What upset Charles the most was how it reflected on him. It always came back to self for Charles and he saw the infidelity as a personal indictment; obviously this was a failure on his part since his parents didn't love him enough to remain faithful and stay together for his sake.

Charles welcomed college as a way to get away from his parents and their faux families. He took with him the selfish secular mindset they had implanted in his brain but his inner most desire was something that would have astounded them. In spite of his hippy dippy, anti-establishment upbringing, the one thing Charles held most dear was the hope of finding his one, true love. In spite of all the disparaging remarks Gerald and Daphne hurled toward Gerald's parents, their example provided a lofty ideal that he secretly harbored; a cherished obsession. In his make believe world, with his wild imagination, he developed quite a strong relationship with the wholesome beauty he idolized from afar, my Syl. She never realized the impact she had on Cane, the intense feelings he had for her even though they had never spoken prior to that one brief encounter. She was the one. He was certain it was true love and that Syl would end his conflict and torment; he could settle into a good and decent life like the one his grandparents shared and live happily ever after in a fairy tale existence. Cane always occupied a private world, his alone, but had secretly prepared it, every aspect of it, to accommodate a partner someday. That day had come at last in the person of Sylvia Adams. It was love at first sight, no doubt about it. With Syl at his side, he would never have to worry about filthy desires. He would never be forced to give into the disgusting lusts his parents had succumbed to with his loathsome, hedonistic, vile step parents. Their love and devotion would be inviolate. When Syl innocently demurred, little did she know that anything and everything that could be considered good in Cane's make believe world came tumbling down.

Everything changed from that point on and Cane was set on a collision course with his unfortunate destiny. Campus life accommodated his lone wolf lifestyle without raising any suspicions. He was just a guy wrapped up in his studies. No one paid attention to a freshman anyway. He loved the freedom of college life. Charles thrived in academia. He had inherited a brilliant, if twisted, mind from his parents and felt comfortable in such an abstract world where no one could challenge his absolute authority. And his professors fawned over him; he seemed so focused and mature for a freshman and possessed a superior intellect that already allowed him to operate smoothly within their lofty circles. Such a talent was given a wide berth and he found that he could express strange ideas that were accepted as advanced and cutting edge. No one could have imagined the bizarre hobbies he practiced in solitude or the insane stirrings that were conjured up by his constant exposure to young pretties flitting about the campus. No longer did any woman evoke feelings of love in Charles Darwin Cane. That once in a lifetime opportunity had passed. Now other emotions were stirred; dark, contaminated malevolent urgings … but tempered with the clinical detachment of a careful, studious researcher. Soon he would be well on his way to becoming one of the most unusual and prolific serial killers of his time.

Cane was not quite ready though; first things first. He had to learn his craft and get in touch with his new feelings to understand the driving force that would replace the longings of love that had been dashed forever. It wasn't all that odd that, as a child, Charles had experimented with bugs. At some point, most boys pulled a leg from a daddy long legs spider to marvel at the way it twitched or pulled the wings off a fly to see if it could survive by walking. But most boys grew out of such cruel pursuits and learned to empathize with the smallest of God's creatures. Not Charles; no it was more than a way to satisfy boyish curiosity for him. He actually derived pleasure from it. Rather than growing out of a bad habit, he nurtured, grew and fed these feelings. For him, there was no satisfaction in dissecting a dead frog or fetal pig. Only live prey thrilled him; their pain gave him intense pleasure. If such behavior was strange for a boy, it was downright bizarre for a college man. He knew it was not only wrong but would be considered sick and demented by his contemporaries. Thus, he went to great lengths to hide his vile passion, taking careful precautions to conceal his monstrous experiments and dispose of the evidence.

What a thrill he derived! He learned early on that the psychological component was the key to his ecstasy. Before graduating from small animals like reptiles and rodents, he actually learned to use the maternal instincts of birds to heighten his pleasure by torturing little babies in front of their mother. Charles was one sick individual. When he graduated to cats and dogs, he used the stray population to avoid raising alarm, inadvertently assisting the Animal Control folks in Columbia. At first, he was content to conduct horrible physical experiments to learn how to maximize and prolong pain. He enjoyed dogs the most because they could register true fright in their soft, expressive eyes. Cane's efforts became more elaborate as time passed. He used his mechanical skills to devise ingenious implements of torture, in some cases trying to duplicate medieval contraptions of the Inquisition on a canine scale.   Still more gruesome than that was the devilish way he employed psychological terror. In a precursor to the level of sophistication he would later demonstrate in planning and cold premeditation, he captured half a dozen rats and caged them until they were famished with uncontrollable hunger. Then he found a stray cat which he somehow restrained with such clever bindings that the poor feline could offer no defense. He even muzzled the frantic animal so it could not attempt to ward off its attackers with hisses or howls. Then he cut into the cat's stomach to release enough blood to pique the interest of the ravenous rats. Cane didn't release the rats immediately but simply moved the cage closer to eliminate any fear they might have retained toward their natural enemy. The cat was enclosed in a wooden border that prevented any timid rats from retreating. At first they were extremely cautious and sprang from any twitch the cat was able to muster but eventually grew bold when it was apparent there was no danger. At first they nipped at the cat and licked up the blood but soon enough tore into the animal with a ferocity which aroused Cane as he witnessed the spectacle of the tormented tabby as it was disemboweled. He quipped, "I guess turnabout is fair play, eh kitty?" Yes, Cane was one sick puppy ... with sincere apologies to puppies everywhere. This is what lurked in the midst of the ivory towers of a peaceful, happy, Midwestern college campus, waiting to be unleashed on the unsuspecting student body.

There's no need to recount the six murders Cane committed while in school. Yes, I learned more details through my careful study of RK's background but nothing that might add to your understanding of the Renaissance Killer. I will spare you and myself from the additional trauma of further chronicling RK's handiwork. Suffice it to say that by the time he graduated from Mizzou, he was more than prepared to advance his *art form* to unprecedented heights in the annals of St. Louis, Missouri. There's also no need to revisit the spate of killings he choreographed from the time he settled in back home as a mild mannered, substitute teacher up to the travesty suffered by Syl and Devon. I was just thankful there was no video or other record of any kind to shed further light on what transpired that night. A blow-by-blow account was locked away in Cane's vaulted brain and would not be forthcoming while he entertained any slim hope of escaping death row. Thank goodness, for I really didn't want to know. My curiosity rested solely in cracking the code to Cane's motivation.

I was unable to draw any reasonable conclusion from my own extensive studies of the facts. For that, I turned to the experts who were not wanting for opinions. Some of the explanations disgusted me, others drove me to anger and many seemed quite foolish, lacking in any common sense. As I studied about serious mental disorders, I was surprised to learn about the seemingly subtle distinctions that differentiated the plethora of maladies that can affect the human mind. At first, it seemed like splitting hairs. I mean, can you really tell one kook from the next with such precision? But as I forced myself to dig deeper, the closer I came to trying to understand the Renaissance Killer. In my ignorance, I would have thought that perhaps Cane suffered from schizophrenia. Even when I first began to peel back the onion it appeared to make sense. There was no doubt in my mind that Cane suffered from a delusion when it came to Syl. And he also displayed personality disorganization when you compared RK's behavior to Charles' everyday demeanor. But that's about as far as the similarities went. Cane liked to play god but he didn't think he was God or felt he possessed any magical powers. He had an extremely elevated view of himself, a grossly inflated ego but his powers were rooted in very real and practical skills: a sharp intellect, steely self-control, superb analytical and planning skills and a mastery of concealment. Cane had tangible talents that could have served him quite well if he hadn't been such a warped creep. RK did not suffer from paranoia either. He took a very rational approach to recognizing dangers and taking appropriate steps to mitigate risks. Cane did not hallucinate. He didn't hear voices or get messages from the neighbor's pooch.

It was pretty depressing to study mental disorders … and kind of scary to think of all the ways we can get screwed up in the head. Come to think of it, it's a wonder that any of us turn out sane. My bitter feelings for Cane aside, I had a tough time buying into a lot of the mumbo jumbo. I guess I'm just a natural skeptic but many of the illnesses offered up by the so called experts to explain Cane's aberrant behavior struck me as pure baloney and poor excuses. There was depression in every form, obsessive compulsive disorders, anxiety, stress disorders, panic attacks, sleeping and eating disorders and every kind of phobia from spiders and mice to crowds and public speaking. To all of them I just wanted to scream, balderdash! Cane felt no anxiety. To him, killing was like a picnic in the park. His compulsion to kill was more than tempered by his keen senses of self-preservation and self-control. Stress? Hah! He was a pampered little brat that was handed everything on a silver platter. There was no sign of panic from this cool, calm, collected killer. RK certainly had no fear of spiders and snakes. It would make more sense to say bugs and mice should have had a phobia about him. There was no shortage of geniuses offering foolish explanations and flimsy solutions for RK: medical, chemical, environmental, physical and genetic. They were nothing but meaningless excuses aimed at explaining away the inexplicable. Maybe it made them feel safer somehow. It was a lot of hogwash.

However, there was one theory that intrigued me: Dissociative Identity Disorder. For lay people like you and me that means a split personality. Contrary to popular misconceptions, schizophrenia has nothing to do with DID. A split personality disorder refers to distinct identities or alter egos that develop as a result of some kind of traumatic experience, usually in childhood. In simplest terms, it means you have two or more persons occupying one body. To me that made the most sense when you compared Charles to RK. The difference was so profoundly pronounced that it had to involve a transformation akin to Jekyll and Hyde. One was a well-grounded, meek and humble public servant dedicated to the care of young children. Charles was pleasant, easy to get along with and, at times, quite charming. For all intents and purposes he was as normal as cherry pie. Then there was RK. They couldn't have been more distinct. But what caused the split that gave birth to a monster inside the body of such a milksop? That's what I needed to know.

There was little agreement among the experts when it came to DID. Many doubted whether it was a legitimate medical condition. Some felt that the symptoms were latrogenically induced by therapists. That's a very fancy way of saying a patient may exhibit split personality characteristics on the basis of the power of suggestion, even if it is not the intention of the physician. Opinions diverged especially when it came to the causes of DID. Some tried to tie it to other medical conditions like epilepsy. Others attributed it to electrophysiological dysfunction ... that's bad wiring to normal folks like you and me. Of all the explanations offered, the most common one was linked to some form of childhood trauma; abuse or more often sexual abuse. There was no documented evidence of direct abuse in Charles' childhood. But it was not too much of a stretch to see how he would have felt abused or traumatized emotionally by his parents' bickering, outright hostility toward one another and eventual split. Could he have been shattered by the acute sense of abandonment he felt when his parents divorced and introduced faux families into his life? Was he inadvertently subjected to a form of sexual abuse by overhearing the sounds emanating from the bedrooms of his mother or father with their new partners? It seemed entirely plausible but I still had my doubts. While Cane clearly exhibited a split personality, he didn't suffer comorbidity with other disorders or any of the associated symptoms that frequently accompany DID: headaches, pains, depression, anxiety, panic, memory loss or depersonalization. No, his memory was, unfortunately, fully intact down to the tiniest of nitty, gritty details. And the last thing you'd accuse him of was depersonalization or a lack of a strong sense of self.

What else did I have to hang my hat on other than DID? Sure, there were some puzzle pieces missing but, all in all, it was the most logical explanation available to me. I eventually chalked up any dissonance to my own inclination toward skepticism. It was just my nature to cry foul and hold myself and others to the standard of personal accountability that Bud and Lilly engrained in me. There were lots of kids from broken homes who didn't morph into vicious killers. Part of me still wanted to scream that there was simply no excuse for Cane; for what he did to my Syl and Devon. I wished for God to drop a lightning bolt on him and end his miserable existence. It was only fair, an eye for an eye, since Cane had torn my family apart like a bolt from the blue and left me rent inside. But then I caught myself again. Would that really settle things for me? Would it reconcile me to God if he were to fulfill my tit for tat desire? Would it bring back Syl and Devon and mend my internal wounds? No, I was still mired in my stubborn rebellion and thus had no choice but to seek a secular solution. Some of my doubts were satisfied when Cane was interviewed by medical professionals who shared new insights they were able to gain. Apparently, according to Cane, he had suffered severe abuse. First there were beatings at the hands of his father, whose temper and wine bibbing combined to provide an outlet for his rage against Daphne and the suffocating confinement of family life. Then later, in the final, shattering blow, his stepmother reportedly seduced him when he was a young teen and filled his head with confusion, oppressive guilt and perverse sexual desires. As this sank in over time, I slowly began to feel something short of empathy but closer to understanding.

5 Mirror Image

My studies had helped to satisfy my curiosity but didn't give me much peace. Over two years had passed since the murders but I was still a basket case and my life was pretty much a mess. A split personality disorder made some sense on the surface but, when it came to causality, I still had my hang ups. I really wanted to think that Cane was inherently good but had come to be dominated by his evil alter ego, RK. Such a thought held the possibility of somewhat restoring faith in my fellow man if not God. I truly wanted to believe that Cane did not start out as a bad seed but had been molded into a monster by unfortunate forces outside his control. It was much too painful and frightening to think that Cane was evil from the get go. That would lead to the unacceptable conclusion that anyone, including me, had the same demons lurking within. It just couldn't be so. I had no choice but to allow my reason to take over and accept a sensible, logical conclusion. But I couldn't remove the stumbling block of my memories of Syl and Devon and the atrocities committed by Cane. And, try as I might, I couldn't lift the suspicions I felt about Cane. What if he was using his intelligence and cunning to pull off a grand charade? What if he had duped the doctors with his stories of abuse to garner their sympathy and aid him in the process of appeals? Finding no solace elsewhere, I came to the conclusion that there was only one way to settle the question in my mind. I had no choice but to see for myself, person-to-person, mano a mano. That was the only way to continue the process of mending the terrible gash in my troubled spirit and making whole my shattered soul.

There was a lot of red tape involved in making the arrangements and it was not easy to get a private, face-to-face audience with Cane. I was almost denied but, oddly enough, it was Cane who influenced the decision. He argued enthusiastically for our confrontation, presumably to make amends and soothe his troubled conscience. Whatever the case, I was relieved to have the opportunity to meet with him and get the chance to exorcise my personal demons. Yet, as the day approached in early 1989, I was very nervous; unsure of how I would handle being up close and personal with such a hellion. The Jefferson City Correctional Center was an old, dilapidated state penitentiary that was on its last leg. It seemed fitting confines for Cane, the worst of the worst. As I was checked in and escorted through the dank labyrinth, my imagination conjured up the worst images of the freak of nature I would soon encounter. Two years later, I would flash back to this moment in seeing Starling approach Hannibal Lecter for the first time when Silence of the Lambs premiered. JCCC was not as gothic as Hannibal's loony bin and didn't have quite the same cast of deranged characters but it evoked the same foreboding sense of danger and its inhabitants, although perhaps less colorful, were more fearsome being in the flesh rather than on film. My mouth grew dry as beads of perspiration began dotting my forehead and I literally grew a little weak in the knees as we approached his cell. My first glimpse was a frightful image with Cane decked out in his prison jumpsuit and properly restrained in a stationary chair, as befitting some wild beast.

The door clanged behind me and we were alone. At least we shared as much privacy as was possible with a guard stationed nearby and a closed circuit camera following our every move. There was an uneasy silence as we awkwardly sized each other up and the room seemed to shrink and separate itself from every other noise and motion in the prison around us. I don't mind telling you that I was having second thoughts and wondered if it was too late to call the whole thing off. Then Cane spoke and broke the spell, "Thank you so much for coming to see me Mr. Newman." I say Cane rather than RK because, from the first utterance, it was clear I was being addressed by Charles Cane and not his alter ego. He was as polite, deferential and pleasant as he could be and put me right at ease. Well, maybe I was not truly what you would call at ease but, relative to the bundle of nerves I had been moments before, it's a pretty good approximation. I suppressed the urge to extend my right hand considering his restraints but offered some show of stilted cordiality, "Please, call me Twain." He responded in kind, "Thank you and please call me Charles." Neither one of us knew how to get to the business at hand so we made awkward attempts at small talk, "Twain, that's an unusual name." "It was my father's idea. It was his way of passing along his love for literature." Cane sensed a snippet of common ground and gestured with his head toward a proud but pitiful little stack of books, "As you can see, I have my own library of sorts and try to keep up on my reading." I cautiously stepped to the reading shelf and thumbed through a few selections, satisfying my curiosity along with the need to avoid painful pauses. It was an odd and revealing collection including mostly novels dealing with DID: Flora Schreiber's 1971 tome, Sybil; Thigpen and Cleckley's 1957 case study, Three Faces of Eve, later immortalized in film and 1954's Bird's

Nest by Shirley Jackson that was also transferred to the silver screen in Lizzie. Topping off the list was Robert Louis Stevenson's timeless classic, The Strange Case of Dr. Jekyll and Mr. Hyde. If I would have been better informed, I would not have passed over Dr. Hervey Cleckley's 1941 novel, The Mask of Sanity. Little did I know that the pioneering psychologist used this book to describe the concept of a psychopath: someone who is able to engage in deviant behavior while exhibiting no outward signs of a cognitive disorder such as delusions or hallucinations. It detailed how someone without any sense of conscience and totally devoid of empathy for the sufferings of others could commit the most heinous acts without a touch of remorse while otherwise appearing completely normal in day-to-day trivialities.

At that moment, in my literary element, with my synapses firing to reclaim recollections from these books, I regained my footing and summoned the courage to proceed. With Jekyll and Hyde in hand to provide a literal segue, I probed gingerly, "Charles, this is awkward for me as I know it must be for you but there's something I'd like to explore; something that I hope will help to put our unfortunate past behind us as much as possible." He nodded with eyes full of shame and repentance and I was encouraged to forge ahead. "As you can imagine, I have been terribly troubled and unable to find any peace for the past two years. I have tried over and over to make sense out of what happened but to no avail, that is, until fairly recently, when reports of your medical problems came to light." He sat attentive and contrite, hanging on my every word and nodding reassuringly. I looked at the book and turned the cover toward him, "How appropriate it is. I'm guessing your choice of books is no accident. You must be searching for answers just as I am. Stevenson masterfully explored the mystery that has intrigued mankind for ages. What is it that drives us to do the things we do? What is it inside us that sometimes lead us to commit the worst atrocities imaginable?" I paused but he remained silent. Cane knew that I was on a cathartic roll and allowed me to spill my guts. "That we commit such acts is proof unto itself that man is perfectly capable of incredible evil. But the question remains, why? Stevenson sought a physiological answer and remedy. But today we know it is not that simple. It's a much deeper, darker and complicated task to unlock and explore the caverns of our minds. Today, we finally may be on the brink of a breakthrough, or so it seems. That, Charles, is my primary purpose today; to hear firsthand what has led you to this tortured existence, with two persons inhabiting one body, one good and one evil."

Cane inhaled and exhaled as though he was preparing to lift a great weight, "Thank you for being so forthright, Twain. I'm truly sorry for the pain and torment I've put you through; you and so many other people. I recognize the unforgiveable, unnecessary hardship I've placed on you. While I know it's of no consolation to you, for what it's worth, it has been unbearable knowing that I am personally responsible for all the heartache and sorrow I've caused." He was overcome with emotion and paused to cover his eyes and wipe away the welling tears. "I too have been horribly disturbed these past two years. Until recently, I lost my will to live. The only thing that kept me from totally losing touch with my sanity has been the doctors. I'm so thankful for their efforts in helping me to understand. I know there's no excuse for what I did and never will be but at least I am starting to see what drove me to such depths. I've come to grips with the incomprehensible truth that there are two people inside me. Thankfully, the doctors are helping me, me Charles, to take a stand and put my *Hyde* in his place; to bury him forever. You see Twain, they showed me that, in order to confront the killer in me, I had to accept my past.

They've helped me to finally admit what my parents did to me and, more importantly, to forgive them and start the healing process." There was another long, emotional pause before Cane could continue, "I don't expect you to forgive me. I can only hope that you will understand somehow."

I was completely floored and had to take my seat again. A flood of emotion washed over me in a cleansing wave and began to erode the layers of cynicism, bitterness and filthy hatred that had caked my soul. Like the Wicked Witch of the West, I wanted to shriek, "I'm melting; I'm melting" but with joy rather than dismay as my stone cold exterior bubbled to the ground. I felt such a relief. An incredible weight was lifted off my shoulders. For the first time in two years, I did not recoil in anger from the bright prospect of peace. I could feel my wounds binding up in a miracle of regeneration. That single, solitary prison cell in the unforgiving confines of JCCC was an odd place to have such a religious epiphany. This was another, more magnificent defining moment in my life, one that would mark the way for a new beginning. I felt such calm and joy that I could only sit back and smile. I had confronted the killer, face-to-face, and was able to smile, genuinely smile. Then Cane smiled back at me. At first it was the smile of someone at peace, someone redeemed. And then it changed. It was terrifying to witness. His eyes squinted with heavy, shadowy lids and his lips curled mischievously at the corners as if they were two dead fish rotting in the sun.

Before he spoke, I was already hurtling back to earth. Just the look on his face told me I had been thoroughly duped. I experienced such dread it was as if I had awakened from my worst nightmare only to have my relief stolen by the realization that it wasn't just a horrible dream but reality. Yes, before he uttered another word, I knew I was in the presence of the Renaissance Killer. My euphoria evaporated in an instant as if someone had pulled a giant drain plug. Like a malevolent spirit, a cold chill descended upon the cell. I reflexively sprang to attention sitting completely erect in my chair. A bubbling cauldron of mixed emotions prevented me from responding: shock, fear, disappointment, revulsion, anger and panic. I gripped the arms of my chair so tightly that my knuckles cracked audibly and turned white as tombstones from the intense pressure. My eyes squeezed shut and I ground my teeth as I gathered myself and summoned what little courage I could find. It was enough to allow me to restrain my deadly urge to lunge at his throat and crush the last breath out of his miserable life. It was just enough for me to stare coolly into his gleaming eyes, not with the mindless anger I had flashed silently at his sentencing but true and just resolve that allowed me to utter one small sentence, "So, at last we meet Mr. Renaissance Killer."

He just stared at me with a sly smirk, relishing how he had fooled me. RK was savoring the moment and, it seemed, basking in the way his vaunted intelligence had triumphed again. RK couldn't have been more pleased with himself. Not only was he locked away in a tiny cell inside a maximum security prison but was completely restrained, unable to raise a hand against me. Yet, while seemingly helpless he presumed he had me totally under his control; the puppet master was pulling the marionette's strings while I helplessly danced to his every whim. Oh how I longed to wipe that smug look from his face. The longer he leered at me, the more strength I was able to gather until finally I was not only able to stand up to him but actually offered a taunt, "I'm surprised RK. I didn't think you had the guts to come out from Charles' shadow and show yourself. I thought you only crawled out of your hole to attack women, children and helpless old men." That didn't rattle him so I hit him where it hurt, "I guess you're not as smart as I thought. All you can do is sit there with that dumb look on your face. Oh yeah, you're some Renaissance Killer alright. You're some master ... the master of stupidity, that is." That one hit home. His smile receded completely and his face became a blank slate; as inexpressive as a corpse. Then a chilling transformation occurred. As if a switch was being flipped back and forth, his countenance oscillated between Charles and RK several times. The *special effects* were so compelling that I was convinced there were two people in the room with me. It was like watching Dr. David Banner become the Hulk, Lon Chaney Jr. the Wolf Man, Professor Julius Kelp the mysterious Buddy Love or ... Dr. Jekyll into Mr. Hyde. But it was happening right before my eyes without the aid of gamma rays, full moons or secret potions.

When the dial stopped spinning, I was alone with unpretentious, docile Charles Darwin Cane. He stared at me as if nothing had happened. I removed my hand from my mouth, heaved a cleansing sigh and asked, "Charles, what just happened?" He responded innocently, "What do you mean?" I probed, "You said you didn't expect me to forgive you but hoped I would understand you. Do you remember what I said to you after that?" He looked dumbfounded, "You just asked me what happened." In amazement, I wondered if it could be possible. I had read how split personalities could be so fractured that never the twain shall meet ... no pun intended, really. As the story goes sometimes, when one personality takes over the other flees so far into the subconscious it is left with a blank; suffering total amnesia toward anything perpetrated by the alter in its absence. That would explain a lot. How could someone like Charles give rise to the abominations of the Renaissance Killer? Perhaps, just maybe he had been totally unaware of RK's deeds the same way he had closed himself off from any memory of the atrocities his parents had committed against him. It was a defense mechanism, the mind's way of coping with something too awful to comprehend and accept. Yes, I was onto something and my reason took over again. That's why Charles was finally able to express contrition. The doctors had unlocked his chamber of horrors and helped him to cope with the terrible reality. But obviously, theirs was just a work in progress and RK was still at large, lurking in the recesses of Charles' mind. Unfortunately, judging from what I had just witnessed, RK was still, by far, the dominant alter. With that realization, an ironic twist occurred. I wanted to rush to Charles' defense, poor victim, and aid him in his struggle against RK. If only I could help him to stand up to RK and take back his life forever! Then Charles could finally find peace ... and me along with him.

In a thoroughly bone headed, amateurish move that I must have lifted from a b movie or some cheesy TV crime drama, I decided to call out RK. What was I thinking? And how would I accomplish this feat, by pulling a gold watch and chain out of my pocket to hypnotize Charles? Without a clue, all I could think to do is take the direct approach in my most stern, professional voice, "I want to speak to the Renaissance Killer." To my complete surprise, almost as if on cue, Charles' eyes began to flutter and rolled back in his head as his lids shut tight. Agonizing moments passed. Then they opened ever so slowly to reveal the killer's gleam and he uttered this snarky reply, "You rang?" Somehow, driven by purpose, I kept my composure in this parallel universe, "What do you want? Why are you doing this to Charles?" The transformation was captivating. Charles was nowhere to be found and I was sharing a dialogue with a completely different person. He spat back at me laconically, "Oh, innocent, little Charles ... poor baby!" It caused me to inch back in my seat involuntarily. He proceeded with spiteful venom, "That little twerp couldn't survive without me. I'm the only thing that keeps the little bugger from going off the deep end." I tried to keep a clinical edge, "When did you reach this conclusion?" "Thankfully for Charlie boy, I came to the rescue when the old man started using his head for a punching bag. If it weren't for me, Charlie would have wound up in a box, either from suicide or at the hands of that creep, Gerald. I also helped him deal with that sicko step mom from hell. I taught him how to grin and bear it and take advantage of the lecherous old dame's uncontrollable urges. Still, he was such a wimp, always wanted to run away and hide. So I let him. I had to take over time and again. And when I did, there was no more door mat Charlie. Since he couldn't take it, I showed him how to dish it out, in style. The jerk has a weak stomach though and would never go along for the ride. So, I'd go it alone, keeping all the fun and pleasure to myself."

The absurdity of the situation escaped me. There I was, talking to a non-person, an alter ego, as plain as day as if we were two blokes in a pub somewhere chatting it up over a couple of dark ales. My busied brain nonchalantly accepted the farcical fact that I had suddenly been endowed with Freudian powers that allowed me to unlock a psychological mystery that had stumped countless professionals. "So, are you telling me that Charles had nothing to do with the murders you committed?" RK blanched, "Whoa, now hold on. I wouldn't go that far. Sure, he didn't stick around for my masterpieces but he was my motivation. I did it for him, the little mouse, since he wouldn't stand up for himself." There was a pregnant pause as I stared at him in skepticism and disbelief, "Okay, okay, I guess it's fair to say he never wanted any part of the killings. But I was only doing it for him; what was necessary." My courage rose with my indignity and anger and I bore in, "Oh, you were only thinking of Charles, were you? You slaughtered innocent people out of your care and concern for Charles, eh?" I was boiling over at the preposterous premise, the unholy defense RK was attempting to push, "How, pray tell, did Charles benefit from your murderous rampage? Did it somehow compensate for his sufferings? Did it provide him safe refuge from the big, bad world? No, that's a load of bull crap and you know it, you sick freak! You didn't do it for Charles ... you did it for yourself!" I guess I didn't realize that reason was no longer my guide or else I would not have tried to debate motivation with a remorseless psycho.

RK kept his cool much better than I, "Say what you want but I know why I did what I did. I'm a product of this big, bad world and I gave it just what it needed, a wakeup call. Where were you, where was the world when Charles was being neglected, scorned and abused? You were all there going along with the program and laughing at his misfortune. There's only one way to teach you all a lesson and that's to visit some misfortune on your own doorstep. That's the only way to get you to look in the mirror. You have the nerve to call what I did a crime, an abomination? Well, I say I did the world a great service. Those people only got what they deserved." That was the last straw and I snapped at his final utterance, barely able to control my emotions, "How stupid do you think I am? You're a complete fool if you think I'm buying into your sick fantasy." My eyes were pointed daggers as I locked my gaze upon his like a laser beam and I trembled to contain the rage. He showed no fear or empathy, only calmly returning my glare. I spoke quietly, as if opening my mouth and lungs further would cause the pressure cooker to rupture and explode, "When you say they got what they deserved, am I to assume you are including my wife and son?" His response gave me pause and puzzlement, "No, they were different from the rest."

I was coming apart at the seams but was somehow able to hold it together a bit longer. It was my intense desire to find the answer to that one, burning question of why, "Go on." RK surprised me, "Hold on, I've got to find Charlie. He's the only one that can explain it." There was another long pause and spellbinding transformation that sucked the air and electricity from the room. When Charles opened his eyes, my blood pressure automatically dropped and fatigue replaced my adrenaline rush. I was back at ease in the non-threatening presence of Charles Cane. Then there was a new revelation that was inconsistent with everything that preceded it. It threw me off completely when Charles calmly advised me, "I just talked to the killer." I blinked repeatedly as if that would expel the confusion that gripped me, "I don't understand." Charles continued, "He filled me in on your conversation and asked me to respond to your last question." I was slack jawed and a thousand questions ran through my mind but could only mutter, "Why did the Renaissance Killer say that my wife and son were different from the rest?"

What happened next was more frightening than anything I've ever experienced, before or since. I was still with Charles but the air of innocence, sorrow and harmlessness was gone. It was definitely Charles, make no mistake, but he spoke in a different tone as he revealed the cruelest, most fiendish hoax of all, "Fun is fun but let's cut to the chase, you poor, dumb chump." As the ruse unfolded and he thoroughly desecrated the memory of Syl and Devon, I remained frozen, unable to summon anger or bring any other emotion to bear in my defense. I couldn't escape this defining moment as he opened his inner sanctum and revealed a truth more terrible than anything I could have imagined. I could offer no resistance but only sat and listened as if in a catatonic state as he disemboweled my spirit. I hesitate to share what he told me but, with my apologies, there is no other way for you to understand what happened to my life from that point forward. Charles continued in matter-of-fact fashion, "First things first, there is no difference between me and the Renaissance Killer. We are one in the same. This DID, split personality nonsense is a lot of malarkey. I went along with it, encouraged it for one simple reason, leniency. But here I sit on death row. Obviously, it didn't work so let's dispense with the charade."

Next, he motioned me toward his cot. "Step over to my cot for a moment, if you don't mind." I moved ever so slowly and cautiously, looking back repeatedly to make sure Charles didn't somehow break his restraints and jump me from behind. I was gripped by an irrational fear as if some cleverly assembled booby trap might await me. As I edged up to his bed he directed me further, "Lift up the back edge of the mattress and take a look. Go ahead, dummy." As I peeled it back, there was a bizarre assortment of spiders, roaches and even a little mouse lined up in the most disturbing, orderly fashion. Each small body revealed the signs of tiny tortures with detached limbs and some removed organs carefully arranged. As I recoiled, Charles barked out a command, "Careful, don't drop the mattress! Set it back down slowly so you don't disturb my guests." I turned and stared at him in disbelief and he belched an evil laugh, "There, you see, even in this place I can still enjoy my favorite pastime. But enough of that ... as I was saying, if you've seen one, you've seen us both. I am RK and RK is me."

Cane was no dummy so he knew he was blowing any chance at clemency but must have reached a calculated conclusion that it was never going to happen. It was that or more likely he had weighed the pros and cons and decided it was worth the risk to experience such pleasure again, the gratification that he could only get through the psychological torture of another human being, in this case me. As he spoke, I could see he was thoroughly enjoying the experience and wanted to savor every drop, "My father never beat me viciously the way I claimed; he was too much of a coward. And my hot step mother never boinked me; I wish. Sure, I had kind of a rough childhood with my parents always bickering. It was a loveless home and it tore me up when they split. But, hey, that kind of thing happens every day and the kids don't run out and start murdering people, right?" I couldn't believe what I was hearing but I just sat there as he chastised the experts and their conventional wisdom, "Those guys are so full of it. It was so easy to put one over on them. All I had to do was tell them what they wanted to hear. They didn't want the truth. It wasn't a big mystery. I was just a spoiled, little brat, a self-centered jerk who always got his way. I always had strange feelings as far back as I could remember; rotten to the core. If you want to fault someone else, you might say my parents didn't do enough to yank me out of the bizarre, little world I created for myself. But that wouldn't be fair either. I liked it there and never listened to them or anyone else for that matter. If you want to know who's responsible, don't look any further than right here."

Charles continued with his fascinating, brutally honest confession, "So now you know. There's no one else to blame. I was fully aware of what I did, down to the tiniest detail." He saved me the time of prodding him with the next question, "The only thing left to know is why; why in the world did I do it?" I nodded slowly as if to say, go on. He shot a rhetorical question, "Did I lack a moral compass? Did I have the capacity to distinguish between right and wrong? You're darn right I did. I fully realized each and every despicable act was evil from the time I planned them, during and after I carried them out. That's why I took such pains to conceal my identity. There you have it, okay? First I knew what I was doing and second I knew it was completely wrong. So, why, why, why did I do it? You want to know the truth? Here it is. I enjoyed it, every flipping second. It was a thrill, power, an ego trip and sex. It was better than sex! It doesn't get any plainer or simpler than that. I did it for my own excitement, stimulation, satisfaction, fulfillment and selfish pleasure. I liked it and didn't care one iota about my victims. If that's evil, then you're looking at it." We were at ground zero and I was shell shocked by the concussion from the bomb he had dropped. He grinned while I stared blankly for what seemed an eternity until the guard broke the silence, "Is everything okay?" Startled to attention,

I assured him, "Yes, we're fine. We need a little more time, please." Then my brain reengaged and I turned again to Cane, "But you said there was something different about my wife and child."

Cane had not forgotten but wanted to save the best for last, "Oh yes; thank you for reminding me." As he continued, he peered at my face and watched carefully for my reactions. I tried not to let him read me because, by this time, I knew it would only feed his sickest desires. It was excruciatingly difficult not to react instinctively and violently to what he said next. I was the mouse to his feline ferocity as he toyed with my fragile emotions and, for the first time, revealed the last moments of Syl and Devon's lives. "There was something very different about my Sylvia," he purred. Just hearing him refer to her as his Sylvia made me wretch and I had to choke back the bile. Just thinking about Syl caused him to take on a different air, a more serious and less self-assured tone, "She was different than all the other victims for I truly cared about her. Sylvia was my one, true love." A dreamy look possessed him, "Oh how my life would have been different. If only she had accepted my love." Then menace returned to his eyes, "But, no, she threw it all away and destroyed my life in the process ... and for what; for you?" I resisted the urge to reason with him. There was no sense to be made of his madness. He would have killed me at that moment if given the chance but, since that was not an option, he wanted to inflict as much mental anguish as possible. He glared as if to say it was my fault, "Her rejection was the spark that started the flame that burned down everything. She set me on the path to destruction and walked away. Every death in my wake could be attributed to her." I refused to respond to the insanity but let him ramble. It was incredibly revealing but I couldn't keep my thoughts from drifting past Cane to a higher philosophical plane. What did this say about God and fate? This showed me that it was more than just a chance encounter gone awry. Cane was not just a love sick freshman when Syl gave him that gentle, thoughtful brush off. He was a ticking time bomb that God had placed in her path or, at least, allowed to cross her path. The disastrous outcome was no coincidence; it was inevitable.

Cane snapped me back to the situation at hand, "When you and Sylvia graduated, it was not quite out of sight, out of mind, but she melted into my subconscious. Sylvia was always a motivating factor but not a driving force. She got the ball rolling but I took it from there. With all of the other victims, I had one thing in mind, to inflict pain for my pleasure. There was nothing personal, really. It was all about me. They were just useful pawns in satisfying my personal whims. The theatrical flair I employed enhanced my arousal and provided a playful outlet for my active imagination but carried no other specific purpose except to cement my legacy and thumb my nose at the police. That's why I was able to control my urges and make such fools out of the authorities. That all changed when Sylvia came back into my life. From the moment I saw her back in St. Louis, I knew that I was at a crossroads and destiny was calling." He shot me a look that was just short of apologetic as he momentarily slipped into trying to justify his actions, "She still had a chance, you know. Things could have turned out differently. My hopes were actually quite high when you left her alone with me on that fateful day." There was a hint of accusation for me as if I somehow shared the blame for taking a business trip that left Syl and Devon unprotected. He drove his point home, "All she had to do was forsake you and the sham that was your marriage and pledge her undying love to me. That's all I wanted."

Cane became deadly serious as he prepared to move to the final act of this perverted passion play. A chill ran down my spine as he pronounced the verdict with the detached finality of a hanging judge, "But Sylvia chose her own fate when she extinguished the flame of our love. She didn't even attempt to humor me. At least she could have feigned conflicted feelings to help ease the blow. But instead, she offered a complete denial and ground my affections into the dust." Knowing what he had done to people when it wasn't personal, I shuddered to think what this monster put Syl and Devon through when such intimate anger was kindled. I didn't want to hear but I had to know. Cane pierced me with the first cut, "It was the first time I lost control." I tried to squelch a sharp gasp but enough sound escaped that it brought a smile to Cane's face. Like a child at an amusement park who boarded a thrill ride against his parents' advice, I wanted off but it was too late. All I could do was hold on for dear life as I gritted my teeth and clung to my chair with a death grip. Cane was at his own amusement park, firmly at the controls, "My urges were different this time, so strong that they drove me to take risks I never could have tolerated under normal circumstances. I didn't care about leaving clues or getting caught. It went way beyond sexual gratification or sadistic thrills. This was personal. I wanted retribution for the unforgiveable transgressions Sylvia had committed against me."

I nearly fainted, literally. Cane was paying close attention and would have none of it. He was so close to pay dirt. He gave me time to catch my breath and motioned for me to take a drink of water. Cane was determined not to be denied the climax, "Pay attention Twain! This is what you've been waiting for, what you need to know no matter how much it hurts." Anger was my friend again. It allowed me to persevere as I steeled my guts for the final twists and turns in this sickening roller coaster ride, "Go on." From that point forward, I suffered through the remainder in silence, taking each piercing lash stoically, staring motionlessly at Cane with death in my darkened, lifeless eyes. Cane the orchestra conductor figuratively raised his baton to bring the final movement to a close, "Listen carefully and take notes if you like for this won't be repeated again. It was so easy to invade your home undetected. I stared at Sylvia for the longest time as she slept peacefully in your bed; a celestial beauty. Oh, but what a startled look she had when I roused her from her slumber. It was pitiful the way she pretended not to recognize me. Even when I told her who I was and shined the flashlight for her to get a good look, she acted as if it didn't register. Of course, I persisted, taking her all the way back to our glory days at Mizzou until she dropped the charade. She calmed down considerably and we actually had a nice conversation."

I felt quiet pride for the bravery Syl must have mustered. It was just like her to keep her poise under the worst conditions. I knew her first thought would have been to remain calm to try to protect Devon at all costs. Cane proceeded cheerfully, "But, alas, we had to cut things short to attend to the business at hand. It was time and, out of the kindness and devotion I felt for Sylvia, I gave her one last chance to set things straight. I told her that if she agreed to leave you and Devon and take her rightful place with me, I would spare her. What a pity … foolish, stubborn bitch! She chose you and Devon over me. She got her just desserts, though. That was the only time I felt such uncontrollable anger. It was all I could do to contain myself enough to orchestrate my greatest masterpiece. With Sylvia as my inspiration, I was able to summon my genius to perform brush strokes like none before. I restrained her by tying her feet and hands to the bed posts before retrieving Devon. The poor, little chap didn't know what to think, being wakened in the middle of the night by his substitute teacher. He was actually pretty calm and cooperative if disoriented, that is, until he saw his mother tied up in bed."

I turned my head aside trying to hide the pain only to prompt Cane to bark, "Stay with me Twain! You would have been so proud of our Sylvia," he mocked. I didn't give him the satisfaction of a reaction and he forged ahead with glee, "She was more concerned with her precious Devon than me, or even her own safety. Playing their emotions, their terror off of each other was the strongest pleasure I have ever experienced. That coupled with my personal attachment to Sylvia aroused me like nothing before or since. I tied Devon to the chair and placed him just right to get a full view. He was so terrified he peed all over himself." Cane laughed out loud before proceeding, "When I began to undress Sylvia, exposing that magnificent canvass, Devon sobbed uncontrollably. She was a trooper though. Her composure really was amazing as I exposed myself and fondled and toyed with her before mounting her. Mind you, I'm not vain enough to think she wanted me or really enjoyed it. No, she didn't fight me at all because she knew it would only make matters worse for Devon. If only she had recited my name in passion over and over but she might as well have been a corpse. Of course, I've had my way with the dead before so I ought to know, right? But forgive me for digressing. The only sound she uttered was to tell Devon, 'It's okay, baby. Mommy is all right.' When I finished with her, I was left with a critical decision since I had not planned things out in advance."

Cane sighed easily as if he was catching his breath in a game of croquet, "It was actually pretty easy. Could I inflict more pain by killing Sylvia or the boy first? Killing Sylvia first would have terrified Devon and scarred him for life ... but what pleasure is there in ruining a life that was destined to end so soon? No offense, but I had no personal connection to your spawn. I cared for him about as much as the rest of my students, which is to say, not at all. But Sylvia, dear Sylvia ... with her it was personal. Torturing her mind was so much more appealing, certainly more pleasurable than the physical pain I could inflict upon her. So I asked her again if she would reconsider and pledge her everlasting devotion to me for the sake of sparing Devon's life. Of course, by that point she was more than willing to do so. But I knew her promise was a hollow one. Two can play at that game. So I gave her a glimmer of hope before killing Devon and dumping his head next to Sylvia's. Oh, if you could have seen the look on her face then! Of course, I didn't behead him while he was alive. I'm not a monster. No, I choked the life out of him while Sylvia accompanied me with a symphony of screams. It was a sweet concerto."

Cane had succeeded in destroying me and the last vestiges of Eden, the life I had known with Syl and Devon. The only thing that prevented me from blacking out or succumbing to my own animal instincts was the single hope that remained. One solitary thought forced me to endure ... the vision of Cane's execution. Cane droned on to the end but it barely registered for I was numb to his ability to inflict more pain. It wasn't so much that I was impervious to his tongue lashing as I was just spent; physically, mentally, psychologically and emotionally. He had put me through a marathon of horror and I was crawling toward the finish line. At the same time, Cane was the picture of vitality, gaining strength with each and every word. If not restrained, I believe he would have skipped with joy and merriment as he achieved his crowning glory. Then Cane feigned resignation and regret, "You know Twain, my pleasure ended before Sylvia's death. It ended with her screams and the petrified look on her face as I finished my work on Devon. After that, it was quite odd. She was mostly mum and unshakeable after that. When I flashed the knife before her eyes she didn't flinch. It was as if she welcomed the prospect of death no matter how grim." Then Cane gave me a look that was as close to sincere regret as was possible for him, "it was such a pity. Poor Sylvia was a fool to the end, placing her misguided hope in the opiate of religious nonsense. She prayed to her God but it didn't help her. He didn't come to her rescue. But, then again, she didn't ask for God to strike me down. Maybe she realized deep down there is no power in myths. You'll be pleased to know that instead she said a soft prayer for you, asking God to keep you safe and steadfast in the faith." Cane guffawed at that one and proceeded to mock, "Then came the best, the all-time whopper. When I placed my hands around her throat to draw the final curtain, Sylvia said, 'Please forgive him, Lord.' Can you imagine that, Twain? Now you tell me, which of us was mad?" He laughed with derision before heaving a dispirited sigh, "She stole my last ounce of pleasure. Normally, when I strangle someone to death, there is an incredible rush as I peer deeply into the frightened, pleading eyes and watch the life escape them. But with Sylvia, it was peaceful repose."

Cane was not quite done. He had to finish this once and for all and share every last detail, "As I said before, it was different with Sylvia. I had no urge to mutilate her body which was still quite beautiful. But my playful side took over and I wanted to demonstrate my sense of humor to the police. You know what they say about all work and no play.

That's when I got the idea to take Sylvia's lovely head off and I carried it along with Devon's and ventured over to your mantle and replaced their likenesses with the real thing. Now that's what I call a family portrait." He giggled and then tried to delight me with a witty pun, "Sylvia and Devon were not the only ones who lost their heads. I was so overcome by the whole experience that I became very sloppy. Although I had used my only condom before, I couldn't resist one more fling with Sylvia's headless body, leaving my DNA behind. Then, since I had not thought to bring a copy of a Renaissance masterpiece, I decided to make one of my own, an RK original. I thought it would be appropriate, as an elementary school teacher, to finger paint on the wall using Sylvia's blood. To get a better feel for my work, I removed my rubber gloves leaving numerous fingerprints. If that was not enough, I stole Sylvia and Devon's pictures from the mantel to decorate my own home. I'm not sure what caused me to overlook such obvious clues. Maybe I wanted to get caught, eh? Perhaps something told me that I might as well quit because I'd never top my last masterpiece."

Cane finally stopped and just sat there peacefully staring at me with the satisfied smile of a triumphant warrior gazing down at the broken body of a conquered foe. I had nothing; there was a complete void inside me. Everything vital had been removed by Cane and the emptiness was overwhelming. But such emptiness leaves a vacuum that must be filled. By the laws of metaphysics, something had to fill that space and, unfortunately, it was anger. From out of nowhere it swirled and gathered like a celestial dust cloud from a distant galaxy. As it spun and twisted and collapsed in on itself, the power and force intensified. Then, with locomotive force, it rushed into me bringing reanimation. I arose from my chair like a phoenix and towered over Cane like a colossus ready to stamp out a bug. A demented smile creased my lips as I placed one claw over his mouth and the other across his larynx. I began to shake with fury. Then I stopped with the suddenness of a meteor crashing into the earth. My reason took control. No, it wasn't the sympathy of a man of faith or the sane logic that two wrongs don't make a right. It was nothing of the sort. I was possessed by the warped rationale of a deadly predator bent on vengeance. A little voice inside my head told me to bide my time. If I acted rashly now, the guards would be alerted and Cane would be rescued before I could complete my task. Then I would be denied access forever. I would never be able to relish the one thing that was now front and center in my life. For now, I would have to be patient. Knowing that someone was at the other end of the closed circuit camera, I released my grip, smiled pleasantly as if I had just been kidding around and playfully patted Cane on the cheek as I stepped back from his chair.

I calmly spoke the following pronouncement, "Charles, don't worry, I'm not going to harm you. That wouldn't be right, would it? No, that might get in the way of the greatest day of my life. I plan to be there to watch them when they stick those needles into you and bring an end to your miserable life. Oh, that will be a glorious day that I will enjoy like no other. Yes, I will be there to send you off to hell." The one thing Cane could not stand was the thought of losing control, especially to someone like me who had been putty in his hands only moments before. His smug look of self-assurance gave way to fear and uncertainty as he tried to regain the upper hand, "Look at you Twain. Take a look in that mirror right there, I dare you." I took him up on his challenge and sauntered over to the mirror with the graceful ease of a man in control. Then I placed myself at an angle where Cane could see me staring back at him from the mirror and I smiled. It was a demonic grin from a face I didn't recognize. Cane still struggled for psychological supremacy, "Take a good look in that mirror, Twain. What does it say? I'll tell you what it reveals, loud and clear. We're both the same; you and me. There's no difference at all. I'll see you in hell, my friend." I turned from the mirror and faced away from Cane. His final rant gave me a slight pause and I didn't want to give him the satisfaction of seeing any hint of indecision on my part. I didn't say another word to Charles Darwin Cane. I kept my back to him as I called out, "Guard, we're finished here."

Part 2 - Final Parting

6 Adrift

The pages of the calendar began to peel off in a blur after that. I had no point of reference in my life to gauge time as the next few years passed by. My career was stuck in neutral and the agency floundered. Instead of being the driving force, I was a drag on the good efforts of others. It took a heavy toll on the business because loyal, talented employees lost heart and began to leave for greener pastures. Losing friends didn't cause me consternation because any sincere, emotional attachment had been eroded by the watershed that occurred during my meeting with Cane. My heart just wasn't in my work. The only time I took a genuine interest was when my personal finances were threatened to the point where I might not be able to sustain myself. But, you might ask, for what? Good question, my friends. There was only one thing that kept me going. I had to survive to see Cane die like a dog! Isn't that an odd turn of a phrase? Who wants to see a dog die? Sadly, I didn't care much about dogs or people but at least dogs didn't deserve to die. There could be no pleasure in the death of a cuddly pooch. Putting down the worst, most vicious canine would never elicit the kind of amusement and delight I would someday experience at the execution of Cane.

There was always a question as to whether I could survive long enough to reach my goal. I'm not sure why we carry on the debate over capital punishment in this country. Hasn't it been effectively wiped out already? That's how it seemed to me. Every day the news was rife with reports of vile crimes, rapes and murders. How often did you hear of a report of an execution? And when you did, on those rare occasions, the story didn't dwell on the crime or the suffering of the victims. It always turned to our inhumanity toward the poor criminal. It made me sick to see the images of bleeding heart, foolish do-gooders marching around and carrying signs on behalf of the monsters. Oh how I wished the shoe could be put on the other foot to give them a taste of what I had experienced. Then maybe they wouldn't be so generous and holier than thou. Every day, the victim's dial spun like a fourth of July pinwheel with the count going ever higher. But the wheel of justice turned at a snail's pace. After waiting at least a year or two for a trial and sentencing, the fun was just beginning. The endless appeal process went on forever. It's no wonder our prisons are overcrowded. When you look at the scale of justice in America, it is pitched completely to one side, the left side. On the high end, you have the pitiful few criminals who receive their just reward. On the opposite end rests a mountain of victim's corpses and the lifeless souls of their surviving loved ones.

Another thing that drove me up a wall was the treatment afforded to such animals. JCCC was no picnic but shortly after I met with Cane, he was moved along with sixty nine other death row inmates to a brand, spanking new facility in Potosi, Missouri in April of 1989. Oh, and by the way, they decided to stop calling them death row prisoners and instead adopted the term capital punishment inmates in order to, I surmised, not offend their delicate sensibilities or cause them any undue distress. Our contemporary prisons have a certain panache with modern conveniences exceeding some of the better hotels I've occupied. It's not a bad gig really. You get three squares and the food's pretty tasty. A lot of thought goes into the menu to ensure variety and nutrition. There are plenty of distractions to ward off boredom and I'm not just talking radio, TV, books and such. The educational opportunities exceed those afforded by many of our dismal public schools. For the less cerebral, there are excellent facilities to maintain one's fitness. We wouldn't want to deny an inmate the chance to maintain a buff exterior and imposing physical strength for their reentry into society; would we? For the ambitious cons, there's also plenty of commerce inside prison walls, legitimate and otherwise.

To be fair, many of these privileges came with strings attached. Some of the perks were only dispensed with good behavior. As long as a bloodthirsty, remorseless murderer kept his nose clean, he could earn all kinds of goodies. Of course, it was different for the capital punishment inmates. But even they could earn most of the same privileges if they gained enough prison bonus points. The only real detriment to being a CPI was the limitation on getting into the social scene. At Potosi, they were housed in two separate wings that surely cramped their style. It must have been hard for a bon vivant to thrive under such conditions. But the ever compassionate authorities who ran the system gradually made amends for this travesty and eliminated the terrible inconveniences it caused the CPIs. At first, they conducted a sociology experiment by allowing them to eat in group settings. Once that proved successful, they expanded the program to include escorted trips to the gym and then, get this, the law library. Eventually, they went so far as to allow the CPIs to take jobs such as working in the prison's laundry room. It got to the point where they said, what the heck, and fully mainstreamed Charles and his CPI pals into the prison's general population in January, 1991.

I knew this because I watched like a hungry hawk. As the sole focus of my miserable life, I paid strict attention to everything concerning Charles Darwin Cane. I'll admit it, it was an obsession. Sometimes it's good to be obsessed with something. If it were not for my one desire to see him executed, I would never have survived. It was a most unpleasant obsession though. The worst thing about it was the uncertainty. There was no way of knowing when the execution would finally take place. And even more troubling was the faint prospect that somehow, if this kabuki dance called justice went on long enough, Cane might just escape the fate he deserved so much. I tried not to let it creep into my brain but that thought brought me more sleepless nights than my worst nightmares. What if the death penalty was revoked in Missouri? Or what if Cane was somehow able to win clemency as time passed and memories faded? That would never happen as long as I was there to provide my testimony. That's what kept me going in spite of everything else. I was no better than an animal in that regard, reduced to a beastly existence driven by blood instinct alone, the instinct to survive and stalk my prey.

Instincts are a powerful force but they cannot produce love. As my idyllic life with Syl faded further in the past, unwanted but inevitable urges returned to my loins. I say unwanted because the prospect of socially reengaging with a woman; or anyone else for that matter; nauseated me. As bad as I needed female companionship to put it in the politest terms possible, I couldn't stand the thought of the courting ritual. I didn't want a relationship, if you get my drift. At times, I actually considered prostitution but couldn't quite bring myself to go to that extreme. It's not that my high morals were impenetrable but I hadn't sunk that far. The remains of my conscience had some effect but, in all honesty, I don't know if I would have been so pious without the fear of exposure, arrest or disease, let alone the cost. Well, you know where the story ends. It was only a matter of time until my lust overtook my aversion to human contact on anything but the most casual level. I bit the bullet and decided to play the game.

All I had to figure out was how to meet a nice girl who had no compunction against casual sex. I ignored every reasonable guidepost and adopted a game plan with the highest odds of failure: bar hopping. To me, it was a no lose situation. If I didn't meet the girl of my dreams, at least I could drink myself into oblivion. So what if it was bad for my health and career? I had no ambition and couldn't sleep anyway so why not while away the hours getting ripped and looking for Miss Right? In any case, maybe somebody up there liked me or I was just one lucky son of a gun because I struck gold right out of the chute. Sally was cute and attractive but not really into the bar scene. What drew me to her is that she seemed so out of place ... and she was. She had been pressured into attending a happy hour with co-workers from her new place of employment. She had been told that such social networking was important for fitting in and avoiding being shut out when opportunities arose at work. It didn't take long for her to figure out she had been fed a line of baloney by guys who wanted to fire on her and gals who needed a partner in crime. Sally retreated into a shell as the group got rowdier and was looking for a polite excuse to take her leave. Watching from afar, I could tell something was wrong and she looked so uncomfortable and vulnerable that I mustered the courage to approach her, "Hi, my name's Twain. This place is awfully noisy, crowded and smoky. I couldn't help but notice that you seem about as happy to be here as me. Would you care to join me for a cup of coffee at someplace a little more laid back?" She was not the type of girl to fall for a pick up line or to run off with strangers but I guess I seemed harmless enough and she saw it as a way to escape without offending her co-workers. Out of courtesy, she stepped aside to let a couple of the gals know she was leaving with a *friend* and they gave her a wink and thumbs up to affirm their understanding as if she was some type of smooth operator.

Once we got out the door, her relief turned into worry as she wondered whether she had just jumped out of the frying pan into the fire. I sensed her concern, "You seem to have second thoughts. Hey, if you just want to leave, I'll understand." The wheels turned as she fret over the prospect of being rude and then smiled demurely, "Oh, I guess a cup of coffee couldn't hurt and anyway I want to find out how you got such a funny name." I laughed at her innocent barb, "Okay, it's a deal. How about if we take my car and I'll bring you back to your car when we're done?" The warning light went on again and she subconsciously gripped her purse tighter which made me wonder if it contained pepper spray or one of those press button alarms. After a moment, she relaxed again and away we went. We hit it off right away. When I told her the motivation behind the name Twain, she giggled and asked me to guess her middle name. Figuring some connection I blurted, "Let me guess, is it Becky Thatcher?" She chided, "No silly, there's no Thatcher but my middle name is Rebecca. What do you say to that, *Tom Sawyer*?"

I couldn't believe my good fortune. Sally was not only pretty but sweet and innocent too. Right off the bat, I could tell she was someone I could admire for more than her good looks. I found myself getting lost in the moment, almost ashamed of the motivation behind this chance encounter in the first place. Then it dawned on me that I had something on my mind other than lascivious longings. To my amazement, I was interested in getting to know Sally better, nothing more. Don't get me wrong though. I was keenly aware of her allure in spite of her modest clothing although I tried not to dwell on her perky figure, silky skin, deep blue eyes, cascading locks or sumptuous lips. Her sex appeal aside, I couldn't go there. If she would have been flirtatious or given to any innuendo, things might have taken a different turn. But she was not that way. Sally was too wholesome; she wasn't a bloody steak and bourbon straight up; she was a glass of cold milk and a plate of warm, toll house cookies. Any remote thought of her turning vixen vanished when she inquired without any trepidation, "So Twain, are you a Christian?" She caught me completely off guard and I fumbled for an answer, "Why do you ask? That seems kind of personal, don't you think?"

I regretted it the moment those words passed my lips. Why in the world did I say that? Sally seemed sincerely disappointed at my overly defensive response, "Oh, I didn't mean anything by it. It's just that we were having so much fun I thought you might want to join me at our church social this weekend. I'm sorry if I put you on the spot." How could I tell her that I was embarrassed at my inability to give a plain and simple response the way I used to and say humbly with joy and thanksgiving, yes I'm a Christian? Still I hesitated awkwardly in introspection. What was wrong with me? Why couldn't I just say yes? I tried to shake the internal conflict this question roiled and ward off my anger against God that was suddenly bubbling up, "Sally, I'd love to go to your church social." She was a bit uncertain over what had just transpired but cheerfully replied, "All right then, it's at 7:00 on

Friday night. You can meet me there or, if you like, I'll pick you up on my way to the church. Here's my number if you need to call for any reason." I gave her my number and took her up on her offer of a ride. My heart leaped at the prospect of spending more time with Sally. Just like that, I had a new lease on life. When I dropped her off at her car, she instinctively saved me from an awkward moment by kissing her hand and sweetly transferring it to my cheek. I tried to keep my feet on the ground until she left but was already churning with anticipation, longing for Friday night to get here as soon as possible. I watched her prance to her car and, at the last second, she spun and said, "Just so you'll know, some of my church friends call me Sal."

I was dumbstruck and just stared in that general direction as she started up her car and drove away. It took me several minutes to break loose and head to my car. I drove home in a stupor and had difficulty getting to the door on wobbly legs as if I had been drinking heavily. When I collapsed onto the couch with head in hands, what a paradoxical image I must have cast. Had my best friend died or did I just meet the most wonderful girl in the world? It was hard to tell from the look of things. I should have been overjoyed at the prospect of developing a meaningful relationship for the first time in years.

This was my chance to pull myself from the morass and wash away all the cynicism, self-pity and hatred that had weighed me down for so long. Perhaps someone like Sally could even help restore my faith in God. But was that my real intention or was I caught up in some sick fantasy, trying to reconstruct my shattered past? It hadn't crossed my mind until she referred to herself as Sal. The similarities were just too vivid to ignore as mere coincidence: wholesomeness, modest beauty, innocent sex appeal, purity, trustworthiness and an open, rock solid faith. These were all the qualities I adored in Sylvia. It was all there, even down to the name ... Syl, Sal. I recoiled at the thought of being unfaithful to Syl with her clone, Sal. Was I projecting Syl onto Sally or had I been drawn by the amazing parallels?

I so wanted to be myself again but it had been so long I couldn't remember what it felt like to be normal. A couple of hours with Sally had done wonders for me. I felt an optimism that had vanished into thin air for more than five years. It was the kind of relief and exhilaration the Tin Man must have experienced when those first squirts of oil were finally applied to his rusty, frozen joints. But why couldn't I just go with the flow, kick up my heels and dance for joy? What was troubling me? The thrill of the long awaited emancipation of my imprisoned soul was being strangled in the cradle. Before my heart could burst into flight, an ominous cloud began to envelop me again. First, there was the weight of guilt. My conscience accused me over and over of betraying Syl and forsaking Devon ... all for my own selfish, sinful pleasure. Then there was doubt. Lust was clouding my judgment for no one could be as sweet and pure as Syl. There must be some dark secret that Sally was hiding that would dash my fledgling hope. Finally, the most powerful antidote for my foolish infatuation was my old companion, anger. How dare she try to coax me back into the church? Was this God's way of trying to tempt me to bend the knee to him again or overlook the tragedy he had allowed to ruin my life? The more I pondered this twisted line of logic, the hotter my anger burned. Before I knew it, I had descended all the way down into my familiar pit of bitterness and loathing. Any breath of hope was smothered in thoughts of Sylvia, Devon ... and Cane. Flashes of rage sprang up as I pictured that demon from hell enjoying undeserved comforts at the taxpayers' expense. I might as well have quaffed Dr. Jekyll's potion judging from the total transformation I had undergone ... from lovesick puppy to an apoplectic fountain of fury. My emotional counter-insurgency to the fleeting hope I had felt was so strong that I came close to completely losing control. But then I got back on track, to that one thought that gave me patience, control and single-minded focus on the only goal in my life that mattered ... the execution of Charles Darwin Cane.

Just then, my laser-like concentration was broken by the phone ringing. I didn't feel like talking to anyone but picked it up by rote thinking perhaps it was someone from the agency, "Hello." "Hey Twain, this is Sally. I'm sorry to bother you but it just dawned on me that I forgot to tell you what church I belong to ... silly me." If I weren't so screwed up in the head, getting a call from Sally would have put me on cloud nine. In one of the most regrettable moments of my life, I left my sullenness in command to offer a sour, spiteful reply, "Let me guess, you're a Lutheran." Sally tried to ignore my sarcastic tone, "How did you know?" Again, I let fly in a lifeless monotone, "Just a hunch." I was painting her into a corner and cutting no slack. Sally tried to be patient with me, "What's the matter Twain, is something wrong? You don't seem like yourself." Then I dropped the bomb, "Oh, you know me so well after all of two hours, do you?" Sally remained prim, proper and polite, trying not to reveal how much I had hurt her, "You know Twain, you're right. It was awfully presumptuous of me and I'm truly sorry. I had no right to invade your privacy. Well, I better let you go … so long."

My righteous anger abated just enough that I was able to realize what a heel I had been, "Hold on Sally, there's something I need to tell you." She was cautious, "Okay, what is it Twain?" I offered an awkward segue, "You're not from around here, are you?" Even after the unwarranted insults I had hurled at her, she still exhibited sweet charm by exaggerating her lilting drawl, "What was yawl's first clue, honey? I moved here for work about six months ago." I continued in a more apologetic tone, "No, what I meant was that you apparently don't know anything about what happened to me five years ago." "No, I'm sorry but I don't," she offered with sincere concern. I went on to explain my difficult past and the terrible misfortune Cane visited upon my family, without all the gory details. Under similar circumstances, many people would have sounded an immediate retreat from someone with such a disturbing past, but not Sally. She reflected the care and concern of a sincere Christian. What I did next could only have been said over the phone. I don't think I could have maintained such a stoic outlook if I had been face-to-face with those enchanting eyes. "Sally, you're the most wonderful person I've met in a long time. I hope this doesn't come across as weird but you're so much like my wife, Sylvia, it's uncanny. There's nothing I'd like more than to get to know you better but I think the timing is wrong. It's very hard to explain but I have a lot of personal problems I just can't seem to shake. My rude treatment of you earlier is just the tip of the iceberg. You would think that after five years I'd be ready to move on with my life but I can't. I'm trapped, living like a hermit, unable to maintain a relationship or even put my heart into my work. Bottom line, I'm a screwed up mess that you don't want, need or deserve in your life. As much as I'd like to have a friend like you again, it's just impossible for me right now. It would be best to say goodbye and move on."

Sally was so kind and understanding, "I'm really sorry for everything that happened to you and your family. I can only imagine the pain you're feeling. I wish there was something I could do to help you. I know we just met but for some reason I feel a real connection; I feel I have a new friend. It's my nature to try to be helpful but I can see that, right now, you need your space and I want to respect that. But if you get to a point where you need something or just want to talk … well, you have my number, right? Or if you ever want to worship, you know where my church is. That reminds me, I don't want to stick my nose in where it doesn't belong but of all the things you've shared, one thought really stands out in my mind. I hope this doesn't come across as preachy or pushy but it seems like you need to get things straight with God. I haven't gone through anything like you but I'm still sure of one thing; God loves you, Twain. Don't forget that."

We said our goodbyes and I hung up the phone, shutting the mausoleum door once again, shutting out the light. What a crying shame. She could have been a godsend, a safe port to rescue me from my stormy existence. However, as God's grace rained down on me, I continued to hold up a huge, black umbrella of resistance and unrepentant defiance and anger. My life still had no moorings leaving me adrift without an anchor in Sylvia or Sally ... or God. The rudder was frozen in place with my ship bound on its lone destination, a collision course with Charles Darwin Cane at his execution. The question remained, how long, and the enemy was time. I fell back into the same hopeless pattern of shutting myself off from the world.

If nothing else, I had learned my lesson about relationships. Never again would I venture out to tread the dangerous territory that led me to Sally.

At first, I tried to again lead the celibate life of a cloistered monk. Like before, that proved to be a losing cause as my sinful lusts grew stronger and, finally, uncontainable. I still couldn't bring myself to resort to prostitution so I gave into the next best thing; the one night stand. Unfortunately, I found our decadent culture to be very accommodating. Somewhere along the line, feminism had triumphed to the point where women gained true equality with men. Of course, they had to take quite a step down to achieve this goal but nonetheless they did. When it came to smoking, drinking, cursing, sleeping around and all other sorts of bad behavior previously in the male domain, the women had finally achieved parity. Let's hear it for the girls! Something about my upbringing still told me this was all wrong but I was able to sear over any remaining conscience with a steady diet of booze. It was incredibly easy to pick up women and even easier to get them into the sack. I didn't have to worry about avoiding meaningful relationships. There were plenty of gals who wanted the same thing I did, gratuitous sex and nothing more. In my debased condition, the irony escaped me. I had jettisoned a possible relationship with Sally over guilt that it would be a betrayal of Syl but somehow it wasn't unfaithful for me to go hopping from bed to bed with nameless partners.

153

In my increasingly rare sober moments, I did experience some guilt and remorse but I became a master of rationalization. If I didn't satisfy my natural desires, how could I focus on my job and other responsibilities? What a joke! If I had an employer besides myself, I would have been fired. My productivity was so lousy, I should have fired myself. And what did I mean by my other responsibilities ... wasting money in bars, trolling for trollops, ignoring my family or barely dragging myself out of bed and failing to shave most mornings? The only lucid thought I ever entertained was how I might best enjoy the execution. And the only productive work I truly enjoyed was tracking every detail in Cane's life.

I had given up any pretense of religion. My attendance dropped to nothing and I became the subject of repeated evangelism calls. It got to the point where I refused them completely and in a last ditch effort, the church resorted to trying to reclaim me through Bud and Lilly. How embarrassing that must have been for them to have the church seeking their help with their prodigal son. Even in my apathetic state, it tugged at my deteriorated heartstrings to see my parents suffer such indignity. But it wasn't enough for me to at least put on a show and get my tail into church on an occasional

Sunday. Instead, I took the coward's way out and requested a transfer to another Lutheran church in the area. I had no intention of attending there either but it would get Bud and Lilly off the hook and the church off my back. Yes, I was only putting off the inevitable but I had a plan for that too. I figured it was kind of like a deadbeat who runs up an unmanageable credit card debt and just opens up a new account with another bank and then another. Of course, that kind of Ponzi scheme will eventually catch up with you and bury you under a mountain of debt or bankruptcy but I wasn't thinking that far ahead. What I should have done was to speak with my pastor and seek his help and guidance for my troubles but no. I'd rather go it alone and bounce from one church to the next like a spiritual flim flam man. That was smart of me, wasn't it?

Growing up, we were such a tight knit family. My parents were such a treasure. Later, we remained ever close with them, Syl and I, and even more so when Devon came along. Shutting out my other relatives and friends was bad enough but the way I treated Bud and Lilly was a travesty. They had always been there for me through thick and thin and had never steered me in the wrong direction. I could always count on them for good advice and a helping hand. As much as I may have chafed at it, Bud's tough love proved to be the best medicine when I was growing up. I realized this most clearly when the tables were turned and I had to discipline Devon. It made me appreciate Bud all the more knowing the type of love it takes to do the right thing when you'd prefer to take the path of least resistance and cut your little buddy a break. Somewhere inside my stubborn, stony heart, I knew the best thing I could do would be to open up to Old Bud and seek his sage advice. But I couldn't help myself. It's no wonder that I was my own worst enemy. Why would anyone expect me to love, honor and obey my dear, old dad when I held my heavenly father in such disregard? Someone with the audacity to shake his fist at God would have no problem in disrespecting loving parents.

They say that drug addicts and drunks have to hit rock bottom before they can wake up and seek help. I was pretty low but not quite at rock bottom. However, the next episode got me a might closer. Bud and Lilly were a long way past being night owls. If they stayed up until 11:00 on a Friday night, it was a special occasion. As for me, I might as well have been back in my early twenties. When they were hitting the sack, I was just getting cranked up. They knew I was no choir boy but the depth of my problem was largely left to their imagination. It was no secret that I had dropped out of church and avoided family except for mandatory appearances on holidays. Bud and Lilly were older now but not stupid. They could connect the dots. Bud peppered me with enough savvy questions at Christmas, Easter and Thanksgiving that he could tell my career was on the rocks. He didn't bother to harbor his old literary dreams for me anymore. Bud would have been happy just to see me on solid footing again. It also wasn't difficult for them to ascertain that my love life was non-existent. They knew the simple remedy I needed: get back into God's word, get my career back on track and find a good woman to settle down with again. But they also knew not to push this too hard. Especially Bud sensed that I was so deeply troubled by Syl and Devon's deaths that too much advice might put me over the edge. So he was incredibly patient and willing to let time employ its healing process. Little did he know how far gone I was; that no amount of time would cure what ailed me. He was about to get a fresh insight.

One Friday, I was staggering through my normal routine. It started by knocking off work early, surprise, surprise. When I stopped for gas on the way home, I'd grab a bottle and a few cold ones to prime the pump. Of course, I couldn't wait until I got home to sample some suds so I'd usually crack open a couple in the car. I would lay into the remainder at home as I got ready to go out. My first stop on that Friday occurred a little prior to when most normal folks were getting ready to leave work; my favorite sports bar. You might wonder why a loner like me would want to get out and mingle. That's an easy one. It was for the booze. Plus, I preferred greasy bar food to cooking for myself. I found that I could be quite sociable when tanked up and felt right at home in a tavern or club filled with the other drunken denizens. Starting early allowed me to build myself up with liquid courage while the bars were still fairly empty and no heavy socializing was required. By prime time, I was flying high and ready to unleash my charming personality on some lucky fox. I liked to bounce around to keep things fresh and avoid conquering the same ground twice. The last thing I needed was a relationship.

I had become such a prolific bar hound and philanderer that it became harder and harder to locate fresh prospects. Normally, I tried to stay away from areas too close to my home or my parents' neighborhood but I had to cast a wider net to find new fish in the sea. So I took a chance and hit one of the spots just a couple of miles from Bud and Lilly's house. I figured it would be safe since they were surely tucked in for the night. The local watering hole was a dirty dive in a strip mall but they booked live music on weekends which attracted the ladies. When I arrived at 10:30 the joint was jumping and it didn't take long for me to latch onto a willing companion. By 11:45 my proposal was issued and accepted and we headed for the door. On the way to my car, she spied the convenience store next to the bar and asked if I'd grab a night cap for later. I mumbled a hearty reply to her slurred request and we staggered into the shop arm in arm. We embarrassed the cashier with our premature foreplay as we selected a bottle of sloe gin as the appropriate aperitif for our upcoming session. Amidst our reveling and alcohol induced stupor, I didn't even notice the other patron who came up behind us. Apparently, Lilly was having a rough night which prompted Bud to rise from his slumber to make a late night run for some Nyquil.

I don't know who was more surprised, him or me, "Is that you, Twain?" I turned around to see Bud right behind me with the foulest look on his face. A sober man would have had the decency to be embarrassed but I was too far gone. The only proper thing to do was introduce him to the bleached blond floozy on my arm, "Hello dad, I'd like you to meet, uh." I failed to suppress a snicker as I pressed my face close to her ear and whispered much too loudly, "I'm sorry my lovely but what was your name again?" Judy, apparently that was her name, sensing my incapacitated state took the initiative and turned to Bud offering her hand palm down as if she expected him to kiss it, "My name is Judith; I'm pleased to meet you Mr. ah … dad." Ever the gentleman, Bud took her hand and shook it and did his best to avoid frowning in disgust in spite of our giggling, wobbly stances and glazed over eyes.

After we paid our bills to the amused cashier, Bud accompanied us out the door and followed us to the car. With all the politeness he could muster, he opened the door for Judy, "It was a pleasure meeting you Judith. If you don't mind, could I borrow my son for a moment?" "Of course, Mr. ah … dad," she said between more giggles. Then Bud turned to me, "Could you step over to my car for a moment, Twain?" I followed behind him like a playful pup, "What brings you out so late dad; is mom okay?" Bud was in no mood for any more nonsense, "Your mother's just fine. Now wipe that stupid grin off your face and listen to me. What in the Sam Hill do you think you're doing with that drunken tramp?" I made a weak attempt at a retort but Bud grabbed me by the collar and yanked me to attention with surprising strength. "Look at you Twain; what's happened to you? You're drunk out of your mind, driving to boot and headed off to do God knows what with a complete stranger! Is this what you've become? Is this why you can't find your way to visit your mother? Is this why you've become a stranger to your own family? Is this why you're a failure and can barely pay your bills? Is this why you won't show your face in church?" I was sobering up fast, at least as much as was humanly possible with the amount of hooch in me, but I didn't dare talk back. "Son, I know you experienced something terrible, something that no man should have to suffer through. But what's done is done. It's time for you to snap out of it and fly right! Do you hear me?"

I nodded but didn't have any concept of accepting a commitment. I just wanted this lambasting to end. Bud could tell I was only sorry about one thing, that I had been caught in the act. I didn't realize it at the time but he was not venting. He wasn't angry ... his heart was breaking. Bud was desperately trying to help me with the only medicine that might work; a heavy dose of tough love. With that, he drove a stake through my heart, "Twain, take a good look at that woman sitting in your car." He wasn't speaking figuratively. He grabbed me by the ear and turned my head, "Go ahead and take a good look." He paused to give me a chance to absorb just how ugly a picture I'd painted, "Now you tell me one thing. How do you think Sylvia would feel about this?" I was crushed. I was too drunk to tell if I'd hit rock bottom but I had never felt lower. Bud had one final dose of strong medicine for me and it was a bitter pill indeed, "I know you're too stinking drunk to think straight right now but I want you to remember what I said. When you sober up, I want you to think about Syl and Devon and ask yourself if this is the way to honor their memories. You're on thin ice boy, thin ice. You're flirting with real danger. I don't know you anymore, Twain. When you wake up tomorrow, take a good, long look in the mirror and then tell me what you see." He turned and left without so much as a handshake or goodbye.

7 Blinded by the Light

Bud had rocked my world all right. Even as boozed up as I was, his admonition hit home immediately. I did something totally out of character. I passed on a night of mindless passion with Judy jiggles. Of course, chivalry is not completely dead so I let her keep the sloe gin. Then I went home and sulked. Self-pity circled above me waiting for the right moment to strike. I would have been easy pickings except that I kept hearing Bud's voice, dressing me down and daring me to man up. As much as I wanted to give up and wallow, I couldn't ignore what Bud had said. I didn't need to wait for the morning light to break. Instead of quitting on myself again, I got off the couch and shuffled into the bathroom and parked in front of the mirror and stared at myself for the longest time. The bright lights of the vanity were harshly revealing. Who was this man in the mirror? Bud was right. I didn't recognize myself. It was a sad, sad picture looking back at me. I had aged so much, beyond my normal years. I looked so pitiful, a complete stranger. The longer I stared, the clearer things became. Images, words began to appear out of nowhere, across my forehead: lecher, sinner, fool, embarrassment, failure and worst of all … lost. The words that didn't appear were perhaps more telling: brother, father, husband and son or … loved and forgiven.

 I'd like to tell you that I took Bud's words to heart and it turned my life around. That wouldn't be exactly true, though. Sure, I cleaned up my act quite a bit. I went cold turkey and quit the bar hopping scene. My heart still wasn't in my work but I did my best to shore up the bottom line. I made a habit of visiting my folks regularly and my siblings once in a while too but I didn't fully reconnect. I even started attending church again but, unfortunately, it was all for show. My heart and ears remained closed to the word. I stopped sleeping around and took another, more determined run at Monkville rather than seeking an earnest relationship with a young lady. I should have tried to reach out to Sally but I couldn't bring myself to do it. To burn off nervous energy and fill the void of my foregone, wayward ways, I took to running and exercising. Between that and my more demanding work schedule, I chewed through the time and actually started sleeping better. With all of these changes, I was much healthier, at least physically. My mental condition still left something to be desired and spiritually, well spiritually I might as well have been a pile of dry bones inside a clean, white sepulcher. At least my keeping up appearances had a beneficial effect on Bud and Lilly. Seeing such dramatic, positive changes gave them a certain peace of mind … except that Bud still sensed something was missing.

Whenever Bud tried to pry into my brain to diagnose whatever was still troubling me, I went into a defensive mode that only raised his curiosity further. When he pushed hard enough, I'd react with just enough indignation to discourage him. Bud knew better than to drive me over the edge. The last thing he wanted was to ever see me in the abyss again. So we played this game in cycles until I figured out how to appease him. To throw him off the scent, I pulled out a favorite old decoy. What did he want more than anything else? You guessed it. I resurrected my literary aspirations and hinted that I was thinking about getting back into writing again rather than just promoting the work of others. It worked like a charm. All I had to do was provide an occasional tidbit about the forthcoming work and offer excuses for the interminable delays in my progress … endless concept development and then research, research and more research. It wasn't a total lie. I did spend a lot of time researching the Renaissance Killer and pouring over all the information I had gathered. In time, I also began to compile personal notes from my encounter with RK at JCCC. As I talked about a book and continued to focus so much free time and attention on Cane, an idea began to take root. Perhaps, someday, I should chronicle the life and times of Charles Darwin Cane, the Renaissance Killer.

It wasn't an ideal life but I settled into a more comfortable, tolerable pattern. I righted the ship at the agency and put my financial house in order. It still struck people as odd; especially Bud; that I didn't develop a relationship with a lady friend but no one made an issue of it since everything else seemed to be going along smoothly. Don't rock the boat, right? Most people were willing to cut me some slack by rationalizing that I just wasn't able to get over my ongoing devotion to Syl and Devon. To them I was just the happy widower, Saint Twain. I had plenty of other healthy pursuits to keep me busy and the years swept by like the spring winds blowing across the Great Plains. I cruised by in the fast lane of life passing the 1990s like they were stuck in neutral. No one else knew that, in spite of everything else going on in my ordered life, I was still driven primarily by one overriding, single minded pursuit: the inevitable if inconceivably slow march toward the execution of Charles Darwin

Cane. Speaking of Cane, things were happening in his regimented life too. Changes were afoot that didn't come to my attention even though I still kept a close watch on him. If I had received any inkling of these changes, turmoil would have erupted in my placid life but, thankfully, I was left unaware for quite some time.

When it came to policy matters such as the changes that resulted in Cane being released into the general population, it was easy to follow things that effected RK's life behind bars. But most things that happened inside a lock up never reached the light of day. Prison officials like to keep a tight lid on everything possible for a lot of good reasons and there's never much of a push from the media unless something really newsworthy crops up like a corruption scandal, inmate riot or high profile execution. Occasionally, you'll see a human interest piece on someone like Manson but, more typically, our serial killers tend to fade into obscurity aside from some significant milestone or an oddity like Gacy selling garish clown portraits. Sadly, our what-have-you-done-for-me-lately attitude extends to our killers and we lose interest when a monster is defanged and locked away in a cage. Of course, that doesn't apply to surviving victims like me. We gobble up any little tidbit of information that meanders our way. In any case, I remained as vigilant as ever but didn't have a clue about how uninformed I really was. While I fumed over my vision of Cane leading the life of Reilly as a pampered house guest, the reality was starkly different. It would be years before I would get the real truth.

RK derived the greatest pleasure from psychological torture so it makes sense that, perhaps, his worst punishment was mental and emotional. It was less than a two hour drive from St. Louis to Potosi, yet Cane's parents never visited him in prison. Gerald was too vain to show empathy for anyone other than himself. Rather than showing pity, he held only resentment for Charles. His main concern was avoiding as much of the embarrassment as possible. He basically disowned Charles in a very public way to try to salvage his standing in the academic world. The last thing he wanted was to accept any of the responsibility for creating a monster. According to his version, everything was fine when he and Daphne divorced, thus implying that she must have been responsible for warping little Charles. Daphne wasn't so narcissistic but she too basically disowned Charles except in a much more private way. She was very hurt by the stories Charles had concocted about his upbringing to try to gain leniency through his split personality charade. Her maternal ties were severed when Charles basically threw her, Gerald and their new spouses under the bus with his lurid lies of childhood abuse. Daphne was livid at what she and her new family were subjected to by the Social Services bureaucrats who combed through their private lives to ensure the children were in no danger. And all because of some selfish hoax! What hurt her the most was the way that Charles disavowed any recognition of the many sacrifices she had made for him and the way she protected him from Gerald. While Daphne's motives were questionable, some of them were not as self-serving as Gerald's. She had a new husband and step children to protect. She didn't want Charles' poison to pollute their tidy, little world and she felt that, if it meant cutting any ties with her firstborn, only biological child, so be it.

Charles felt completely abandoned by his parents which might not sound so bad for a loner who had tried to avoid them as much as possible as a teen. But their rejection of him cut deep. During his childhood, especially his early years, they had doted over him and constantly lavished him with praise to build up his self-esteem. Now they were deconstructing his ego with the devastating efficiency of a professional demolition team. Even for a monster like Cane, prison can be a very scary place and he longed for some outside connection, a psychological sanctuary from the daily danger he faced but none was forthcoming. His was the face that even a mother couldn't love.

It really was an odd turnabout. The reclusive killer, who shunned any meaningful human connections after his disastrous fantasy flirtation with Syl, now longed for something, anything. But Cane didn't fit in with anyone. Just about everything in prison society revolved around one clique or another. He couldn't hang with the homeys or bros and didn't want any part of the white supremacists. Cane didn't click with any of the outliers either. There weren't a lot of college educated preppy types in the joint. It was too bad for him because there's safety in numbers. Being the odd man out was not only lonely but extremely dangerous, especially for someone with Cane's criminal background. There's an odd moral standard in most maximum security prisons and the cons have their own code of justice. Certain crimes, especially violent ones against rivals, authority figures or society's privileged leeches are held in high esteem. There's also a lot of respect for perps who have demonstrated guts or ingenuity in committing their malfeasances. Stupid crooks, a category netting the majority of cons, are lower on the food chain but pretty much get a pass. It's frowned upon if you had the good life and simply blew it. In that case, you're liable to wind up as someone's female dog but probably won't suffer deadly violence. But there's one thing that won't be tolerated and that's a crime against children.

Sickos don't last long. Charles didn't catch onto that at first. Early on, he was quite pleased with the policy changes that brought what seemed like highly desirable privileges. If he would have been more plugged in, he might have sensed the danger and opted out. Not only did he not have an ear to the grapevine but everything seemed safe and secure with the escorts and all. Of course, prison officials don't go broadcasting an inmate's background for their own protection. Also, Charles was not the chatty type. He was generally wary of the other, bigger beasts in the jungle. Nevertheless, it was only a matter of time until the rumors wafted to the wrong ears. Charles had two very big strikes against him. First, he was a major sicko with a rap sheet full of disgusting deeds including the physical and psycho-sexual torture of a little boy. Then, on top of that was the kiss of death of being a celebrity. Criminals resent being upstaged by someone with the star power of RK, someone so undeserving.

The Potosi Correctional Center's grand experiment with mainstreaming was about to suffer its first major setback and no one saw it coming; not the guards or Charles. Prison subculture is very effective at maintaining secrecy and incredibly efficient at meting out justice. Charles was very sly and had pulled off so many clever ruses on his helpless victims; yet he was caught completely off guard. First there was the diversion, a ruckus between two inmates that materialized out of nowhere, galvanized the guards' attention and evoked an immediate response. Then, with lightning quickness and military precision, two burly cons grabbed Charles and held him tight while a third stabbed him repeatedly with a nasty shiv that had been fashioned from a pork chop bone. The wounds were not deep or well-placed enough to take Charles' life but delivered with such piston-like ferocity in a matter of seconds that they left him a bloody mess in need of intensive care in the prison infirmary. Oh, there was one well-placed blow in the middle of his crotch that was aimed at sending a clear message of their disdain for sexual predation involving children, even if it was only as a witness like with Devon.

Charles was overwhelmed with shock from the devastation that had swooped down on him in such a blur of violence. For someone who had inflicted so much pain upon others, Charles was a neophyte when it came to being on the receiving end. Regarding his own physical suffering, he had led a pampered existence. Now it made it that much worse for him. His discomfort was so intense that he vomited before passing out. It took some doing for the doctors to put Humpty Dumpty back together again. He had a long recovery in the infirmary but still did not receive a visit from Gerald or Daphne even though they were promptly notified. This only added to his pain. Being bed ridden in this condition gave Charles plenty of time to ponder. For the first time in his life, he thought about someone other than himself. Yes, most of his thoughts were centered in self-pity but, from time to time, his mind wandered off to his victims. He didn't feel remorse but he wondered what they must have felt. Finally, he had a personal point of reference from whence to gauge the enormity of his evil.

Charles received another healthy epiphany. The frightener became the frightened and, for the first time, he was gripped with genuine terror. The self-assured, cocky killer was in fear for his own life. Once he got past the initial shock and pain and began to feel his body mend, Charles began to

173

dread his release from the infirmary. He knew he was a marked man and it was only a matter of time before this or something worse happened again. The prison officials promised him that he would be returned to solitary confinement where they could ensure his safety. It was little solace to Charles, the scared little rabbit. At the end of his rope, Charles then received the most gratifying and unexpected surprise; he had visitors. It was not mom and dad but Gerald's parents, Grandma and Grandpa Cane. In days gone by, Charles would have turned up his nose at the prospect of spending time with them. Although he had at one time come close to growing fond of them, his parents had poisoned his feelings and caused him to reject them and everything they stood for. As the Renaissance Killer, the personification of evil, he had eschewed every good and foolish thing they represented. But beggars can't be choosers and he welcomed them with open arms.

How ironic it was that the two people who had been rudely and heartlessly shut out of Charles' life were at his side while his parents stayed away. There they were, showing genuine concern for his well-being. Grandma reached out and touched him tenderly, "We were so worried about you. How are you doing Charles?" Charles actually choked back

174

tears, "I'm just so happy to see you. It's been very lonely in here. Look what they've done to me." He exposed his ugly, purple wounds, "Believe it or not, I'm doing much better than I was when they first brought me into the infirmary." Charles hesitated causing some concern, "What's the matter Charles?" "Grandma, Grandpa, why are you here? You must be so ashamed of me. Mom and Dad won't even speak to me. They've never visited me, not once. You must feel the same way, so why are you here?" They looked at each other sadly before Grandpa answered, "Charles, we know that you've done terrible, unspeakable things and we regret everything that has happened. We wish with all of our hearts that none of this would have ever taken place. But we can't change the past. We are ashamed, very ashamed of everything you've done. But that doesn't mean we don't love you."

Grandpa lowered his head to hide his tears and Grandma reached over to wipe them away. They must have sensed, as I found out the hard way, it's impossible to read Cane. Was the moisture in his eyes just the tears of a crocodile or did he have some tiny, dried up remnant of compassion buried somewhere inside? You know my opinion; he has no more compassion than the devil himself. But if anything could warm up this Grinch's heart, it might have been the unconditional love demonstrated by his grandparents. "Charles, as long as you are living and breathing, we will never lose hope in you. Do you know why?" Cane was truly perplexed, "Grandpa, I can't think of one single, solitary reason. I've never spent much time with you. I never listened to you. I'm an evil man who has never raised a finger to help you in any way. The only thing I've done is to bring the worst kind of shame upon your family name. No, I can't comprehend any reason why you'd place any hope in me." Cane's tone was not one aimed at garnering pity. He was matter of fact, almost accusatory as if he suspected a con game, an octogenarian swindle.

Grandpa reached down and picked up a Holy Bible and extended it to Cane as a gift, "Charles, this is why we have hope." Cane looked like a vampire staring at a silver cross and declared with perturbation, "Grandpa, I have no use for that book." Undeterred, Grandpa advanced, "Charles, this book has power, *the* power." Cane sneered as he delivered his retort, "What power might that be Grandpa; the power to lull me to sleep at night like Grimm's Fairy Tales?" Grandpa sidestepped the affront, "This book has the power to transform. It has the power of love. It has the power of forgiveness. It has the power of salvation. It has the power of God. Charles, this book has the power to wipe away everything you've ever done as far as the east is from the west." Cane scoffed, "I doubt that. You don't know everything I've done. There's no book in the world that can make what I've done go away." "Charles, believe me, if you'll just read it, you will see that there are plenty of people who've done terrible, despicable things that God has forgiven. People like King David and the Prophet Moses, pillars of the Bible by God's grace, were terrible sinners … they were murderers too." Cane crossed his arms in defiance but remained silent. "Please Charles; you don't have to read it if you don't want to but I beg you, please take this book and keep it; please keep it close." Perhaps he just wanted to shut the old man up but, in any case, he took the Bible and set it aside.

They chatted a while longer before the old couple took their leave. Charles was still harboring skepticism and had his nose out of joint a bit over Grandpa Cane's insistence that he accept the unwanted gift. But he was glad that they had visited. It gave him a lifeline … a sliver of a connection outside the antiseptic confines of the impersonal infirmary and beyond the imposing walls and fences of PCC. He had a link to something

177

intriguing, something he had never experienced before and couldn't understand. It was unconditional love, a concept he couldn't grasp but had a chance to observe. His grandparents didn't talk about it, they lived it. They gave Charles a living, breathing example to consider. Cane didn't have the capacity to fully incorporate something so foreign into his being but it kept the wheels turning inside his head. He thought; what if there wasn't a catch? What if they didn't want anything in return? What did they have to gain and what did he have to lose? As boredom set in again and he braced for another long evening, he stared at the Bible resting on the night stand. He huffed and turned away in disgust but stopped suddenly when something caught his eye. There was a slip of paper peeking out from between the pages. Curiosity got the better of him and Charles reached for the Bible and retrieved the notebook paper to discover that Grandpa had taken the time to jot down some suggested readings. Charles was such a stranger to the Holy Book that he had difficulty making sense of the numeric scripture references. At first he clutched the book in an attempt to prove he was up to the intellectual challenge presented by Grandpa's outline. He fumbled through the front pages until he happened upon a listing of the sixty six books of the Bible in order. Then it didn't take long for him to figure out the numeric reference system within each book.

So, it was nothing more than curiosity and intellectual snobbery that drew him into the word. He had no idea of its true power and the transformative impact it could have on him. He looked at the first listing and started in at Acts 21:8. The story, totally new to Cane, fascinated him. The Apostle Paul was warned not to go to Jerusalem but did so anyway in order to comply with God's missionary will for him. Paul, a former leader of the Jews, had been called upon to witness to the Gentiles. He preached a message that was anathema to many of the Jews, claiming that their old ceremonial laws no longer had any force and effect under the new covenant of Jesus Christ, the fulfillment of the law. That was bad enough but then he made the grave mistake of taking several Gentiles into the Jewish Temple in Jerusalem for the rite of purification. When the Jews discovered this transgression, they were incensed that Paul had polluted their holy temple and a mob formed with intent to kill him. In the nick of time, Paul was rescued by Roman guards who took him into custody for his own safe keeping. He then became entangled in the Roman judicial system and was transferred to a prison in the provincial capital of

Caesarea. He was held there for two years by the Governor, Felix, who hoped to receive a bribe in exchange for Paul's freedom. This was juicy stuff that whetted Charles' appetite just as Grandpa had hoped.

The next reference, Acts 25:9-11 showed how Paul exercised his right as a Roman citizen to appeal his case to Rome. Then it was onto chapter 27 and the harrowing tale of Paul's shipwreck in route to Rome. Finally, chapter 28 recounted Paul's two year term of solitary confinement in a Roman prison. Charles imagined the harsh challenges Paul faced at the hands of the Romans in such a bleak setting. He marveled at the way Paul never let his imprisonment get in the way of his evangelical mission. That's when he got the point of Grandpa's outline, or at least he thought he did. Grandpa thought Charles would relate to a fellow prisoner's story, right? Maybe yes, maybe no; but it didn't matter because it was a good read nonetheless. The only problem was that it was a King James Version and the language was a bit challenging. But Charles was never one to shrink from an intellectual challenge. So he forged ahead to the next reference back in Acts 16, another prison story. This one was better than the first two but Charles wondered why Grandpa had taken this earlier occurrence out of its historical sequence and saved it for last. The account read like something out of a tabloid. First, Paul, with some guy named Silas as his sidekick, came across a young woman possessed by a demon and, doing the only thing befitting a gentleman and a man of God; exorcised the evil spirit. She was undoubtedly grateful but some of her handlers were not so pleased. They had been making a good living off of her fortune telling abilities and didn't appreciate Paul and Silas taking their money maker out of commission. These guys were really ticked. They leveled all kinds of false accusations at Paul and Silas and raised such a ruckus that they were stripped naked, beaten with rods and thrown into the pokey in Philippi. It was a nasty place and a bad situation but Paul and Silas took it all in stride and prayed and sang praises to God well into the night in such a loud voice that the other prisoners heard them. Maybe they were happy because they knew the fix was in from God because later that same night there was a miraculous earthquake that was not strong enough to level the place but packed just enough punch to spring loose the doors and shackles. It was a capital offense to lose charge of a prisoner back in ancient Rome so the guard, fearing horrible torture before an agonizing death drew his sword to kill himself. Paul stopped him and laid the gospel on him right then and there and he was converted. When the guard asked what he needed to do to be saved, Paul didn't exhort him to some form of penance or good works. He simply told him to believe on the Lord Jesus Christ, nothing more.

Charles laughed and wondered if old gramps was encouraging him to engineer a prison break. The next passage listed settled that question but raised another. He turned to John 8:31-32 where it quoted Jesus saying, "If ye continue in my word, then are ye my disciples indeed; and ye shall know the truth, and the truth shall make you free." Charles understood all the prison references and the obvious parallels to his predicament. He also had no problem grasping the value of freedom now that his was completely gone. But he didn't get what Jesus was saying about freedom. Sure Jesus wanted everyone to believe he had a monopoly on the truth. But, even if you believed that, how in the world would that set you free, especially if you were rotting away in prison like him? Should he pray for an earthquake? What Cane didn't realize is that Jesus was providing a spiritual message that couldn't be discerned by someone thinking in worldly, temporal terms. For that, he would need some help.

If I was stubbornly holding up an oversized umbrella against God's grace, Cane was encased within a solid steel death star impervious to all the elements. Thumbing casually through a few Bible stories had about as much hope of penetrating his granite heart as a bb gun piercing Kevlar. Still, the next reference on Grandpa Cane's outline, Romans 1:16, proclaimed, "For I am not ashamed of the gospel of Christ: for it is the **power** of God unto salvation to everyone that believeth." Charles snorted with cynicism for there was apparently a footnote that had been omitted: "Everyone that is except for the murderous maniac, Charles Cane." His grandfather had spoken eloquently of hope but what hope could there be for a man like Cane who probed the Bible for his amusement but surely was not seeking after God? I would submit there was none, but who can deny the power of God? Something seemed afoot though, first with the surprise visit from Grandma and Grandpa Cane and then another twist of fate. When Cane was returned to solitary, a new neighbor was awaiting in a nearby cell, a most unusual tenant.

The Reverend Floyd Hartzenberger had been a man of God and was an unlikely candidate for capital punishment, that is, until he snapped and shot his wife to death. In a murder-suicide gone awry, he got cold feet when he turned the gun on himself. The less charitable among us might say he chickened out. More accurately, his Christian upbringing and years of training and service kept popping up as his life passed before his eyes. By the grace of God, he was unable to commit that final, blasphemous act of suicide; the most dangerous, damnable sin this side of sinning against the Holy Ghost. So actually, as strange as it sounds for a man who just killed his wife, his cowardice was really an act of fleeting faith in what was otherwise an abomination. I'd like to think that God stopped him short because he had another calling in mind for Rev Floyd. The only problem is that anything inuring to the benefit of Charles Cane was an unholy endeavor in my mind. But one couldn't deny that Rev was perfect for Cane. Who could be better for Charles to relate to than a fellow murderer? This one just happened to have the theological background that Cane lacked.

The visit from his grandparents had left Charles with a wholly unfamiliar longing. Although he was terrified by the prospect of being exposed to the baboons in the general population, he now craved social interaction, a safe sounding board for the thoughts and questions cropping up in his head. Within the confines of the solitary wing, there weren't many worthy prospects. Rev Floyd was really the only one. He was tall and gangly with a chrome dome surrounded by a monk's half halo of hair. In spite of his size, pronounced features and imposing, raw boned frame, he didn't strike any fear in Charles. There was something about his nature that was meek and humble. Never mind that anyone in this neighborhood was obviously capable of violence. Charles was drawn to him and was curious to find out how a man of the cloth had wound up in PCC's CPI wing. Rev Floyd actually initiated the first contact when he noticed Charles perusing his Bible, "You don't see many of those in here." Charles was caught off guard, "What's that?" Rev tried again, "I was talking about your Bible. I couldn't help but notice. You don't see many people with their nose in a Bible around here." Charles nonchalantly dismissed the new guy, "Oh yeah, it's a gift from my grandparents." "Very good... they must love you a lot." Charles was miffed by the unwanted intrusion, "Whatever fella ... now, if you don't mind, I'd like to get back to my reading." Rev was unfazed by the curt dismissal, "Oh, sorry to bother you. I'll let you get back to your studies. By the way, my name is Floyd. I'm a bit of a Bible buff myself ... you know, if you ever feel like comparing notes." Charles had had enough and blew him off rudely, "Whatever, Floyd … got it … don't call us, we'll call you."

Charles was not about to let just anyone into his tight circle of trust; not without doing a little homework first. But Floyd had some potential so Charles checked with the guards to get the scoop. Charles couldn't believe his ears … a Christian minister who blew his wife away? Now that's something worth looking into. At the next opportunity, Charles worked up the courage to ask for an escort to the CPI wing's common dining area. He was very skittish in spite of the screening that was required before a CPI was deemed worthy of even this small taste of freedom. There were still some very scary dudes out and about but the heavy presence of the guards provided some comfort. The Rev was sitting alone when Charles approached with his tray, "Do you mind if I join you?" "Oh no, please do," he replied cheerfully. "Hey Floyd, I'm sorry about the other day. It's just that I got jumped recently and have been leery of strangers ever since." "I'm sorry to hear that. Are you okay? By the way, may I ask your name?" "Oh yeah, sorry … I'm Charles. Hey, speaking of names, Floyd, I understand you're some kind of minister. Should I call you Reverend or what?" A touch of discomfort creased Rev's otherwise contented look, "I used to be an ordained minister ... before ... well, that's in the past. You can just call me Floyd, if you like. Or, some people took to calling me Rev at my last stop before being transferred here." Charles smiled, "I like that, Rev. So you weren't kidding when you said you were a Bible buff." It was the beginning of an odd but fruitful relationship. The once faithful, now disgraced man of God and the demonic serial killer searching for answers in, of all places, the Holy Bible ... yes, quite the odd couple. They were polar opposites but shared one all important patch of common ground, the word of God. One was a skeptic of the worst kind while the other was a faithful believer but both were terribly flawed. One was a broken and contrite man filled with remorse and repentance while the other didn't even recognize the concept of sin much less harbor any regrets other than his own capture.

They had to get one thing behind them before they could plow the common ground together. Charles took the first stab, "I'm sure you've heard all about me. You'd have to be some kind of hermit to have missed the saga of the Renaissance Killer. So there's not much to figure out about why I'm stuck in here. But you ... how does a man like you end up in a place like this?" It was visibly painful for the Rev to recount his fall from grace but he didn't hold back. He explained how his devastating tragedy was the culmination of a steady sojourn down a twisted path that started with one seemingly harmless, small step in the wrong direction. That first voyeuristic peek into the tantalizing world of pornography didn't seem dangerous at all. He just wanted to satisfy his intellectual curiosity … yeah, that's the ticket. The Rev bared his soul and admitted he knew it was wrong from the start. But he had plenty of excuses. He and Brenda had grown apart. It's tough enough being the wife of a pastor but when they found out they could not have children, disappointment grew into depression. Brenda's passion evaporated and the romance departed leaving their bedroom cold and loveless. That's how he justified his tiny transgressions at first; it was just a harmless diversion to appease his masculine urges and take his mind off their marital problems. But pornography soon sunk its claws into Floyd and his diversion became an obsession.

From there, he was caught in a deadly spiral that led to adultery and prostitution. Brenda knew what was happening and finally had enough. She threatened to divorce Floyd and publicly expose him as a vile hypocrite. The next part was the most difficult for the Rev to share, "I was caught in

Satan's snare. There was only one good way out, to turn to the Lord. But I listened to that other beguiling voice instead. You could say I panicked at the prospect of my life and career collapsing in a crescendo of shame and embarrassment. However, there's no excuse for what I did. I decided to take the coward's way out and end our miserable lives. I knew better than to play God. I knew that life and death were in his providence. But I tried to take matters into my own hands anyway. My only comfort is in knowing that, in spite of my sinful act; God turned my evil into good and took Brenda home at his appointed time.   He didn't let me take my own life though. I'm ever grateful to him for that. All I can do now is try and serve him and his good purposes in any way that I can." Charles was perplexed, "But Rev, why would God use you, a murderer, to do anything for him? There are plenty of good people out there for that; aren't there?"

Something changed in the Rev's pained expression in the blink of an eye. Charles' question took him from the confessional to the pulpit in a heartbeat. The Rev looked at Charles with compassion and earnest concern, "Charles, don't you know that there aren't any good people?" Before Charles could object, the Rev reeled off Romans 3:23 from memory, "For all have sinned, and come short of the glory of God." Without missing a beat he then launched into Romans 3:10, "As it is written, There is none righteous, no, not one." Finally, Charles interrupted, "Okay, if you say so. But you can't say that some of us aren't much worse than the rest." The Rev smiled and again demonstrated his amazing recall, "That's not what God says … he tells us in Matthew 5:48 that we must be perfect to meet his standard, 'Be ye therefore perfect, even as your Father which is in heaven is perfect' and he goes on to proclaim in James 2:10 that we're all in the same boat when it comes to sinning, 'For whosoever shall keep the whole law, and yet offend in one point, he is guilty of all.' God sees you, me and all the so called saints in exactly the same light, as miserable sinners deserving nothing but an eternity in hell." Charles was truly flustered, "Jeez … what have you got, a photographic memory or something? Very impressive … but you still haven't answered my question. Why would God use a lousy murderer like you?" The Rev took the slight in stride, "Charles, God delights in using broken tools like me to do his work. And, do you know what? He can even use someone like you."

Charles just about blew a gasket, "Yeah right … me and God are real tight, BFFs. Rev, I think you've got a screw loose. I guess maybe you haven't heard about me or else you'd know I've been working for the other team." The Rev remained calm and pastoral, "Charles, I know all about you and your exploits as the Renaissance Killer. From a worldly standpoint, I agree that it doesn't get much worse. You take the cake. But you need a little history lesson. Apparently, you're not aware of some of the really bad characters that God has made good use of throughout the ages. Some of them are just as despicable as you, in some ways even worse." Charles was still in an argumentative mood but intrigued just enough to hold his tongue, "I'm all ears, Rev." Then the Rev started Charles on a journey that would take him to a most unexpected destination. He took a piece of paper and jotted down a long list of Bible references, again all from memory. He left Charles with the following instructions, "I'd like you to read about these two fellows and see what you think. Pay close attention to where they started, where they ended up and what happened to them along the way. Then let's get back together and talk."

It would still be almost four more years before I'd get wind of what had transpired between Cane and the Rev. But, in due time, I'd get a blow by blow account from the man himself, Charles Darwin Cane. He would share everything I've passed along above and then some. Cane would explain that his first assignment from the Rev really wasn't about two men but only one; a man who started as Saul and wound up becoming Paul. That was the breakthrough that led to Charles' transformation. He liked to say that Manfred Mann got to him. Or he would quip that a funny thing happened to him on the road to Damascus. If one were to believe a consummate con man, a master liar like Cane, he was blinded by the light; the light of Jesus that knocked the Apostle Paul from his horse and shone all the way from the Damascus road to Potosi, Missouri across 2,000 years through the pages of a book.

8 Face Two Face

Cane's transformation was not nearly as immediate or dramatic as Paul's. It remained a work in progress under the radar screen for a long while as he journeyed through the Bible with his travel companion, Reverend Floyd. Eventually, like any convert to Christianity, he was compelled to share the good news with others. A jailhouse conversion almost always provides grist for the tabloid mill, especially when the convert is a monster like Cane. There was a time when I was optimistic about such transformations and had faith in God's ability to change the darkest hearts. That's how I felt in 1987 about the news that the Son of Sam had come to Christ. That was just weeks before RK came into our lives and gave me a whole new perspective on such things. When I heard the first report of RK's amazing turnaround, I cursed aloud. All the angels in heaven could have been singing for joy over one lost sheep being found but I was certain it was a sham. I was convinced it had taken him almost ten years to figure out that every other legal and procedural avenue was closed before he opted for the spiritual route. I was sure he had taken plenty of time to study, rehearse and perfect his latest role.

The media loved it and ate up his performance. Observing such a stark example of the aging process was fascinating in and of itself since fifteen years had passed from the last time Cane was newsworthy. The physical transformation, I guess in their minds, was proof of his spiritual makeover. Not everyone jumped on the bandwagon since a lot had changed in the way people viewed religion, especially Christianity which was really getting a bad rap in many circles. So the prospect of someone so despicable claiming to be saved by Jesus Christ raised a whole range of emotions, many of which were not very healthy. You can put me on the sickest end of that spectrum. With the Renaissance Killer back in the limelight, I was naturally caught in the spotlight's glare too. I was more than up to the task and took every opportunity to denounce Cane as a charlatan. It didn't take long before my mission took on a whole new outlook. I rather enjoyed being the center of attention and began to see a silver lining ... I started seeing dollar signs.

At first, I only hinted at a forthcoming book as a way to legitimize my crusade against Cane and the accusations I was leveling without any shred of hard evidence. I was surprised at how serious people took my idle threat and how they began zeroing in on the promised tome with voracious interest. It got out of hand really. First, I started receiving inquiries from ghost writers offering to help me with the project. Then there were solicitations from publishers and other literary agents. I was even approached by screen writers, TV producers and studios interested in converting the prospective book into film. I began to wonder, why not? The more I pondered, the more sense it made to me. I had the literary skill, mountains of background and, unfortunately, personal knowledge of the killer. The only thing that gave me pause was the guilt of profiting from the terrible misfortunes of my dear, departed loved ones, Syl and Devon. Any such fleeting thoughts vanished when I received a sizable cash advance from one bullish publisher. It was easy to rationalize at that point. I wouldn't be profiting from the deaths of Syl and Devon; I'd be extracting just retribution at Cane's expense while doing the righteous work of exposing the real Renaissance Killer and blocking him from attracting a following on the basis of his phony conversion. It also was a big plus to see Bud so invigorated by the likelihood of his vicarious literary dreams finally coming true. For me, there was something more important than money or gaining my father's favor.

If it helped ensure that Cane's sentence was carried out, it would be worth any price.

I began my work in earnest but progress was painfully slow. Working the talk show circuit and newscasts was easy with little preparation or effort involved. Writing a book takes more than imagination and talent … it also requires strict discipline and a lot of mental elbow grease. Years of neglect had left me lazy and intellectually out of shape. Feeding the media's appetite was so much easier and, frankly, more fun. I was great at marketing the book but all I did was create more demand for something that wasn't coming together. Rather than taking responsibility, I blamed my failure on Cane. Of course, there were plenty of media types out there still willing to give him a voice to carry out his cruel and disingenuous ruse on a gullible public. It drove me up a wall and constantly broke any concentration I was able to raise toward my work on the book. This time, I wasn't just facing disappointment and the accusing eyes of friends and family that could so easily be shut out. Since I had accepted an advance, there was real pressure for me to perform. I was trapped like a rat in my own lethargy and lies. Resourceful rodent that I was; I didn't buckle down and get to work but instead found a way to wiggle through a tiny crack to make my escape. I told my publisher that I'd need to meet with Cane again to keep the book current. They agreed and provided the resources and connections to make it happen.

Of course, Cane could have blocked any meeting with me. That was my hope. It was a legitimate one too since Cane had every reason to rebuff me after I had leveled so many accusations and publicly disparaged his faith as a cleverly premeditated forgery. What a perfect excuse I would have if I was unable to conduct a fresh, personal interview of Cane! Unfortunately, there was only one problem. Cane welcomed the opportunity to meet with me. Now real panic began to settle in. Not only would I have to make good on the book but, even worse, I'd have to come face to face with that two faced, manipulative devil's child again. Sweat started pouring from my brow at the prospect of facing Cane again. Terrible fear gripped me as the old memories flooded my head ... the way that Cane had toyed with me and had so easily been able to strip me bare and salt my wounds. I was like a child who didn't want to confront the boogey man under the bed. Unfortunately, I had really painted myself into a corner and had no other way out.

To have any chance of surviving the ordeal, I had to summon an old friend: my anger. Anger was the only ally I had in this fight. But I was afraid because anger hung out with some unsavory friends. Anger had saved me before but when he departed his friends stayed around: despair, apathy, moral decay, dependence, cynicism, hatred and self-loathing. I really didn't want to go down that road again but I had to find courage somewhere so I was willing to welcome anger back with open arms. Locating my anger was a painful process because I had to dredge up all the visions of Syl and Devon that I had tried to bury as deeply as possible. This time, the visions were worse; enhanced as they were by Cane's revelations during our first meeting at JCCC. As the day approached in early 2005, I readied myself as though I was training for a prize fight. While this was great preparation for going into battle, it left me devoid of one of a writer's essential tools, objectivity. The new surroundings were lost on me at first. The stark contrast between JCCC and PCC didn't register immediately. This place was a veritable country club in comparison to Cane's former confines. It was much more modern and so much less foreboding. But all I could think about was Cane.

As we entered the cell, I was so keyed up that I took no note of the surroundings at first. My defenses were on high alert and I could barely contain my aggression as I focused solely on his face. I was ready for a stare down and was determined not to let him wrest control from me this time. But he had changed. No, I don't mean the gray hairs that peppered his head, the gaunt face or craggy lines that displayed the inevitable ravages of time. Cane had a peaceful, serene look on his face. His expression was open and friendly and held no traces of the haughty smirk or condescending grin I had expected. By all appearances, he was a changed man. But I was not about to be fooled again. I recalled clearly how he had been able to transition so effortlessly between RK's evil aura and Charles' contrite persona. Still something seemed different this time. It caught me off guard and broke through my defenses just enough to give me pause to scan the surroundings in Cane's cell. On one wall, there was a cross and the opposite held a picture of Christ knocking at the door. Behind Cane, there was a poster of the Apostle Paul upon which he had taped a piece of paper with a reference to Romans 7:14-25. The cell was neat and clean, with no evidence of the tortured remains of bugs or rodents. He still maintained a small library but the contents of the shelf had changed. Gone were psychiatric works and fictional accounts of killers and troubled souls. Now the shelf was home to the Bible, several commentaries and assorted scholarly theological works. I stepped silently toward his new collection and thumbed through it to get a better feel. He had a copy of Martin Luther's Bondage of the Will with a book mark picturing Luther in front of his Bible which was illuminated by a ray of light. It contained a reference to Romans 1:17, the just shall live by faith.

Cane waited patiently and, I guess, expected something inquisitive or an intellectually motivated observation from me. What he got was quite different, "You've got all the trappings, don't you RK? I'm surprised you haven't replaced your sink with a baptismal font. Do you keep any wine and wafers around the place?" His only reaction was an involuntary one; his pleasant smile was replaced with a look of shame and sorrow. Otherwise, he held his tongue and didn't rebut my sarcastic challenge. "Oh, are you going to do the Christian thing and turn your other cheek? You can spin your head clear around for all I care but I'm not buying." I was itching for a fight but he just sat there and took it as I hurled one invective after another. When it was apparent that my harsh words were falling on deaf ears, I lost control and angrily swept my arm across his library shelf and scattered his books in every direction. When this outrageous behavior was met with quiet acquiescence, I had to take stock of the situation. In my suspicious mind, I had been duped again. Somehow without lifting a finger or saying a word, Cane had made me lose control which, in effect, opened the door for him to take charge just as he had done during our first encounter. That's the last thing I wanted In the presence of my bitter nemesis, so I sat down, gathered my thoughts and regained my composure.

Cane sat patiently for several minutes until I was ready to speak, "As I'm sure you've been told; the reason I'm here is to interview you in conjunction with a book I'm writing. Just so you'll know; I intend to expose you for what you are. I have no intention of painting you in any light other than red … bloody, demonic red. If that doesn't suit you, then we might as well end this interview before it starts." Cane swallowed hard, "Mr. Newman, I wouldn't expect you to do anything different. I'll answer any questions you have as honestly and straightforwardly as possible." I took out a note pad to help me concentrate, "Let's get right to the point then. Why should we believe that you've suddenly come to faith in Christ after fifteen years? Isn't this just a thinly veiled attempt to seek clemency from the death penalty?" "If I were in your shoes, that's exactly what I would think. After everything I've done, I don't have an ounce of credibility and there's absolutely no reason to trust anything I say. But if you want the truth, I didn't come to Christ suddenly. This is something that happened over many years." "Oh, so you didn't just get hit by a lightning bolt, shout hallelujah and, voila, were born again?" Cane remained serious and patient in the face of my sarcasm, "No, it wasn't like that at all. I can remember the day my life changed, when my grandparents visited and left me with a Bible to read but I remained skeptical and defiant for the longest time. The Bible says in Romans 10:17 that faith comes by hearing and comprehending the word of God. I read from the Bible over and over so I was hearing but I wasn't able to understand. It didn't sink in because I rejected the word as a pack of myths, written by sinful men and full of errors." Cane paused out of courtesy but he had my attention to where I just said, "Go on." "I met a friend who changed my life. I'm convinced this was no chance encounter but a godsend. Somehow, Reverend Floyd wound up here in Potosi on death row with me. How does that happen to a man of the cloth who knows the Bible backwards and forward by heart? There's only one way, in my opinion. God sent him here for my benefit. He showed me the way and illuminated the Bible in ways I couldn't have imagined on my own. The most important lesson he taught me early on is that God's forgiveness is so great, so infinite that it can even cover the sins of someone like me."

I recoiled at the very thought. Forgiving Cane would be tantamount to atoning for Hitler or Stalin in my book; unthinkable. Cane saw the look on my face, "I know; it doesn't make any sense. How could a just God forgive someone like me? I committed unspeakable sins and had absolutely no excuse. As I confessed to you before, I was not the victim of society or the product of my childhood environment. I couldn't pass blame onto a chemical imbalance or psychological malady. When I committed those murders, I was in full charge of my faculties and derived an evil pleasure from my deeds. I was my harshest judge because I knew firsthand of the evil that lurked inside me." My furrowed brow relaxed and Cane proceeded, "Then I saw the light, so to speak. Reverend Floyd guided me on a journey through the Bible and we stopped along the way to admire the great heroes of ancient times, the giants of the faith: Moses, Elijah, Abraham, David, Joshua, Peter and many others. They all shared a common thread that we often overlook. The Rev showed me how they were all terrible sinners, some murderers, and they were all horribly flawed. He explained to me, using the Scriptures, how we're all worthy of hell in God's economy. Yet, God delights in using his broken tools to accomplish great things for his kingdom."

I couldn't hide my indignation at such a notion, "So you, the Renaissance Killer, are comparing yourself to Moses, Elijah and Abraham?" "At first, I could only relate to them on one level, their sinfulness. Moses murdered the Egyptian, Elijah ran from Queen Jezebel like a scared, faithless rabbit and Abraham fathered a child with his wife's maid, Hagar, instead of trusting in God's promise. I couldn't get past the feeling that my sins were much worse than even theirs. Then Reverend Floyd led me on an in depth study of the Apostle Paul and my outlook changed completely. As Saul, the Jewish Pharisee, Paul had been in his own words the chief of sinners. He not only murdered but specifically targeted Christians. Saul held the cloaks of the executioners who hurled the stones that struck down the great martyr Stephen. Saul was such a prolific persecutor that he traveled far from Jerusalem to stamp out the church of Christ and visit death upon its early adherents. And yet, this was the man God chose to be the greatest evangelist in history; the Apostle who penned so many epistles under God's inspiration. What really convinced me to see things in a different light was the way Paul admitted and lamented his sins even after his conversion."

It had been a very long time since I was sincerely into God's word but I knew my Bible and hadn't lost track of everything I had been taught and the beliefs I shared with Bud and Lilly and Syl and Devon before I became shipwrecked by RK. As what Cane said sank in, I couldn't shake the feeling that there was something genuine and true in his words. I kept waiting for him to thrust his finger in my face and throw his head back in maniacal laughter. As I've said before, once bitten, twice shy. Nevertheless, Cane was making sense so I kept my peace and listened some more. Cane continued with an excitement and joy that seemed so out of place for him, "It helped me so much to see how God's mercy could extend to someone like Saul, a devoted enemy of Christ. But I couldn't really understand God's economy until Reverend Floyd showed me the enormity of the price God had to pay to satisfy his own divine justice. The Bible has so much to say on this topic but I think it's best summed up in II Corinthians 5:21, 'For he hath made him to be sin for us, who knew no sin; that we might be made the righteousness of God in him.' I was finally able to see that God, in the person of Jesus Christ, who lived a perfect, sinless life that none of us ever could, offered himself up to pay for all of our sins. I finally realized that when John 3:16 said 'whosoever' it included me, Charles Cane."

An old flame flickered inside me. I felt joy over hearing the gospel proclaimed so plainly and openly … even coming from someone like Cane. But there was always that stumbling block, a bushel basket ready to cover the flame and snuff it out. This was the man who had raped my wife and tortured and murdered her along with my son. As if right on cue, Cane was full of remorse, "I don't mean to offend you with any of this. I feel ashamed and unworthy to express the joy of the gospel. But as unworthy as I truly am, it is my privilege to spread the good news of the salvation that extends to me because I have the merit of Christ as the free gift of God's grace. I have no righteousness of my own but my Lord and Savior, Jesus Christ, has imputed his perfect righteousness to me. He has rescued me from this body of corruption and death." Once again, his face showed a roller coaster of emotion from joy to remorse, "Mr. Newman, I know you're here because of the book and I realize I will be and should be cast in the worst light possible.

Nevertheless, I'm happy to assist you in any way possible. There's only one thing I'd like to accomplish if you can permit me. I have a message to get out … something I'm compelled to convey to whomever will listen. That message is the gospel of Jesus Christ."

My heartstrings were so calcified they resisted all tugging, "Oh, I see where we're headed. You'd love that, wouldn't you? Why don't I just let you write the foreword to my book? While we're at it, why don't you handle the epilogue? I bet you'd do a wonderful job of penning a happy ending. Why not just gloss over your crimes and get right to the moral of the fairy tale: Charles Darwin Cane the man of redemption. And they all lived happily ever after, right? Let's kill two birds with one stone and rush a copy to the clemency board. I'll deliver it personally and make a tearful plea for leniency. That should do it, right?"

Cane's demeanor never changed. There was no surprise to be sprung this time around. If this was an act it was a convincing one. He really seemed like a changed man: peaceful, joyful, full of contrition and humble. And the depth of his knowledge of scripture was impressive. He hadn't just scratched the surface but had mined the treasure trove extensively. His whole philosophy and outlook on life was radically changed; or so it appeared on the surface. He responded to my outburst as a Christian would, "I can't blame you for the way you feel. There are no words to express my deep, heartfelt regret for everything I've done other than to simply say, I'm truly sorry. I won't ask you to forgive me but I can say with all confidence that God, in his divine, unfathomable mercy, has forgiven me. God has given me a new life, one that will last for eternity. But that doesn't mean he's released me from the consequences of my sins in this life. I know I have been a liar and I have misled you in the worst, most sadistic way in the past. But I want to ask one thing of you. Please believe me when I tell you that I am not seeking an escape from my punishment. I will not utter a plea for leniency. There is no cause for which I seek your enlistment. For everything I've done, I deserve to be put to death and more. I am no longer afraid of death. That is because God has released me from the sentence of the second death. What awaits me beyond the grave is something I long for thanks to the grace and mercy of God and the merit of Jesus Christ, his Son, our Lord."

I didn't know how to respond to Cane. Suddenly, I was not so resolute as to blast him with a vindictive tirade again. My sentiments were torn by conflict but I didn't want to reveal the struggle occurring within. In the back of my mind, as unlikely as it seemed at that point, I cringed at the thought of ceding control only to be hoodwinked by the sadistic killer once more. Was Cane a different person now; had he really turned over a new leaf? Could such a monster possess an ounce of sincerity? Or was he still the vilest hypocrite ever to walk the earth? Would he make me the foil for his amusement and sick pleasure just like before? Finally, I simply spoke from the heart, "I honestly don't know what to make of you. For eighteen years, I've set my mind on one thing and one thing only ... to see you executed for your crimes. That one desire has dominated every waking moment of my otherwise worthless life. You not only took my wife and child from me but you destroyed my life. I've been living in a prison that, in my mind, is every bit as real as the bars that confine you. Now, you tell me you've changed and you're a different man. I would really like to believe you. I wish I could trust you enough to accept your apology. But I can't erase the vision of your cruelty ... what you did to my precious Syl and Devon. Are you a new man? Is your grief genuine? Or are you still the worst, two faced serpent that has ever slithered out of hell? There's nothing you can say to ease my mind. I'll just have to live with these feelings for the rest of my life … or should I say; the rest of your life? At least there's apparently one thing we can agree on … you deserve to die for your sins."

9 Clemency

My second meeting with Cane didn't go as planned. I regretted that my anger had abated because it had given me a single minded purpose and iron clad certainty. That was gone now; replaced with confusion and doubt. My furious salvos had not been returned in kind. Even though my rage lost its head of steam, there was no acquiescence to Cane's control, no gotcha moment like the shocking twist at the end of a horror movie. My life seemed more aimless than before, if that's possible. Then I read a news item, just weeks after interviewing Cane that raised my antennae. The execution chamber was being moved from Potosi CC to a different facility in Bonne Terre, Missouri with the ridiculous name of the Eastern Reception, Diagnostic and Correctional Center. It elevated my ire to a familiar level to think of this latest example of political correctness gone mad. Whatever happened to calling a prison a prison? Why not call it a penitentiary? The ERDCC … what a bunch of bull puckey!

The ERDCC was designed for the incarceration of male offenders in the eastern region of Missouri and would be the only facility to carry out death sentences. There were sixty two executions carried out at PCC between 1989 and 2005 but there would never be another one performed there. It boggled my mind to think that there were only sixty two executions in sixteen years. How many rapes and murders had there been in that time span? For some reason, ERDCC was not designed to house CPIs. Cane and the others would remain on death row in Potosi or elsewhere until their date of execution and then be transferred to ERDCC for the big finale. Was this designed to make their stays more pleasant; to remove the constant reminder of their impending deaths? I wasn't sure but it made me worry nonetheless. Was this just another step in the process of gradually eliminating capital punishment and robbing people like me of some sense of justice in the world?

I used this latest affront to common sense and my personal sensibilities as a motivating factor. What else did I have? My life was basically a sham. I was walking the straight and narrow path and putting on airs just to make Bud and Lilly feel good and keep everyone else off my back. I didn't really derive any satisfaction from my work or relate to anyone on a personal level and was still shutting God out of my life despite the pretense of visiting his house regularly and following all the necessary rituals.

Leading such a charade was tough enough without losing the driving force of my anger and desperate desire to see Cane suffer and die. Thus, I welcomed my anxiety, real or imagined, over the possibility of Cane's sentence being overturned by a legal technicality or misguided grass roots movement. I wanted to stoke the fires that kept my furnace running and consequently let my emotions boil over until I was back on a collision course with fate; waiting for doomsday for Charles Darwin Cane.

For months, this would sustain me and I would be carried along on a rancorous river of molten malice. I was a willing slave to my daily routines as I took comfort in the swift and steady passage of time. I did not know when the execution would be carried out but took heart that each turn of the calendar brought me another day closer. Try as I might, I couldn't bury the confusing feelings I'd been experiencing ever since my second meeting with Cane. Disturbing sentiments of doubt, pity, grief, guilt and even compassion laid siege to my fortress of hatred and revenge. What if there had been a miraculous transformation and Cane was a new person? What if he was truly sorry for the abominations he had carried out? Every time these invaders threatened my defenses, I'd charge to the ramparts and drop torrents of boiling oil to try to repel them. I'd think back to Devon and Syl. Then I would force myself to imagine again what was going through Devon's mind as Cane brutally raped his mother. Or, what misery Syl experienced as she watched RK strangle the life out of our poor little boy. These terrifying treks down memory lane would always win the day and stave off any foolish, sympathetic thoughts.

It was self-serving and dishonest of me to use Syl and Devon in this way. Syl never would have allowed me to sink to such depths of bitterness. She was the most optimistic person I ever knew. It was impossible to remain down in the dumps around Syl. When my bowl of cherries turned to sour lemons, she was there to sprinkle her own special brand of sugar to produce tart, refreshing lemonade. When the dog dumped some you know what on my shoes, she'd find a way to turn it into shinola. Her love was bottomless and warm as a morning muffin straight from the oven. Syl's cheerful outlook was infectious and could cut through my gloom like a lighthouse beacon on a stormy, sea swept night. As for Devon, his dimples could hold an ocean of delight. A smile and a hug from our little man could fuel me all the way to the moon and back. A simple word of encouragement from Devon could propel daddy to the top of

Everest. That's how I wanted to remember them ... as they lived, not how they died.

I couldn't help but think of how ashamed Syl would be of me right now. She had a way of always putting the best construction on everything, from the good to the bad to the worst. When difficult times would get my dauber down, Syl would tickle me under my chin and say, "I see a gold mine forming." It was her way of lending her amazing faith and reminding me how God uses afflictions, trials and testing to refine us like gold, make us stronger and draw us nearer to him. Ah, Syl's faith ... it was so rock solid and constantly inspired me in her humble, inconspicuous way. If only I had some of her faith to draw upon now. I shuddered to think of how disappointed she would be if she could see me in my current state. Where she would be hopeful, I was suspicious. Where she would gladly offer the benefit of the doubt, I was heartless in my condemnation. Her forgiveness was only matched by my hatred and thirst for vengeance. Where Syl had zeal, I possessed apathy. Worst of all, my heart was full of resentment and rejection where Syl had absolute trust and faith in God.

I had imagined a speck in Cane's eye and accused him of being two faced. But now when I looked in the mirror, I started to see the reflection of the beam in my own eye. I could almost see two faces looking back at me. One was hard to recognize. It was the man I used to be ... a father, husband, son, brother ... a believer. The image of the man who loved and was devoted to his family and relished the opportunity to pursue a career that might bring some joy into the lives of others was obscured. And out of the shadows was another visage; this one now more prominent, easier to discern. It was an ugly, grotesque face, twisted by hatred and filthy with obscene, corrupt, profane obsessions. This was not the man that Syl loved or Devon looked up to. *Mr. Hyde* would have been a complete stranger to them. It weighed on my conscience more and more that I had given myself over to this interloper.

My fits of rage provided enormous firepower that allowed me to unleash incredible devastation in the heat of my internal battles. But this was turning into a war of attrition, one that I could not sustain forever. Ever the fool, I refused to give into my better, purer instincts but instead sought out mercenaries to reinforce my flagging anger. I turned to my neglected book and attacked the project with a new fervor. I figured this would help to keep my mind and time occupied. Also, it would force me to maintain a level of intellectual awareness of Cane's dastardly deeds that would surely feed my anger and play upon my greed. It had gotten to the point where I had to make some measureable progress or relinquish the cash advance which was already largely spent. My publisher had even started to drop hints about legal action. Oh what a blow it would be to Bud if I had to admit my ensuing blockbuster was a fraud, dead in the water. I wondered what Bud would say if I had to go crawling to him for relief to pay back the portion of the advance I had squandered. Such a thing was unthinkable and provided all the motivation I needed.

As I threw myself back into the book in earnest, I was pleasantly surprised at the wealth of information I had collected. The most challenging aspect of the work was organizing and making sense out of all the background data I had amassed. This took an incredibly and laboriously long time, more than a year, but I was at least back on track and able to show meaningful signs of progress to my publisher. Things were coming together and had worked out much as I had anticipated. My greed and keeping the wolves at bay provided powerful incentives. The work kept me occupied and chewed up the passing time. Most importantly, in my screwed up mind, was that it forced me to constantly relive Syl and Devon's deaths and revisit the psychological torment I had suffered at the hands of RK. It helped me to keep my eye on the prize, revenge, and ward off any silly feelings of regret or sympathy. Then I ran into a roadblock that threatened to derail me. My progress served to reveal certain gaps in the story that I needed Cane to help fill. I couldn't stomach the prospect of another face-to-face meeting with Cane. Instead, I decided to correspond with him to keep things detached and impersonal. Luckily, true to his last words to me, he was more than willing to help me. Unfortunately, I didn't realize that these letters would serve as a Trojan horse in the battle for my conscience.

Cane didn't dodge my questions or hesitate to answer even the most specific inquiries although he must have known that he was indicting himself further and destroying any slim chances he might have had of getting his sentence reduced. I'm sure he could tell from the context of my questions that I was following through on my promise to cast him in the harshest light possible. He didn't try to sugar coat things or make excuses but had this bad habit of apologizing and claiming remorse. I had no interest in hearing these things but didn't object for fear that he might cut me off from my most essential source of information. While other chroniclers often had to rely on analysis, assumptions and suppositions, I was able to gain crucial insights into the mind of the killer. For example, I was able to capture the essence of his mega-sized ego when I asked him what bothered him most about the police's response to his first letter. He got right to the point, "I was really incensed that they referred to me as a copycat killer. All they gathered at first was that I wanted to duplicate Jack the Ripper. They missed the whole point of the name Renaissance Killer. I can recall how livid I was that they were too dense to appreciate the painstaking work I had done, not only in matching the Ripper but exceeding his exploits. They missed the finer points … the subtleties of the psychological torture were lost on them."

As he continued on, chilling aspects of RK's nature resurfaced but he constantly sprinkled in hints of the new man who had supposedly emerged. "In my former state, I was actually insulted at their apparent lack of understanding about my choice of moniker. They didn't comprehend that the Renaissance Killer was bringing serial killing out of the Dark Ages, so to speak, and elevating the art to new heights. They showed no gratitude for my painstaking attention to detail and flamboyant style. In my depraved mind, I determined that they would have to learn their lesson the hard way and I'd force them to gain an appreciation for my talents. I'm sorry to say but this demented thought served as my motivation for cutting out the heart of Claudette Perlmutter. I was so jealous of the Night Stalker, Ramirez, that all I could think about was getting a leg up on him and succeeding where he had failed with poor Mrs. Zazzara. Can you imagine that? I was so out of touch with reality and human decency that the pain and torment I put that poor woman through never entered my mind. I was that obsessed with my own legend and my sick desire to elevate myself above Ramirez and all the other deranged killers out there. It was a blessing from God that I was viciously attacked and stabbed repeatedly by those animals in the general population at PCC. Finally, I received a taste of my own injustice and was forced to consider the type of pain I caused so many people."

Another time, I asked Cane to tell me more about his parents. I used open ended questions to allow him plenty of leeway to take his response in any direction. This, I figured, would reveal as much about Cane as his parents. His reply surprised me. He didn't use this as a forum to point fingers or transfer the blame for his actions. However, he was objective and didn't mince words. Cane demonstrated a very cogent grasp of reality. "My parents didn't set out to raise a monster. They were just horribly misguided. You couldn't fault my grandparents. They provided my parents with about as traditional an upbringing as you could imagine. I don't know why but my parents just went their own way and wound up living inside a bubble world where their topsy turvy outlook went unchallenged and, thus, made nothing but sense. Their approach to child rearing was well intentioned but went way overboard in coddling and protecting me. I wasn't allowed to see both sides of the story and make up my own mind. They were so intent on blessing me with self-esteem that I never learned to consider anyone else's feelings. Before I go further though, I want to stress that none of this turned me into a serial killer. I became the Renaissance Killer because I wanted to … I cultivated and gave into the evil that existed within me. Call me a bad seed if you must but don't blame Gerald and Daphne for my misdeeds. I watered, pruned and fed that poisonous plant all by myself."

Cane continued to unload his burden, "It wasn't anything my parents did that made the biggest difference. It was more of what they didn't do. I never received any discipline. When I was a child, I never so much as received a pat on the bottom. I got time out. That really helped … not! This was exactly what I wanted, to be left alone. Make no mistake, I had a reasonable concept of the difference between right and wrong … call it conscience if you will … but there was no outside reinforcement or guidance. Left to my own devices, naturally I gave myself a pass and rationalized away my bad behavior from the start. By the time I finally received justice at Gerald's hands, I was at the age where the effect was only negative. And Gerald wasn't correcting me. He was venting his own frustration. That's not at the heart of my problem though. My greatest regret is that my life was completely secularized by design, totally devoid of God and his word. I know there are plenty of atheists and agnostics who lead normal, crime free lives so I'm not making excuses. But I wish I had been closer to God all my life. I just have the feeling that everything could have been so much different and all the pain and suffering could have been avoided." Then he said something that sounded so self-serving to me at the time it made me mad, mad enough to spit nails. "I guess it was somehow all a part of God's plan. I'm just thankful he didn't deal with me as I deserved but showed me such incredible mercy and favor." It was a good thing that we were not sharing this dialogue face to face. I would have slapped him with all my might. How dare he say that Syl and Devon's pain, suffering and murder were part of God's plan? What conceit for someone to think that his murderous rampage was necessary for carrying out God's will! I guess he thought Syl and Devon were just useless pawns in some grand, diabolical scheme.

Looking back, I wonder if my temper flared up involuntarily or by design. Maybe I wanted to shed my objectivity. It was much easier and simpler to compartmentalize Cane and assign motives according to my narrow view as if I had the ability to read hearts and minds. Furthermore, I have to admit I enjoyed my sore state of mind. Anger was familiar and comfortable, my best friend really. It was too much work to try to think through things calmly and patiently with an open mind and consider the broader context. Perhaps Cane didn't mean to sound so incredibly insensitive toward Syl and Devon. Hadn't he said plenty of other things to express this regret and deep remorse? What would it look like from Cane's point of view; if I were to take Bud's advice and walk around in his shoes? How would I feel if I had committed such damnable sins only to be forgiven by God? How would I reconcile such a paradox and live with my own guilt? No, these types of questions were much too complicated … and unnecessary. The real answer was obvious. In the midst of all his false contrition, Cane had slipped up and showed me what was still behind the curtain … a heartless monster trying to dupe me and the penal system.

I knew how to smoke him out, the questions that could unmask him. First, I probed him on why he had been so sloppy with Syl and Devon after such meticulous work beforehand. It took Cane longer than usual to reply, "This is something I've thought about a lot and I'm still not certain. I know for sure that I was not trying to get caught even though it must have looked that way. Maybe I was so full of myself, so cocky and self-assured that I thought I was invulnerable. But I don't think I was that out of touch with reality. Unfortunately, I'm ever so sorry to say, I knew exactly what I was doing. I could never honestly plead insanity even though my actions were completely irrational and inhumane. It's hard to explain. You couldn't call me insane because I was fully cognizant of my own actions and in control but I was not in my right mind. I had been living in a fantasy world so long, my reality was terribly skewed. In my world, Sylvia had maliciously spurned me. I know that sounds crazy but it was one of the main pillars propping up my make believe world. Without that notion, I would have had to admit that I was a weak, sniveling, impotent freak who was too petrified to pursue a normal relationship with a young lady my own age. That's the last thing my bloated ego could tolerate. So I let this bizarre lie take root and grow for years."

As I read the words on the page, I could feel that Cane was struggling for the truth, "Somewhere inside I knew; I must have known, that I was living a lie. But I buried that feeling deeper and deeper. When I attacked Sylvia I was truly conflicted. I was at a crossroads and my world was coming apart. In my sick mind, I thought everything would be all right if only Sylvia would apologize and pledge her loyalty to me. When she didn't, I became unhinged. Then, unfortunately, I was no longer conflicted. I was given over completely to the evil within me as my romantic fantasies evaporated. I still don't know why I lost control and left the clues that led to my demise. It was such a pivotal moment with my fantasy world colliding with harsh reality that I just snapped. Twain, I wish I had a better answer but I don't. There's just no explaining evil, what I did to Sylvia and Devon. I am eternally sorry."

When I read this first part of his response, I regretted the second question I had asked ... what message had he intended to convey with the bloody artwork, the finger painting on the wall? Cane dutifully answered in spite of how painful it must have been, "It was meant for nothing more than to serve my ego, my pure evil ego. In my haste and mental disarray, I had not prepared like always before with a well thought out piece of classic art to compliment my murderous work. This was completely out of character for me … an unscripted drama. My unholy ego took over and gave me the evil inspiration to operate on the fly. Reality deserted me and, my madness combined with my zest to confound the police with what I foolishly considered my towering intellect, produced the reprehensible collage of blood I scrawled on the wall. It's no wonder that none of the authorities could grasp its significance. Not only was it a crude depiction substituting finger and blood for brush and paint but the imagination of the artist was much too deep and twisted for plumbing by conventional minds. Of course, to me, despicable, deviant me, it all made perfect sense. The two figures on the left represented Wood's classic American Gothic. It was a metaphor for how I saw me and Sylvia, the quintessential American couple forever frozen in an immortal pose as was my fervent longing. Fashioning the man's pitchfork brought out my sick humor and I added horns and a

226

tail. The halo I added to Sylvia was, I guess, my repressed admission that she was, in reality, good while I was the evil one."

Cane again bared his soul and offered profuse apologies and regrets before finishing this dreadful task I had put him to, "The likeness on the right side, I think, was a way of showing a modicum of hidden remorse, however reluctant, for what I had done to Devon. Again, I could only do so in the context of my cruel and disgusting sense of humor. I found it deliciously amusing to be in the ludicrous position of caring for young children as an elementary school teacher. That was the reason I chose finger painting. To further mock the absurdity of parents and administrators giving charge over small, defenseless children to the Renaissance Killer, I thought it would be comical to include a nursery rhyme alongside Wood's masterpiece. It may not have been distinguishable to the police but I thought I gave a pretty good rendition, under the circumstances, of a haystack, little boy and a horn. Little Boy Blue was one of my favorites from childhood and made me think of poor little Devon when I recalled the last stanza: 'Will you wake him? Oh no, not I, for if I do he will surely cry.' I was such a monster." More apologies and soul searching torment ensued. Finally, Cane closed with this explanation, "Twain, it can never be excused or properly explained for there is no justification, no rational purpose within anything approaching the bounds of human decency. But this Bible passage from Philippians 3:19 helped me to understand how helpless, hopeless and doomed I was in my former state: 'whose end is destruction, whose God is their belly, and whose glory is in their shame, who mind earthly things.' I was glorying in my shame ... taking pleasure and pride in the worst kind of damnable behavior and abomination before God. As the scripture says, I was dead, spiritually dead, in my trespasses and sins. And everyone knows that a dead man can do nothing ... move nary a finger to raise himself from his tomb. Only God can raise a dead man and grant new life."

Cane's brutal candor served me in two ways. It provided priceless insights for my book. No one else had ever been allowed such entry into the heretofore tightly sealed chambers of the Renaissance Killer's mind and memories. If I could maintain my discipline and apply my craft masterfully, the book would surely be a success both critically and commercially. I wondered if Cane knew he was giving me this windfall and, if so, was it a payoff aimed at garnering my forgiveness. The other effect of Cane's unfettered, contrite

228

confessions was like that of a sharp probe being inserted deep into my brain; causing involuntary stimulation of atrophied regions of my gray matter. As much as I wanted to cling to my hatred, anger and cynicism, I couldn't help but feel a measure of creeping, grudging sympathy toward Cane's pitiful, tormented condition. Something was trying to pry open the vault where my objectivity was locked away and lend credence to the veracity and sincerity of Cane's impassioned pleas. Could I be so wrong? Was there any possibility that the Renaissance Killer was, in effect, already dead? I tried to deny these unwelcome feelings by focusing on the book and closing the gaps that Cane had obliged to help me fill. However, against my best efforts, progress on the book stalled and I couldn't escape my troubled conscience.

With the wealth of information at my disposal, pulling the loose ends together and forging ahead should have been easy. At least, it should have been simple to plug and chug through the detailed outline I had developed earlier. But that outline was constructed from a strict and narrow mindset with clear and tidy conclusions that now lacked the absolute certainty I previously possessed. How can you finish a book without a proper conclusion? Was it enough, as I had envisioned previously, to fully expose the monster and bring him to his fitting end; the final justice of the death penalty? Or was there another story to tell, a more optimistic moral of repentance and redemption? The latter had been unthinkable and was still beyond my grasp but I couldn't shake the haunting questions and resolve the dilemma. More time passed. We were now well toward 2008 and I was slipping back into the pit and my problems abounded: professional gridlock, a disgruntled publisher, concerned, prying relatives and apathy toward church and my false piety.

Then a wind came along to push me past these doldrums. I received notice of a pending clemency hearing in early 2008. My earlier suspicions came flooding back and washed away my sympathetic doubts. I immediately rushed to the conclusion that this was proof positive that, somehow, Cane had been manipulating me and the system all along and was now ready for the coup de grace. My indecision and lethargy was replaced by a locomotive of single minded purpose. The train left the station and headed down one track. I dropped everything else including any thought of completing the book and focused my entire being on blocking Cane's scheme to avoid his death sentence. There was a lot of work to do. I had to get up to speed on the process of clemency. How could I defeat the enemy without understanding the foe?

The first thing I learned was that it would be a state matter. The FBI had played a major part in the case of the Renaissance Killer but technically had done so in a supporting role. The local and state authorities never officially relinquished jurisdiction. All of Cane's murders occurred within Missouri's borders except the one in Illinois. That could have changed the case to a federal one but the prosecutors never pursued Cane for crimes committed across state lines. In fact, they only pursued one case in earnest, the first degree murder counts against Cane for the deaths of Syl and Devon. There were a long list of assorted other charges including rape and breaking and entering but capital murder was the key focus of the entire investigation and indictments. RK had been so successful in covering all of his tracks with the other murders and left such a dearth of evidence that it would have been next to impossible to win convictions. The time and expense was considered unnecessary as long as the prosecution could obtain guilty pleas against Cane in Syl and Devon's cases and, most importantly, secure the death sentence. Surviving loved ones of the other victims could take solace in seeing ultimate justice done to Cane if only on two official counts of murder.

I was the only relative of a victim to be notified of the clemency hearing since the other cases technically remained open. However, I took the time to track down and notify all the others since, official or not, they had as much at stake in this game as I did. I was still very anti-social but was compelled to break out of my shell in this instance knowing firsthand what kind of suffering they'd experience if Cane's sentence was reduced. I even took the very uncharacteristic step of creating a web site where everyone could follow the process and proceedings to, hopefully, a successful conclusion. I posted updates as my research continued. In general the process was set to start at the prison board level and work its way up. If the prison board came up with an affirmative recommendation, the clemency plea would proceed to the Attorney General's office for a complete and thorough review and then, if accepted, would be passed along to the Governor for granting or denial. My participation would take place at the prison level where, hopefully, I could help to nip this in the bud.

I was nervous because I was the only person who would be allowed to speak on behalf of the victims. It would have been a slam dunk, in my opinion, if dozens of surviving members of all the victims' families could have pleaded our case in unison. Cane would be given an equal chance to make his case but beyond that I didn't know for sure. I assumed that he would bring others to bear witness of his transformation; probably Reverend Floyd and Cane's grandparents. Knowing that so much would be riding on my testimony, I was able to gird my loins for battle and drive out any foolish thoughts of sympathy for Cane or doubts about the sham he was perpetrating. There would be no conflict or uncertainty to deter me from the mission.

This gave me confidence but not the total assurance I longed for so I began looking into back up plans, just in case. The other family members and I agreed that we could pool our resources and pursue one or more of the other open cases, if necessary. That possibility was more frightening than soothing because we were at such a disadvantage in terms of hard evidence. The admissions Cane made to me were not likely to be considered admissible in court. If we could prove guilt beyond a reasonable doubt which was not probable, it seemed less likely we could secure the death sentence. We thought that, perhaps, it would help to reopen the Southern Illinois murder case. Would there be any advantage to having a federal prosecutor involved? Everything about this process and the interminable three month wait until the hearing wracked me with constant worry. I don't know about the other victims' family members because a whisper was never uttered but I assumed they were starting to entertain some very disturbing thoughts, like me. I pursued every angle in thinking about what to do if clemency were granted and no other convictions could be secured. This is something I don't like to admit but I even pondered the possibility of hiring someone to kill Cane. I was sure that, with the right connections and financial wherewithal, arrangements could be made to enlist the services of a jail house assassin. My faith had been fluttering, nearly extinguished, for the longest time but I think I reached the nadir in contemplating Cane's clemency. I hadn't prayed to God in years but I finally bent the knee and pleaded with God to end Cane's miserable life. I was taught that vengeance is mine sayeth the Lord, but I didn't care at that point. I'd break every commandment and pay whatever the consequences just to see Cane dead. Mine was not the prayer of a righteous man and, thus, would availeth nothing.

10 Star Crossed Witness

I decided to stop corresponding with Cane. In terms of completing the book, I had lost all interest. It had become an unwanted distraction since I was totally absorbed with blocking the clemency request. Beyond that, if I wanted to kick start the project, I didn't need RK anyway. The information I had already amassed with his help was surely more than enough. There was no reason to take any chances. I feared that, if I continued to correspond with Cane, he might be able to cast another one of his spells on me. A more confident man would have trusted in the strength of his convictions but I had been through this too many times before not to remain wary. Cutting myself off was the only sure fire way to avoid being manipulated. There was only one problem … nobody told Cane. He continued to correspond with me. We had graduated from snail mail to email. Access was granted on the basis of good behavior but, of course, everything was routed through a screener to block anything untoward or sniff out any coded messages that might present a security threat. There were no first amendment rights in maximum security prisons. Driven as I was, I was able to hold my curiosity at bay and didn't open the emails from Cane. However, I couldn't quite push myself to press the delete button and instead dropped his messages into a folder.

The last month before the hearing was extremely hard on me. I had gone over my preparations again and again to the point where it was useless to review something which I had firmly planted in my memory banks with total recall capability. With nothing to occupy my time, my mind began to wander. To ward off the demon of empathy, I'd snap myself back in line by replaying the remembrances of Syl and Devon over and over. My nerve endings never numbed no matter the number of repetitions. The pain was fresh and intense each time. This self-flagellation served its purpose in keeping me from embracing any desire other than revenge but it took a heavy toll on me otherwise. I could hardly sleep and when I did it was usually cut short by fitful nightmares. It got so bad that I considered popping pills or hitting the bottle but, thankfully, was able to avoid going down that path again.

How could I bargain with my own conscience? I had presented every conceivable argument in support of retribution and yet my unyielding scruples would not be swayed. World War III continued to rage within me. If I could not subdue my conscience through drugs and alcohol or push it aside by filling my time with work and other daily pursuits, then how might I tame it? Perhaps nostalgia would be a worthy substitute. With that thought in mind, I dug through my basement in search of mind soothing nostalgia. When I first began mining my memorabilia treasures, it did have a positive impact on my outlook. It not only consumed idle time but provided a means of escape. It felt good to recall the happy, idyllic times and think of Syl and Devon as they were before the tragedy. My heart grew lighter and my sleeping habits improved. Unfortunately, this proved short lived because my conscience is a sagacious fellow who saw through the smoke screen and pressed his case anew. After going through the photo albums, trinkets, baby baubles and Devon's kindergarten heirlooms, I made the mistake of reading some of the letters Syl and I exchanged when we were first dating and later when we were just married and I had to travel a lot.

Ah, young love makes a man say and do some silly things. The letters took me back to a time when I was a different person. It was kind of embarrassing to read the mushy things I penned to Syl during those weak, lonely and frivolous moments. I guess absence does make the heart grow fonder. Boy, would I have been mortified if my buddies would have gotten their hands on some of those letters back in the day. It would have done major damage to my macho image. Yikes, I even resorted to poetry on occasion! My discomfiture aside, these letters gave me a warm feeling. Oh, how I missed those halcyon days. My playful pining may have lacked maturity but, even after all these years, the sincerity still came through. We were truly, deeply in love, Syl and I. Long dormant feelings stirred as I indulged in fond retrospection. This was what it had been like, I recalled, being totally open and carefree with no prickly defenses to lock everyone else out. This was what it had been like to think about someone else much more than one's self. With Syl, I only strived for her happiness and didn't need to give a thought to my own. She always took care of that so effortlessly. I never needed to be suspicious or on my guard.

Our old love letters brought back another memory which should have been fond but caused more guilt and shame than anything else. Syl had this habit of closing with a scripture reference. She had a knack for finding just the right passage to match whatever encouragement I needed. If I had a doubt, she would supply God's sure promises. When I was feeling guilty, there would be God's great mercy, patience and forgiveness. Afflictions were met with God's fatherly comfort and closeness. And if I was joyous over some good fortune, she would always remind me how God was the source of our blessings and urge me to be like the tenth healed leper who turned back to Christ in thankfulness. Most of all, she constantly inspired me to put my trust in God in all things and spurred me to always turn to God's word for guidance, edification and strength. If Syl were to have seen me now, she would have been more than distressed. She would have been crushed by my lack of faith and anger toward God. But she would have never let it happen. If Syl were alive, she would have kept me in the word no matter what. The fact that I had given into bitterness and hardened my heart against God spoiled my trips down memory lane. I realized that I was a different person now … one that Syl would not have liked.

I cut myself off and locked myself inside my lonely, dark room to suffer in virtual solitude. There were only three companions to keep me company, all with the last name anger. I was viciously angry with Cane, raged against God and hated myself for spurning the memories of Syl and Devon. It's a wonder I didn't go mad but somehow I survived to reach the day of the clemency hearing. It felt

239

liberating to have such a strong sense of purpose and the opportunity to act upon it. I was so geared up for this confrontation I was in a near frenzy. During the drive to Potosi, I had to dial myself back to a state of control. I practiced along the way, reciting my lines and working on my delivery. It would not be enough to summon all the terrible recollections. I was determined to convey the heart rending emotions so that the review board would feel my pain and be able to put themselves in Syl and Devon's shoes. Call it a performance if you will. I don't mind. I guess, in a way, I was preparing for an important role and I would definitely employ classical method acting techniques. I had no problem tapping into real thoughts and emotions. It was an easy role because I never really stepped out of character, whether on stage or not.

Perhaps I should have turned the radio on to occupy the time on the drive to PCC. Once I had my part down pat, my mind began to wander again and I found that my conscience had stowed away for the ride. It asked whether our lives were star crossed, Cane and I. While I was never a believer in astrology and the notion that events in our lives were governed by the stars, I had often pondered fate. From a Christian theological perspective, this notion was wrapped up in a most perplexing treatise known as the doctrine of election. That is, if you're bound for heaven, it's totally due to the work and will of God and was determined before creation. Yet, on the other hand, if you wind up in hell, it's all your own doing. God did not predestinate anyone to hell. He justified all mankind through Christ's atoning sacrifice on the cross but many people stubbornly reject his grace, the free gift of salvation, to their own doom. It truly is a matter of faith. This doctrine is a divine conundrum that is beyond man's finite reason. I guess it's like we're told in Deuteronomy 29:29, the secret things belong unto the Lord our God. So, were Cane and I star crossed, destined to cross paths in such a tragic way? This raised another basic theological question. Are our lives just a string of random occurrences happening willy nilly by chance? Or is there a higher purpose? If, for the sake of argument, I accepted the latter as posed by my conscience, what was my purpose in all this? Was I God's tool of retribution, some kind of avenging angel on a mission to seal Cane's doom? Or was there some divine task of forgiveness and salvation at hand? This seemed impossible, inconceivable. If Syl were along for the ride she would say, "C'mon, Twain, don't you remember what Jesus said in Matthew 19:26? With men this is impossible; but with God all things are possible."

Yes, Syl could have forgiven anyone for anything. But could she have forgiven Cane for Devon? I doubt that even Syl had that much in her.

The sign said Potosi 10 miles. Thank goodness for that! I couldn't wait to hear what Cane and presumably others had to say in his defense. Just the thought made me indignant and helped push my troublesome conscience into the distant recesses of my mind. I was poised for a battle royal when I entered the hearing but was disappointed by the unexpected surroundings. The small, stark conference room was much too informal to represent officialdom as I had expected it. There was no grand dais or separate witness chair; no gallery filled with witnesses. The four of us sat together around the same plain conference table in close proximity with everyone seated on the same nondescript chairs. The only other person in the room was inconspicuously off to the side, there only to record the proceedings. I came in with an attitude of me-against-the-world but the board members were anything but confrontational. They were polite, courteous and more than objective. All three of them seemed sympathetic toward my plight and went out of their way to make me feel comfortable.

There wasn't a cross examination from some antagonistic defense attorney as I had imagined and the opposition was not present during my testimony. This sidetracked some of the dramatics I had envisioned with me pointing the finger at Cane and laying my charges to him personally. The three members of the review board could have been a doting aunt and my two favorite uncles. They weren't stiff, heartless bureaucrats droning on about rigid procedures and legal technicalities. They basically gave me the floor and let me speak from the heart. At first, I spent a lot of time talking about Syl and Devon. I wanted them to get to know my wife and child and really grasp their memories. It was important, I thought, to put a face with the names and bring them to life in the minds of the board members. Syl and Devon couldn't be two ordinary human beings now dead and long gone. The review board needed to assess their value and assign worth as I did.

They were very patient with me even though I went well over my allotted time. Once satisfied that I had set the bar as high as possible, I launched into a condemnation of Cane. I was careful to avoid a hateful diatribe to maintain the victim's high ground but was able to draw a glaring comparison between Syl and Devon's lofty heights and Cane's bottomless pit of depravity. I pleaded, "What kind of human being would do this? Rape was not enough for him. No, he had to rape my wife in front of my seven year old boy. Murder couldn't satiate his bloodlust. He had to physically torture them and psychologically terrorize them. And this was necessary for what reason? Was it justified because Sylvia turned down a date with a college freshman she didn't know from Adam? Even all of that was not enough to satisfy Cane. In death, even in death he had to desecrate their bodies. And he violated my wife's lifeless, headless body!" They knew all of this as well as I. Each of them had dutifully read the case files again. But hearing it from me and being exposed to such raw emotion was different. I knew that it had hit home with them. They were each armed with a legal pad and pen but no one bothered to take any notes. It wasn't necessary. My words were like hot irons that were branded into their memories.

There was no rebuttal from them or opposition of any kind other than the requisite question from the designated chairperson, "Mr. Newman, we assume you are aware of Mr. Cane's purported religious conversion. " I nodded in agreement and tried to hold back a smirk. "That being the case, do you care to comment on its pertinence in your mind?" I had to clinch my gut to avoid an unpleasant reaction. This was not the time for bombastic railings against Almighty God. The review board members struck me as Christian folk who wouldn't take kindly to such an affront. I looked down, as if in prayer, to contemplate and gather my thoughts. "It's okay Mr. Newman, please take your time. We know this is difficult." Little did they know that I was trying to shut my conscience out. It was screaming at me, yes Twain, yes it makes all the difference in the world! I was at the point of no return. Should I give into the fleeting compassion I had felt when I met Cane the second time and was exposed to the new man? Would I succumb to the emotion that gripped me when I read Syl's letters and recalled her loving, forgiving nature? Or was it time for the avenging angel to strike a final death blow?

The remains of my fleshy heart wanted to break its iron fetters and forgive. I knew deep down that it was the right thing to do; not only for Cane's benefit but my own peace. And yet, I didn't follow my heart or Syl's cherished example. I took the low road. The gutter I traversed flowed with filth and wretchedness. It carried me along with its malignant current to my reply, "I would like to believe Cane; I really would. As you know, I met personally with him after his reported conversion to see for myself. He gave a convincing performance. If I didn't know better, I would have believed that God performed a miracle on his black heart. But I do know better. When I met with him the first time, he gave an even more impressive portrayal of a man helplessly plagued with Dissociative Identify Disorder. He had me believing that part of him was inherently good but our bad, bad world and corrupt society had created an evil persona that took control of his life and actions. In that case, he admitted the sham in an effort to psychologically terrorize me for his own sick pleasure. His conversion, I believe, is no less a farce but he would never admit it with so much at stake. He must keep the mask firmly in place to have any chance of avoiding the death penalty."

I continued to drive nail after nail into Cane's coffin, "Will executing Cane do any good? I'm sure we would all prefer to spare his life if there was the slightest chance he could be reformed and have any hope of having a positive impact on our world in any small way. I'm sorry to say though that every breath from Cane's lungs can only pollute our world. He lives for only one thing; to perpetuate evil. For Cane, death is the only way to bring this to an end. Sadly, the world will be a better place without him. We may not be able to say with absolute certainty that Cane's conversion is just a clever ruse. However, we know beyond the shadow of a doubt that he is guilty of the most heinous crimes imaginable. We have a solemn duty; justice must be served. Sylvia was the kindest, gentlest, most loving Christian I ever knew and Devon, my sweet, precious Devon, had the purest heart any person could possibly possess. Did that make any difference to Cane? Was there an ounce of mercy in his heart? Did he show them a crumb of compassion? I submit to you that Cane's execution will be infinitely more humane and merciful than anything he showed to Syl and Devon."

There was no doubt from the looks on their faces that they were in my court. Nevertheless, I had no way of knowing how Cane might yet sway them so I drove the final nail home, "I know this is off the record since Cane was only convicted of killing my wife and child but I am compelled to speak up for the others. It may not be admissible in a court of law but Cane has confessed his other crimes to me. He not only admitted them but reveled in them. What he did to Syl and Devon is more than enough to warrant the death penalty. But let us not forget the others. There are dozens of other victims with stories just like mine. A storm tossed ocean of pain still washes up on the shores of dozens of other households because of Cane. I've talked to them and shared their sadness. They all want the same thing, peace and justice. So many lives will remain shattered as long as Cane is allowed to live and breathe and menace others with his evil from within the confines of this prison. On behalf of Sylvia and Devon and all the others, I implore you with all my heart to do what is good and right in God's sight and deliver Cane up to him in justice."

There was a long silence as we waited for the tension to dissipate. Then *Aunty* said, "We thank you so much for your time and candor, Mr. Newman. We know this was not easy for you. We will take everything you've said into consideration before making our recommendation. Before we close, is there anything else you'd like to say?" While it seemed like a slam dunk, I couldn't help but worry about Cane and gave into my curiosity, "Can you tell me, have you spoken with Cane or any others yet or is that still to come?" "Oh, I almost forgot. You haven't been privy to any of the other details regarding our proceedings. I can tell you now that this hearing was conducted according to state protocol and not at the behest of Mr. Cane. When we notified him of the opportunity to speak with this panel, he declined. We advised him of the importance of hearing his personal testimony but he refused. There were a couple of other witnesses who wished to speak on his behalf but Cane discouraged them." I was dumbfounded and it must have shown on my face. "We were just as surprised as you. We thought there must be some catch. Perhaps it's part of some clever strategy that his lawyer helped him to hatch but, for the life of me, I can't imagine why. So, we're effectively done here." When the other two panel members left, *Aunty* pulled me aside and whispered, "I'm not supposed to say anything but, off the record, I'm sure we'll recommend denial. It may take a few weeks before it's official but, rest assured, there will be no clemency for Mr. Cane."

In spite of the assurances given to me, I was on pins and needles until the official word came down. Just as *Aunty* had promised, clemency was denied. As an added bonus, they finally set a date for the execution, October 10, 2010. I wasn't perturbed by the fact that I still had to wait almost two years because I was so relieved to have an end in sight, an unambiguous, firm appointment for Cane's date with destiny. It was enough to put me back on an even keel for a while. Then curiosity got the better of me. Why had Cane refused to testify? If it was a scheme, it certainly backfired. I knew Cane was no dummy; far from it. Also, with his notorious notoriety, he was able to attract a top notch attorney, not some rookie public defender. It seemed to me that, if nothing else, he would have allowed Reverend Floyd or perhaps his kindly grandparents to testify on his behalf. They surely would have had some impact on the panel. It just didn't make any sense but there was no place to go for answers. The review board had been as clueless as me. Well, there was one person who could help me if I wanted to know bad enough.

I was reluctant to contact Cane. Since I had for all intents and purposes pulled the lever on his execution, it seemed wholly out of place for me to ask him to confide in me. As an alternative to such a last ditch effort, I retrieved Cane's unopened emails from my file with the hope that they would reveal some hint as to his motive. I was stunned by what I read as I've summed up for you in the following excerpts:

> Dear Twain,
>
> By now, I'm sure you've heard about the pending clemency hearing. First, I want to assure you that everything I told you in our last meeting is true; including when I said I didn't want to seek clemency. I remain

genuinely full of the deepest remorse for what I did to you and your family. I've continued to seek solace and answers in the Bible. One thing I've learned is that the Fourth Commandment extends beyond father and mother to all legitimate authority and, thus, I know I should be subject to the just sentence I've received and do nothing to impede it from being carried out properly.

I cannot deny or make any excuses for my grievous sins. I am guilty of the charges brought against me and have been fairly and rightly convicted. My sentence is appropriate and I deserve to die. To try to skirt God's justice would be a denial of the new man in me. I have new life now and, by the grace of God, have been freed and am no more a slave to sin. By the power of the Holy Spirit, I have been emancipated and empowered to do the right thing. Yes, I know it sounds ludicrous but I have never been this free in my life, even as I am rotting away in this prison within the executioner's long shadow.

Nothing is the same anymore. I can see everything in a different light. Everything has been turned upside down. Before I didn't know God and spent all my time doing the work of the devil. Now, all I want is to know and do God's will. You see, I've been purchased with a price, an incredible price that only God could afford to pay. I'm happy that my life is no longer my own for I am a bond slave to Jesus Christ. It makes absolutely no sense but perfect sense to me … I've been set free by becoming a slave. My former life has been lost but I've gained eternal life in the process.

I hope that you will attend the clemency hearing and do everything you can to condemn what I've done. By telling the truth, you will be serving our Lord and Savior and me in turn. If God wanted to set me free from these bars, he could and would do so. You should commend me to God's care and mercy and then carry out your duty without guilt or remorse. Just tell the truth, Twain.

Your suspicions were totally warranted and you had every reason to doubt me. It is my fond desire that these words might bring you some comfort and peace. Still, I know that it may take more than words for someone with a past like mine. Thus, I want to buoy you with my actions too. My attorney has advised me vigorously to the contrary but nevertheless, I am compelled to set the record straight. Under separate cover, I am sending you a hard copy of my full confession to all the crimes and murders I've committed. It will be notarized and duly witnessed by my attorney and fully admissible in a court of law. I do this with the full knowledge that it will countermand any affirmative recommendation regarding my clemency hearing. It will leave me open to multiple convictions with death sentences and expose me up to federal prosecution for my crimes in Illinois. Hopefully, clemency will be denied and further actions by the courts will be rendered moot. I could wait to see what the outcome of the hearing is first but I want to do this anyway. I owe it to the other families. There's nothing I can do to make up for their pain and losses but, perhaps, this will grant them some closure.

Twain please do not feel bad about my execution. I have no fear of death anymore. When that day comes, you can take heart in knowing that I will have finally been completely freed from my old, corrupt, evil self. There shall be life beyond the grave. Until then, I have one thought in mind; to serve the Lord in any small way possible. I shall, God willing, proclaim the gospel of Jesus Christ to anyone who might listen. As for you, may God grant you peace and purpose. Stay in God's word where you will find power, spiritual nourishment, healing, faith and truth. God has started a good work in you with your book. I wish you continued success. May it bring more than the condemnation I deserve but also hope in the power of God to save; even a chief of sinners like me. If there is anything I can do to help you with the book, I am at your service.

In Christ's precious blood and righteousness,

Charles

Would it have made a difference if I would have read his emails before the hearing? Perhaps I was too jaded to escape my cynicism anyway. The compassion and warmth I felt now may not have materialized if the outcome of the clemency hearing was still in question. I wondered if I was only feeling charitable because my foe was vanquished and his fate sealed. Could I be that callous? Or was I experiencing a change of heart because the veracity of Cane's claims now seemed to be beyond question? It was impossible to answer these questions but maybe it didn't matter. If I had opened the emails and had a change of heart, would it have made a difference in the outcome? Cane had only encouraged me to do the right thing and tell the truth. Then I wondered if it was possible this was one last effort by Cane to fool me into helping his cause. Could it be a grand scheme of reverse psychology by urging me to do the opposite of his true bidding? Any such thoughts were put to rest when I went back and opened the hard copy letter from Cane. True to his word, he provided a full confession; documented, authorized and fully admissible. He had come clean and sealed his own fate. I didn't give the confession to the police but shared it with all the victim's families.

Now I finally had a new lease on life or so I thought. I decided to do two things long overdue; get back into my manuscript and take a fresh run at developing a meaningful relationship with someone. The latter was easier said than done. Where do you start at my age after being out of circulation so long? I didn't want any part of the bar scene ... been there, done that ... and couldn't bring myself to faking shopping cart collisions at the super market. Online dating services were all the rage but seemed a little scary and weird to me. The best place to find a nice gal would be in church but I still couldn't shake my demons there. Being cut off from friends it was tough to get referrals and I wasn't desperate enough to ask Bud or Lilly for prospects. Also, I knew better than to soil my own nest and frowned upon workplace romances. I figured it would just have to happen naturally in the course of my normal daily routine outside of work. More often than not when I ventured out in public it was to hit the gym or frequent one of my favorite running trails. I was too committed to fitness to interrupt my normal workout for the sake of romance but I got into the habit of people watching when I finished jogging. My favorite spot was Creve Coeur Lake. After a good run, I'd cool down on one of the park benches where I could watch passersby with the backdrop of windblown waves lapping against the shoreline. It was a peaceful setting with a panoramic view of the sand, water, foliage and a majestic tree line covering the steep surrounding hillsides and cliffs.

It was actually pretty silly even though there were plenty of prospects. But everyone was on the move, blading, biking, running or walking. Variety was not a problem though. The Lake was a melting pot of cultures with just about every nationality imaginable from Middle Eastern to Asian to Eastern European. All the major religions were covered and the gals came in all ages, shapes, sizes and colors. There was something for every taste. Still, I didn't have a good plan of action. What would I do if I saw someone that interested me? Would I jump up and start chasing after them? A more devious fellow would have borrowed a dog or a baby; sure fire ways to attract women. But I had neither. I also lacked the confidence to approach women even if they weren't scurrying past so quickly. One day an attractive lady who looked to be about my age caught my eye. She was jogging alone so without thinking I jumped up and began to trail her. As I followed, it dawned on me how foolish I was. Should I run up alongside her and breathless say hey baby, what's shaking? Maybe I'd try to pull her over and say, would you mind stopping so I can catch my breath and hit on you? Did I still have enough left in the tank to tail her until she finished her run? If so, could I avoid looking like a stalker to prevent from having her rush to her car or seek out the nearest patrolman or park ranger?

Granted it was a bad idea but I kept at it anyway. Even if I didn't engage anyone in a live conversation, it made me feel good to be a part of the crowd with a faint hope of a felicitous encounter. Then one day it happened. I had finished a good, hard run and was enjoying the sunshine and cool breeze while lolling peacefully on my favorite lakeside perch. I wasn't really paying much attention as I casually gazed down the path at the gaggle of oncoming enthusiasts. At first it just seemed like a mirage, a product of my aimless daydreaming. But as she approached more closely within my field of vision there was something oddly familiar. I couldn't see her face clearly yet so it could have been her gait, something about her shape or the color of her hair. Whatever it was, I locked in my tractor beam as the mystery guest drew nearer. Luckily she wasn't paying attention and didn't notice me staring. Then it clicked and just about knocked me off the bench to the ground. It was Sally! I was sure of it … I'd know her anywhere! My heart leapt like crackling flames from dry kindling. She was shapely as ever and pretty as can be. The years had been very kind to her. Sally had a bounce in her step that fit her effervescent personality. In an instant my mind whooshed into the future: we were married and living the life of perpetual honeymooners. I was so carried away, my inhibitions vanished and I prepared to spring into action. In my haste and excitement, I almost didn't see the young man on roller blades up ahead, circling back, "C'mon, mom, you're slipping … better pick up the pace." "Don't you worry about me. Go on with your roller blades, Mr. Hare, and let this walking tortoise be. I'll catch up eventually," she said with a bright smile.

I might as well have jumped off the cliffs above the Creve Coeur waterfall like the Indian princess of lake lore. According to legend, the Lake of the Broken Heart was formed by her fall when she leaped to her death over the unrequited love of a French fur trader. My hopes and dreams were similarly dashed as quickly as they had been resurrected by Sally's presence. I was so deflated, utterly crushed that I didn't even stop her as she passed. There would be no point in renewing our old acquaintance. It would just swell my bitterness and pain. Any reminder of what might have been would just torment me. Why had I let her go before? What was wrong with me? Another man had taken my place forever. I imagined she had a wonderful family and, hopefully, the type of idyllic life I had shared with Syl and Devon. I burned with resentment toward myself like the slow embers from a waning fire that linger well into the night. I was a victim of my own stubbornness and stupidity.

After that, I lost interest and became resigned to loneliness and despair. I turned my attention to my long neglected manuscript which brought Cane back into focus. It seemed my whole life had been committed to seeing him die. Or would it be more honest to say I had wasted my life? Now I had lost my fervor. Cane seemed to be genuinely contrite and intent upon willingly paying the price for his evil deeds. With my vengeance about to be fulfilled it had lost its allure. It dawned on me that God had been right all along and I should have left vengeance in his hands. Then I recalled an old, familiar Bible passage where God claims no pleasure in the death of the wicked. Thinking about Cane and my former lust for his execution cast this truth in a whole new light for me. Was it too late to make amends? Did I even want to? While those questions remained unanswered, I took to corresponding with Cane again. I used the convenient excuse that I needed help in putting the finishing touches on my research but the truth was that I wanted to somehow peer into the man's soul for answers.

Cane didn't question my motives but openly shared his deepest insights and feelings as October 10th approached. No matter where the dialogue took us or how many times we corresponded, he was consistent to the end. His newfound faith never wavered and he always took every chance to share the good news and tried to build me up in the faith. He was never preoccupied with his pending execution and seemed genuinely more concerned about my well-being. Cane never dwelled on death but instead spoke volumes about the glories of eternity that awaited him. Talk about role reversal; as October 10th drew nearer, his joy increased while I was the one filled with foreboding. Instead of me consoling him, he was offering encouragement to me. He only had one request of me. Cane pleaded with me to use his example to get the word of God out, "Use the book to do some good, Twain. Treat it like John's Revelation; not a message of gloom and doom. Move past that and shine the light of hope. Please give it the happy ending that God's work deserves."

After more than twenty years of waiting and focusing on one single event, I now had serious reservations. The culmination of all my thoughts, longings and most consuming desire were about to be realized and I was having second thoughts. I didn't want to attend the execution. I could not foresee deriving anything close to pleasure by witnessing the death of Charles Darwin Cane. Instead, a crazy, wild thought bored into my brain. Did I have enough time to finish a rough first draft of the manuscript ... as a gift to Cane? Something told me he was right and that I should steer it to the happy ending he suggested. This notion possessed me and I tackled the manuscript with every bit of resolve I could muster. The first thing I needed to do was read the entire manuscript and edit here and there to facilitate the transition to a new closing. As I launched into it, the consequences of my good intentions were totally unexpected. As I reread the original, it conjured up old ghosts, the malevolent spirits that had haunted me for so long. My depictions of the murders were so graphic, so real that I couldn't avoid stirring up my old, destructive emotions. Before I knew it, I was clasped in their tight, suffocating grip again. How could I have any compassion for such a heartless monster? How had I fallen under his spell? As my past anger was recycled, it flushed every other feeling I had for Cane from my system. A new man, is he? Hah, bah humbug, I Scrooged! My mind was made up. I would see Cane die with my own eyes.

I did my best to maintain my resolve for the last few days leading up to the execution. The drive to Bonne Terre was the longest trip of my life. I tried everything to drown out my conscience from ear splitting music to CD books to blathering talk radio but to no avail. You can fool a lot of people but it's hard to deceive yourself. How could I fall for my own bluster? I knew I was sustaining my anger with false bravado. My ears were deaf to my own bombast. The self-inflicted pain of recalling RK's account of Syl and Devon's deaths over and over was the only thing that sustained me. When I finally approached the entrance to the ERDCC, it was from that point just like a succession of scenes from a movie. The security precautions, clueless protesters, red tape, strict procedures, stoic prison guards, somber officials and stark surroundings were so stereotypical it almost seemed like I had been through this before. It offered some momentary relief when I realized some of the other victims' family members had made the trek too. But, in this case, having company did not ease the misery and tension.

We were finally ushered into the witness room adjacent to the execution chamber along with various prison officials and other sorry souls with the abhorrent duty of covering the joyless event. It was deadly silent and no one dared to utter a word. The curtains covering the execution chamber remained closed for the longest time. We were sheltered from all of the procedures and preparations being carried out behind the scenes. Capital punishment is a very precise business. With every slow tick of the clock, a little more air seemed to be sucked out of the claustrophobic room. When the curtains were finally pulled back exposing the brightly lit chamber, it had the startling effect of a bolt of lightning.

There was Cane, strapped to a gurney, helplessly restrained with a series of tubes running to and fro between his arms and the contraptions set to deliver death to his veins. You would think that one tube and needle would be enough to get the job done but it's much more complicated. First, there's a backup system just in case the primary delivery system experiences a failure. Then there is a control module to mimic the empty shell introduced somewhere within a firing squad. It's designed to assuage the guilt of the executioner because there are two control panels with manual switches and neither one knows which will deliver harmless saline versus the deadly dose. Even the drugs administered were designed with a particular sequence of effects in mind, ostensibly to ease the discomfort experienced by the condemned.   First a heavy barbiturate induces sleep, then a paralytic agent stops the breathing process and lastly a potassium solution shuts down the heart. This can take several minutes before the monitors allow death to be pronounced.

I was getting squeamish. Cold beads of sweat sprang from my forehead and my stomach churned like a bag of maggots. This is what I longed to see for some twenty years? This was one horror show I didn't want to watch. I couldn't stand to see my dog put to sleep much less the execution of another human being. I wanted so badly to get up and walk out but I was trapped, frozen in my seat. No one looked at each other and, I think, like me, most everyone tried to avoid eye contact with Cane. That changed when Cane was given the chance to offer his final testimony. I've never seen someone in such a pitiful, hopeless situation, bear up to the inestimable pressure with such dignity and fortitude. His face was a portrait of peace, not panic and tranquility, not terror. Surely his faith was genuine to face death with such confidence and

serenity. As he spoke, you could hear a pin drop.
First, he expressed his regrets for everything he had
done and the pain he had caused to all the families
in attendance. Then he gave a beautiful witness to
the salvation of Jesus Christ and thanked God, his
Lord and Savior. I'll never forget his last words …
"Twain, I'm so sorry. Please forgive me. I leave the
message for you to carry now. Stay in the word.
Please put your trust in Jesus Christ, my friend." He
smiled meekly and closed his eyes before the
switches were thrown and he passed into eternity
peacefully.

Part 3 - Reunion

11 Dark Dungeon

I sacrificed twenty years of my life to the cause. My one and only mission had been to see justice wrought to Charles Darwin Cane. The other families had suffered even longer and were equally as determined if perhaps not misshapen by obsession as I was. The anticipation built slowly over so many years and reached a crescendo on 10/10/10. It reminded me of one of my favorite poems, the classic Casey at the Bat. It seemed all hope was lost for the Mudville nine, down two runs in the final inning. When the first two batters went down, the somber mood went into free fall since there were two feckless hitters in the lineup preceding the hometown hero, Casey. But one reached first unexpectedly and the second miraculously ripped an extra base hit. Now with runners on second and third with two out, electricity ran through the crowd as Mighty Casey approached the plate. In his arrogance, the great slugger let the first two strikes go by sending the crowd into a frenzy. The time had finally arrived and Mighty Casey would deliver them. Well you know how it turned out and after similar twists and turns our emotional sojourn ended differently but oddly the same. We realized the long awaited victory but then ... there was no joy in *Mudville*.

There has never been such melancholy at a victory party, if you can call it that. There was no celebration at all. At first there was only silence and introspection. Then brief, awkward conversations followed. Most of the comments went something like this, "I was stunned by his final testimony. It was so moving and seemed so genuine. This was the man who tortured and slaughtered our loved ones?" A few people tried to console each other with the words, "I'm just glad it's finally over," but I'm certain that everyone felt the same underneath it all. It was a hollow victory. The guilty had received justice but we the just felt somehow guilty. There were hugs and a few tears then everyone departed quietly, draped in sullenness. The very next day, I shut down the web site dedicated to Cane's victims and their surviving family members. I would never see or hear from any of them again, this side of heaven.

Perhaps the executioners maintained a clear conscience since each could cling to the hope that they had only administered a harmless injection of saline solution. I was not so fortunate. Of all the survivors who witnessed the execution, there was only one who was responsible for Cane's execution. I acted alone in eagerly blocking the clemency request. No one else had ever met Cane face to face. The only insights they had into Cane's soul and character prior to the execution were supplied second hand by yours truly. Would the others have been so cynical had they been given the chance to see the new Cane like I had? Or would they have had a change of heart and been moved to support the clemency request? Only God knew. God ... why did God have it in for me? Would my torment never end? Cane's execution brought me no satisfaction or closure.

My name, Twain, never seemed more appropriate than after Cane's execution. Before, my family had been torn apart and my soul troubled for so many years but at least I had been given over to single minded intentions, although base and cruel. Now I was split in two and horribly conflicted. Wasn't I justified in finding some peace and fulfillment in the death of Cane? He had confessed to the vilest, most unforgiveable sins any man could commit. He welcomed his punishment and took every step to ensure his sentence was carried out. So why then did I feel so guilty? Why was there a huge, unseen, mountainous weight of self-reproach crushing the life out of me? Should I have forgiven him and allowed him that peace before his appointment with eternity? Should I have collaborated with an evil murderer and comforted him with the promise that I would use my book about his life and deeds to tell a tale of redemption? What had seemed outrageous in the context of my former condition when I was beset with blind anger now took on a different tone. In hindsight, part of me said it was at least plausible if not laudable. However, it was too late. I had shown no mercy, only judgment and condemnation.

I was unwilling to openly admit what was at the heart of my troubles but deep within I knew. It was not a chemical imbalance or psychological deficiency. Nor was it a fractured conscience although that was certainly a primary symptom of my ailment. No, my affliction had to do with one looming obstacle that partitioned my soul like a Berlin Wall. It was the barrier I had erected between me and God. Here, in my dark, dank dungeon, I had tried to shut him out of my life completely but still he seeped through the cracks driving me ever deeper into its lonely bowels seeking refuge from inevitability. That's the true folly of atheists, isn't it? They spend their lives going here and there, huffing and puffing about the nonexistence of a God that they know, in spite of all their protestations, they will eventually have to face. The only people more pitiful are the agnostics who try to hedge their bets by saying it's impossible to know if God exists. Agnostics lack common sense because, apparently, they don't realize that the word agnostic literally means without knowledge. Would they be so quick to wear the badge if it meant stamping the word ignorant across their foreheads? They'll get no pass from God on judgment day due to stupidity. I suppose I was worse than the atheists and agnostics combined because I had been raised in the church and properly educated about God from the Holy Scriptures, yet I was trying to deny him too. I had the truth but chose to ignore it.

Yes, I knew God existed. However, I was trying to paint him with my own brush … with the colors of a capricious, sadistic, harsh judge full of wrath and vengeance. Part of me realized how foolish I was being. If you can't fight city hall, how can you expect to enter a battle of wills with Almighty God and come out on top? I guess hubris is part of being human but then so too is humility and unfortunately I was lacking in the latter. Luckily, I was in short supply of another commodity, endurance. I had wasted the better portion of my life pursuing Cane's execution with the hope that it would free me from my cursed chamber but his death brought no emancipation to me. My war of attrition against God had taken its toll on me. I couldn't maintain my will to fight while staring at the prospect of living out the rest of my meaningless life in such a wretched, worthless condition. "Okay," I thought, "You win God. I'll tear down the wall that has separated us and come back home."

I was a lousy prodigal. I went to church and read my Bible but it went in one ear and out the other. There was no problem with my hearing but the comprehension part was lacking. I even tried praying but I didn't pray the prayers of a righteous man. A truly righteous man knows that his righteousness comes from outside, not within. My prayers were self-centered. I wanted this or needed that by my own estimation. The thought of seeking God's will never entered my mind. God always keeps his promises but I didn't deliver on mine. I may have taken down the wall by, I thought, seeking God in his house but I was wearing an invisible coat of armor that shielded me from God's gracious love. Recall the Prodigal Son. He had rejected the advice of his father, taken his inheritance and squandered it on booze and broads. After bringing nothing but shame to the family and being so destitute he had no other choice, he returned to his father to beg for crumbs and the lowliest, most menial job on the family estate. To his amazement, the father welcomed him with open arms and gave him the best of everything including a huge homecoming celebration. Now, imagine if the Prodigal Son would have declined the father's invitation to the welcome home party, doffed the fine attire for his old, filthy, ratty clothes and said, "Hey pop, if you don't mind, I'd rather just relax on the couch over here in front of the TV. By the way, would you grab me a cold one on your way to the kitchen?" That was me … a prodigal recidivist. My heart was not in the right place and I still didn't get it.

My outward religiosity may have been a boon to Bud, Lilly and a few others but didn't amount to a hill of beans for me. It was more like Chinese food. You know, it filled me up for a while then left me running on empty again. My fluttering faith was not boosted in the least. I should have recalled Hebrews 10:4, "For it is not possible that the blood of bulls and of goats should take away sins." Alone, I was impotent. I had no more power to strengthen my own faith than a gnat has to move an elephant.

273

But I was still cut off from the real power source, the word and sacraments. When I went to Holy Communion, I might as well have been guzzling Strawberry Hill and munching on some Wheat Thins because I wasn't receiving the body and blood of Christ. I was surely an unworthy recipient of such great gifts and was too ambivalent to recognize the danger of taking the sacrament to my own condemnation. Why didn't I just commend myself to God's gracious will and let him take the helm of my life? Why didn't I plug into the power plant of Holy Scripture and feed my soul with the Bread of Life and spring of living water? There's no one to blame but myself. I knew better but was still harboring resentment against God.

I had other problems too. My publisher had finally given up and began resorting to legal remedies. In an effort to appease them, I returned the remainder of the advance I hadn't blown but it amounted to less than half of what I owed them. Their attempt to recoup their remaining loss through garnishments against my flagging business only served to bring about the agency's inevitable collapse a bit sooner. Things were so bad I was on the brink of bankruptcy and losing my home. The thought of being left out in the cold and crawling back to Bud and Lilly on my hands and knees to seek shelter within their abode was enough to prod me into feverish activity. I had to generate some revenue ... I desperately needed to finish the book; my last lifeline. I entered my final charge toward literary immortality with great gusto. Don't get me wrong; I loved Bud and Lilly. Nevertheless, there is no motivation more powerful than the distress of facing the prospect of being forced to move back in with mommy and daddy at the age of fifty three. I would have preferred confinement in JCCC or PCC instead.

In spite of my dogged determination, my progress quickly ground to a halt. I could have easily completed the book in a few weeks but that had been true for years. It wasn't the distance that stood in my way but rather the direction. Should I travel east or west, north or south? The two choices had been apparent for the longest time. The life and times of Charles Darwin Cane could be a tale of retribution or redemption, not both. I kept conjuring Syl's voice as if she were whispering in my ear, "Do the right thing, Twain. Forgive those who have trespassed against you as God has forgiven your trespasses." Part of me wanted to follow the latter path so badly I could taste it ... and it was hearty, sweet and savory and the aroma was as inviting as Christmas dinner with all the trimmings.

Always, a stern, thunderous voice would shout Syl down, echoing the wrath of God first from Jeremiah 17:9 and then Matthew 15:19, "The heart is deceitful above all things, and desperately wicked: who can know it? For out of the heart proceed evil thoughts, murders, adulteries, fornications, thefts, false witnesses, blasphemies." Yes, Cane's heart was desperately wicked and he had maliciously deceived me in the worst way. His was a coal black, murderous heart. Cane got what he deserved. That was the moral of the story.

It was a stalemate. I was as conflicted as a two headed serpent with one on each end tugging in opposite directions. You would have thought that my self-preservation instincts alone would have forced me to decide and move on but my conscience and ego were deadlocked in a struggle to the death. I fiddled while Rome burned. Indecision had me so paralyzed I was helpless to lift a finger in my own defense as my world crumbled around me. My faith, however weak, was not dead. In spite of my apathy and resentment, I never doubted God's word no matter how hard I worked to shut it out of my mind. Good words of wisdom would come back to me now and again. I could hear Christ calling me to cast all my cares and burdens upon him. Still my stumbling blocks, vanity and pride, wouldn't allow me to heed his loving invitation. So, I did nothing while my life spiraled toward the abyss; faith and reason were pitted against one another, spinning, whirling, out of control.

I never doubted God's existence or his power but I was a master of selective memory. When it came to God's goodness, mercy and grace, I drew a blank. There was no denial of God's plan of salvation or Christ's fulfillment. Turning to false gods or man-made religions was not an option. I knew and still believed that Jesus is the only name, under heaven, given among men whereby we must be saved. I never doubted that Jesus is the only mediator between God and man. I simple chose to ignore those things. All I wanted to focus on was my pain and suffering, my loss. Never mind that God lost his one and only begotten Son and willingly sacrificed his perfect, sinless life to serve as a ransom for our sins. Like a petulant, spoiled child, I could only see things from my point of view. I still blamed God for Syl and Devon's deaths. The mass of undeniable evidence from creation to Calvary be damned. I, the one who had been forgiven everything by God, was standing in judgment of God, unwilling to forgive him for a transgression he had no part in. I was a hypocrite of the highest order but too stubborn and foolish to admit it.

I remembered the times earlier in my life when I wondered if I had hit rock bottom. I was sure it hadn't happened because the bottom was fast approaching me now. What could be worse than no wife, family, home, money or visible means of support? Sure, old Job had health issues on top of everything else but he never had to contend with the Renaissance Killer. On I went with my lament. Instead of being a blessing to my mother and father in their old age, I was an embarrassment but, of course, I worried more about my own humiliation than the indignity I had caused them. Beyond that, my faith was heading toward shipwreck but, thankfully or unfortunately depending on your point of view; I lacked the courage to end my pointless life. Speaking of Job, my health wasn't so good either, at least not mentally and emotionally. Talk about feeling sorry for yourself … you know it's bad when you're trying to one up Job! That's how self-absorbed I was; I missed the whole point of Job's story … his faith wavered but never left him and, throughout his whole ordeal, God was in his corner even when it seemed God had deserted him along with everyone else in his life including his three finger pointing pals: Eliphaz, Bildad and Zophar.

If there was a silver lining to my life coming apart at the seams, it was that it left me plenty of time to think. Sometimes that was more a curse than a blessing. The worst part was that I never reached a conclusion or came to any kind of resolution. I kept spinning round and round, always stopping at the same place. It was like that movie, Ground Hog Day, only this was no comedy. It was more like an episode of the Twilight Zone. One day, a new thought popped into my head and I kept coming back to the date of Cane's execution, 10/10/10. I couldn't accept it as a coincidence. It seemed to have fate or God's providence written all over it. Ten is a big number in God's mathematics. It is used over and over to denote completeness. The triple effect had God's signature all over it too. How could the Trinity not come to mind? So was 10/10/10 God's appointed day for Cane? And, if so, what did God complete on that October day? As I pondered these questions, it spun me round and round again and spit me out at the same maddening, inconclusive spot. Had God completed his work of just retribution and cast Cane's spirit into hell or did he finish a miraculous work of redemption? If I could figure that one out, there was no doubt in my mind that I'd be the author of a best seller.

Some days, I wondered if I was going insane. You know what they say; insanity is repeating something over and over and expecting the outcome to be different. I was either the dumbest man alive or the most stubborn. Twenty four years earlier, the answer would have been obvious to me but time had passed and I was a different person. I tried to think back to what the old Twain was like but he seemed such a stranger to me now. The words of Jeremiah 17:9 and Matthew 15:19 crept back into my head. What do they say about a man's heart? I once knew the answer. We're all evil by nature and everyone is capable of the most horrendous acts. We're tainted by original sin from our very conception and deserve eternal damnation in hell. Our very flesh is corrupt and, left to our own devices, we're doomed to evil. We have no choice in the matter for we're dead in our trespasses and sins. Not one of us is different from another. The heart of Hitler, Stalin … or even Cane resides in all of us. Only God can rescue sinners. Any goodness, any love that resides within us originates from God alone and is a gracious gift for which we can claim no credit but only be thankful.

At least that's what the old Twain believed. Somewhere along the line I had fallen off course onto a different path. I knew I wasn't perfect but I was nothing like Cane. I'd never think of committing the senseless, heartless acts of gratuitous violence that he thrived on. There are a lot of bad people in the world but few, if any, could match the evil of Charles Darwin Cane. I was sure there had to be a special place in hell reserved just for him. If only they had executed him earlier, I wouldn't be gripped with these ridiculous doubts. When we met the first time and he subjected me to that cruel hoax; when he revealed the true depth of his evil, I would have thrown the switch myself and never given it another thought. Why did I correspond with him? Why did I visit him again? What good had it done to try to satisfy my curiosity? Why in the world did he have to go and change?

This was a sobering thought. Did I resent God for allowing RK to kill Syl and Devon or was I angry about him letting Cane off the cosmic hook? I really didn't know. Could I be that shallow? Abraham trusted in God so much that he was willing to sacrifice his only son, Isaac, if that was what God required. Abraham had faith that somehow even death would not prevent God from fulfilling his covenant, not through another but Isaac, the child of the promise. I was a far cry from Abraham. Then I thought, I was a lot more like Jonah. He knew the truth, as did I. It wasn't that he didn't believe God could save the dreaded Assyrians. Rather, Jonah hated Israel's murderous neighbors so much that he didn't want to see God's grace extended to them. He tried his best to resist God and run the other way. We all know how that turned out. In the end, with much prodding from God, Jonah completed his calling and shared the good news of the coming Messiah and his salvation with the Assyrians whom he despised.

Was I a modern day Jonah foolishly trying to resist God's will and plan? Looking back on my life it seemed so. I might as well have been in the belly of a great fish because no matter how hard I tried I couldn't escape my conscience. God's word, upon which I had been nurtured since childhood, kept coming at me like a battering ram, shaking the foundations and walls of the castle of apathy and despair I inhabited. Then a grisly coincidence dawned on me. The Assyrians were renowned in the art of torture and mayhem and, as far as I knew from ancient history, were the first people to employ impaling, the glacially slow and painful, unthinkable method of death used by Cane against our favorite Santa. Was there a lesson for me? If God could send his prophet to bless the bloodthirsty, vile, cruel and heartless Assyrians, could not his grace and mercy extend to someone like Cane too? No ... the voice boomed in my head ... no, no, no! My reason reared its ugly head and lashed out in blind rage, sending my compassion hurtling into the stratosphere. The Assyrians were despicable alright, but their damning deeds were at least conducted in the context of war against enemies who had some chance to defend themselves or flee. Never mind the atrocities committed against their vanquished foes. Those were the spoils of war. Cane slunk in the shadows like a coward and attacked the helpless and the innocent. He killed my Syl ... my Devon!

Was I suffering from DID, my own split personality? Weren't there two different people fighting tooth and nail for control of my soul? In one moment, I was absolutely certain that Cane got what he deserved and was hopefully writhing in eternal torment in the undying pain of the fires of hell. My lifelong commitment to sealing his doom was surely a good work. Then, without warning, insidious doubt would trickle back in until my brain was flooded with its tepid waters. Was I angry at Cane or God? Was I thinking about Syl and Devon or myself? Did Cane, with God's help, destroy my life and banish me to my miserable existence or was that just an excuse? Wasn't it I that threw my life away in a childish, twenty year tantrum of self-pity and loathing. Wasn't I the coward? Did God turn away from me or was it the other way around? Then, in spite of all the barricades I had erected, the spiritual ramparts that littered my soul, the question I had tried to avoid for so long, forced its way into my consciousness. Was my inconsolable, unrelenting pain a result of my self-pity or the lingering thought of Syl and Devon's suffering? Wasn't it the ugly truth that I felt sorry for myself rather than Syl and Devon? I was bemoaning my own loneliness and wretchedness more so than their tragic deaths. Twenty three years had passed! Reason rushed to my defense and loudly objected. But my conscience silenced the counter-offensive with the one question my reason dreaded the most, "Were not Syl and Devon in heaven?"

There, it was out in the open; the question that I had exiled to the lowest level of my subconscious for all those years. If Syl and Devon were so pure and innocent as I claimed and their faith so stout, surely they were in heaven. And if they were in heaven, there was no pain or suffering, only eternal peace and joy. To deny this would be to deny everything including my own flickering faith. This I could not do under any circumstances. However, this twisted reason's logic into a knot from which it could not escape. If Syl and Devon were in heaven, then what charge could I lay to God? Wasn't it by his grace that they had entered into heaven. Reason was not foolish enough to pose that they were worthy of heaven on their own merits. I knew better; even Syl and Devon were sinners like the rest of us although they occupied a higher plane in my scheme of things. And what would it mean for me if eternal life in heaven depended in some small part on my own goodness and merit? I knew that was a dead end in hell for sure. What kind of heaven would it be for Syl and Devon to live with a god who sanctioned their murder or was filled only with wrath and hard justice? Reason had let me down and my logic was crumbling into dust. God had brought me low, to the rock bottom so he could finally raise me up. But I was not finished resisting quite yet. Anger rushed to my defense to fill the void left by my reason's cowardly retreat. Anger did not rule by logic. He was blind and brutish, armed with fear, intimidation, ignorance, conceit and greed to battle my conscience. How dare anyone accuse me of thinking more about myself than Syl and Devon? I sacrificed my whole life to bring their killer to justice!

Rage won the day in a rout taking the field by storm. However, I knew the victory would be short lived because my conscience would not surrender. It would retreat for a time and melt into the woods and hedgerows waiting patiently to lay its next ambush. I couldn't take much more of this turmoil; possessed by two warring factions locked in mortal combat. I believed I would go stark, raving mad. I desperately needed to reach out to someone for help but my guilt, foolishness and stubbornness would not allow me to turn to God. Bud and Lilly were my next best option but I felt as though I had already caused them too much embarrassment and distress. In a near panic, I jumped into the car and headed out, driving aimlessly at first. Then, I decided to venture to the one place where I might find some peace. It was not far but you would have thought it was a million miles away since I had visited so infrequently. It wasn't the distance but rather the painful memories that kept me away from Laurel Springs Cemetery.

It was near dusk when I arrived and the cemetery was empty except for a couple of unseen souls in the small hovel which served as an office. Not many people made their way there on a weekday evening. It was not in a good neighborhood. Laurel Springs was technically in the county but butted up to the northern reaches of the city proper, one of the heavier crime areas within the region. This had been a depressed area for many years but I consented to Syl's wishes that we be buried there where her parents and Grandpa and Grandma Adams rested. Back in their day, it was a thriving neighborhood with the only stigma being that Laurel Springs was more of a blue collar resting place populated largely by simple grave stones rather than ornate headstones or elaborate mausoleums. As I stepped out of the car with the sun dipping down below the horizon, there was an otherworldly feel to the place. Graves stretched out as far as the eye could see in every direction and I couldn't help but wonder about all the lives and history captured there as I made my way toward Syl and Devon. The graves were packed so tightly together that it was impossible not to step across them here and there. Each time it happened I wanted to offer an apology to someone. It was easy to find Syl and Devon since their graves were marked by headstones that seemed impressive in the unobtrusive surroundings. Since I had come on the spur of the moment, I had no flowers and felt ashamed that there were no adornments to brighten up their bleak plot.

I stared at their names and the dates on their tombstones. All I could think was they died much too young. Tears moistened the corners of my eyes then gathered until finally torrents flowed and I sobbed openly. Then I was clutched by guilt over my self-pity and abruptly stopped. I didn't trust my thoughts so I spoke out loud, "Syl, Devon, I'm sorry that I cried. I know I should be joyful that you are both enjoying the glories of heaven. It's just that I miss you so much. Syl, I'm glad you're not here to see what a mess I've made of my life. It's been so difficult without you and Devon. You were always the strong one, especially in matters of faith. You wouldn't recognize me now. Sometimes I don't know myself. I'm always angry, bitter and full of hatred. I don't know what to do anymore. I can't go on like this. I've turned my back on God and can't seem to find him without your help. God promises not to test us beyond what we can handle and make a way of escape if it becomes too much to bear. I'm at that point now, Syl. What should I do?"

I knew Syl couldn't hear me and certainly couldn't respond. That would be some kind of lousy heaven if we still had to be troubled by the cares of this sinful world, wouldn't it? Still I carried on this imaginary conversation because it was a cathartic release, one that hopefully would help me maintain my sanity. It was just a mind game but when my conscience answered my questions, it came in the soothing sound of Syl's voice, "Twain, you've got to let go of your anger. It's time to forgive." Again, I spoke audibly, "I've tried to forgive, over and over again but it doesn't seem to help. How many times can this go on before I admit the truth and throw in the towel?" Syl's familiar voice echoed in my brain with an answer that was so Syl-like, "C'mon Twain, who are you fooling? You know what the answer is. Jesus says, 'until seventy times seven.' In God's algebra, that means infinitely, as many times as it takes." Then Syl, I mean my conscience, put the icing on the cake with a big cherry on top, "Twain, you stop worrying about me and Devon now, okay? We're doing just fine, better than ever, perfectly if you don't mind me rubbing it in. Just work on getting your life in order. Don't forget, it starts with forgiveness. And stop all the childish nonsense and run back to God. He still loves you, you know. Get back into his word. Everything will be fine." I smiled contentedly, "Thank you Syl, that's just what I needed to hear."

Then I was startled back to reality, "Are you all right, sir?" I nearly jumped out of my skin. I was so deep in thought and *conversation* that I had lost

289

track of the time. The attendant wanted to politely shoo me so he could close the gates and go home. "Oh sorry, everything is fine. I was just getting ready to leave, thanks." It took a while for my heart to settle down so I could think about what had just transpired. Syl was right in everything she said. Okay, okay … I know it wasn't Syl but give me a break. It's hard enough to admit I've been a stubborn fool and wasted over twenty years of my life. At least give me the satisfaction of attributing this long overdue epiphany to Syl's memory. Thanks to the mental gymnastics which credited her with my inspiration, there was no counter attack from within. Syl's power of love overwhelmed my embattled soul. I headed home to log into my PC. There was something I needed to know. Where was Cane buried? I desperately needed to have one last *conversation* with him.

What would we do without the internet? Within minutes I not only found the cemetery but was able to pull up a directory mapping his exact plot location. I hit print and then raced out the door as if I was late for an appointment with destiny. It was dark now and ominous storm clouds had gathered and the horizon was splintered by fingers of lightning as if heavenly hands were signaling me to turn back. Cane's grandparents had made the arrangements for his burial in a modest, affordable location near their home. It was about a forty five minute drive west toward Warrenton which took me directly into the storm. Rain began to fall and then pounded my car so fiercely that I had trouble seeing with the wipers running full tilt. Some of the few other fools out on the road were at least wise enough to pull over to wait it out. I wasn't thinking. The cemetery would surely be closed but I was obsessed with the thought of making my peace with Cane before my demons rose up to halt me, so I drove on gripping the wheel with both hands. Sure enough, the cemetery was closed for the night when I arrived. Then, as if I needed further evidence that I was losing my grip, I did something truly crazy. Like some scene out of a horror movie, I jumped the fence and proceeded on foot. Thankfully, it was not a large cemetery and, once I got my bearings, I was able to locate the grave before my plot map was drenched beyond recognition. The modest headstone had a small cross etched above the name, Charles Darwin Cane.

 I stood there in the monsoon, soaked to the bone but oblivious to the downpour. I spoke aloud at the top of my lungs as if the volume would help Cane hear me over the whistling of the wind and splattering of the rain, "Charles, I have something I want to say to you. This is much too late in coming but it's something I need to do for my own peace. I've hated you with every ounce of my being for twenty three years. Your professed conversion made no difference to me. I didn't consider it for a moment. As judge and jury I was as heartless as you. Your apologies and remorse fell on deaf ears. Can I forgive you now for killing Syl and Devon? I don't know but I'm going to try. There's one thing I am sorry for though. You're likely burning in hell at this very moment and you'd probably be the first one to admit you deserve it. That doesn't justify the way I've longed for you to languish there in everlasting torment. No Christian man should ever wish that on another soul, for any reason. It is the providence of God and I should have commended you to his good and gracious will long ago. I should have prayed for God to extend the mercies of salvation to you. Forgive me Charles."

Thankfully, I left before anyone passed by and reported me to the police. I climbed into the car sopping wet with mud up to my ankles. It was just another imaginary conversation but I had never felt so relieved in my life. The cloudburst had not abated but I drove on anyway. To make matters worse, I drove seventy miles per hour as though I was in a hurry to get somewhere. Perhaps I was in a rush to put my pitiful past behind me. Finally emancipated, I was running away from my old slave master as fast as my feet could fly. I wanted to get home, out of my wet clothes and not waste a minute in restarting my life on the right path. In fact, why wait until then? I began to pray to God to seek his forgiveness for everything my stony heart had conceived. Thankfulness spilled from my renewed, fleshy heart. I lauded God with thanksgiving and praise for never giving up on me and releasing me from my dark dungeon of gloom and hopelessness. God's warmth enveloped me and I felt such tranquility … I was so serene that I didn't notice the abandoned vehicle sitting on the shoulder in complete darkness with no warning flashers. I was unaware that I had drifted over to the right. By the time I caught the faint reflection coming back from my headlamps off of the dark tail lights through my rain splashed windshield, I barely had time to hit the brakes as I slammed full force into the back of that pickup truck.

12 Dead Repose

What happened next was beyond me or perhaps better said I was beyond it. I didn't see the passerby stop to inspect the devastating accident or call 911. I was oblivious to the arrival of the police. They had to use the Jaws of Life to retrieve me from the snarled, smoking wreckage. The paramedics arrived, checked my vitals and administered CPR. I was not there when they placed me on the gurney and loaded me into the emergency vehicle. Nor was I present when they rushed me into the ER. Their frantic efforts to revive me didn't bother me in the least. I couldn't have cared less when they pronounced me gone and began unhooking me from all the wires and tubes. No, I was far away, on the journey of my life.

When I awoke, I was in a strange, wonderful place. I might as well have landed in Munchkin Land but that wouldn't do justice to the awe inspiring surroundings. It was like I was in a different dimension … you know, weird, as if there were more than 360 degrees when I turned myself around in a circle. The horizons seemed endless. Although it was completely foreign, it felt like home, all warm, cozy and inviting. There were mind blowing vistas in every direction and I turned my head ever so slowly to soak in each captivating view. Everything was lush and emerald green and full of life. The grass all around was silky and soft. To my left, the open field stretched toward what, I guess, you might call a garden. Behind me a forest sprouted humbly then ascended gradually to magnificent heights with trees that would dwarf the tallest redwood. On the right there were rolling plains that climbed gently then raced upward into towering peaks that resembled majestic steeples splashed across the horizon. As I turned round, new visions seemed to replace the others in a never ending panorama except that one remained constant … a far off city skyline. From the mountains the mists gathered into a stream that formed a river that took a sharp turn nearby and flowed onward from there toward the distant city straight ahead whose skyline was so vast and enchanting that it mesmerized me. In height and breadth, I don't think one hundred New York Cities could match its grandeur. The river, which ran directly into the heart of the city, must have been incredibly deep because the waters were so calm and still as they ambled off into the distance. It was much wider than the Nile, Amazon, Missouri and Mississippi combined and had the sheen of pale blue crystal. The city's elegant, soaring spires were impossibly, breathtakingly tall but seemed twice as high due to the clear and perfect image in the river's glassy reflection.

As I looked about, I noticed a dramatic change in my senses, as if the dials had been amped up ten times. My eyes were keen as an eagle's, stretching my vision far into the distance while at the same time revealing the finest details of tiny, nearby objects. I marveled as I counted the dots on a lady bug some twenty paces away then gazed upon a stately heron preening itself along the river bank over a mile away. My hearing was no less amazing. When I concentrated, I was able to pick out the whirring wings of a humming bird hovering in the adjacent garden at least one hundred yards away or the trickling of water far upstream where the river was a mere brook tumbling across the rocks of the foothills. My nose was no less perceptive for I could draw in the same sweet honeysuckle scent the humming bird was enjoying. All the while, I was able to instinctively meter these powers with such speed, pinpoint control and accuracy that I was not simultaneously bombarded with a cluttered collage of sights, confusing cacophony of sounds or acrimonious assault of aromas. I took in the beautiful surroundings in peace and tranquility.

Then I experienced the most amazing sensation. When I tried to move about and explore the inviting landscape, it seemed as if I was floating. It was like gravity had been cut in half. As I moved about cautiously at first then more purposefully and finally with great vigor, I learned to my delight that I had boundless energy and didn't experience the least bit of fatigue. I felt so light-hearted I wanted to do cartwheels ... so I did. When I leapt for joy, I bounded like a gazelle. Michael Jordan would have been green with envy. Not only did I feel like a world class athlete but there was something even more liberating. With all of this extreme action and motion, there was absolutely no pain or discomfort of any kind. Somehow, I had discovered the fountain of youth and then some.

I paused to take further note of the glorious settings around me. The climate was indescribably flawless. It put San Diego to shame. It was neither warm nor cold but perfectly comfortable under every condition. As I had scurried about in my glee, I did not become overheated but remained fresh as a daisy. I sensed there was some type of hyper-sensitive climate control that kept the dial permanently on sublime no matter what conditions prevailed. Peering at the lavish gardens, dense forests and vaulted mountain tops, I suspected there would somehow be no accompanying extremes of heat, cold, humidity or pressure and I planned to test my hypothesis soon enough. The humidity or lack thereof was also uncanny. Everywhere there was a perfect balance between arid and moist. The air was mostly still but never stagnant with the slightest breeze to gently tickle the senses. It was fresh, clean and completely pure.

The sky was uninterrupted azure with nary a cloud or hint of dust or other particles. Only the flight of birds and bees happily dotted its endless tapestry. It seemed to me an optical illusion because the sky was at the same time a model of blue consistency while also reflecting unknown spectrums of color from the ground below like a polished, mirrored dome. There was something else very odd about the sky. What was it? Ah, now I know … there was no sun beaming above. Yet, there was light. It was bright but gentle and had no apparent source, emanating from nowhere but everywhere. That was evidenced by the absence of any darkness. I'm not kidding; there was not even a shadow anywhere. The light bathed everything from every angle. This seems like a very weird thing to say but being in this light was like being enveloped in goodness. Is that possible; can light be good? In any case, it made me feel safe, like a baby being held in its mother's arms.

Where was I? I was either in heaven or a dream, a dream unlike any other. In many ways it seemed much too real to be a dream but was also so surreal it had to be a dream. I wasn't about to worry. If it was a dream, then please don't wake me up … just let me go on enjoying it for as long as possible. One thing puzzled me. Where was everybody? Other than the cute little bugs and warbling birds, I was completely alone. How could this be heaven? Surely it wouldn't be so lonely. Then, just as if on cue, I was greeted by the most cheerful ambassadors imaginable. Four bottle nosed dolphins jumped out of the river in unison to catch my attention before plunging back into the deep. To my delight, when they resurfaced, they danced on their tails and welcomed me with their own unique version of Yakety Yak. As if that was not impressive enough, they summoned one of their pals, a huge orca who, pardon the pun, made quite a splash. For their big finale, the dolphins formed a line and spun around in unison before exiting stage right. There's nothing like the Cheshire grins of four performing dolphins to make one feel right at home!

I couldn't imagine what other surprises were still in store for me but I didn't want to wait to find out so I embarked on a self-directed tour, starting with the garden environ off to my left. It wasn't a man-made garden in the sense of having plants, flowers and vegetables laid out in neat rows or squared patches. But there was a certain symmetry which revealed the touch of a master designer. Everything appeared natural but well-manicured. The foliage was plush and plentiful but not dense to the point where I had any difficulty moving carelessly through the greenery. The garden was expansive, roomy and well laid out for easy enjoyment. The first thing that struck me was the variety of plant life, then the sheer size of some species. The sun flowers were as large as colorful kites and the geranium boughs were as big as basketballs. There was no apparent sign of tending but no weeds were present, not one. Absent also were any types of thorns, thistles or sharp barbs. Only velvety smooth leaves caressed me. Some plants were quite familiar while others appeared as species heretofore unknown. What stood out most were the colors. Trying to share what I saw is like asking a blind man to explain color. I don't know how to describe it other than to say, there are other spectrums beyond the ones known to man on earth. Walking through the garden, I was treated to an artist's pallet filled with a myriad of colors beyond imagination. The only thing that topped this experience was the thrilling display put on by what I'll call the charming sentries. These tall flowers lined one far-reaching pathway like endless palace guards standing erect, at full attention. They were solid green with narrow stalks that accentuated the disproportionate nature of their bulbous heads. As I passed by, the bulbs popped open in succession like well-arranged falling dominos and flashed brilliant colors illuminated like the glow from a fire fly's tail and sprayed out puffs of pollen that shined like glitter as they fell effortlessly and then melted invisibly into the ground. No king had ever been feted so royally.

The forest was no less impressive with the hand of a mighty creator stamped everywhere in glory. The deeper I ventured, the greater the majesty. The trees reached monolithic proportions that made me feel as if I were standing among the skyscrapers of Manhattan. Then something new grabbed my attention. There was no sense of danger anywhere in this beautiful place but my curiosity was aroused by a sound. My keen eyesight could not look behind trees but my ears caught hold of something unusual. There was movement out there … I was not alone. I hushed and stopped in my tracks and trained my ear toward the direction of the sound.

At first, it seemed to approach cautiously then suddenly bounded directly toward me with a burst of speed. Through the trees, I saw it. It was quite large and looked like a wolf. As it came into the clearing near me, it hesitated and I could see that it was a dog; a German Shepherd. Could it be … was it my old childhood pal, Buddy? No, it wasn't. There's something about the bond between a boy and his dog that is unmistakable. Every dog seems to pick out one member of the family as its favorite and I had been Buddy's. He slept in bed with me until he became too big but even then would still only sleep in my room with his snout tucked between the floor and box spring as far as his girth would allow. No, it wasn't Buddy but he could have been a clone. He made me feel just as Buddy would have when he jumped up, laid his massive paws on my shoulders and licked my face with gusto. Surely this was heaven!

I made my way out of the forest and headed toward the mountains with my new Buddy in tow. We followed the river upstream until the waters became narrow, swift and shallow. I paused for Buddy to quench his thirst and I caught a glimpse of something very large shimmering in the water. Upon closer inspection, we discovered that the brook was not inhabited by a single leviathan but rather was teeming with a school of fish that seemed to form one large, shining body; another welcome sign of life. A bit further ahead we came around a sharp bend only to come face to face with a large, orange tabby that had also come to drink and admire the trout and salmon. Instinctively, I reached out to restrain Buddy remembering violent encounters from my childhood. But to my surprise, Buddy did not try to pull away or even offer a low growl. Neither did our feline friend arch his back or hiss. Instead, Buddy's tail began to wag and the kitty purred contentedly. I released Buddy and, incredibly, the two of them exchanged sniffs and rubs and began cavorting like old chums. Onward and upward we went following a natural trail that allowed us to safely reach the heights that touched the sky. As I had suspected, the temperature did not drop as the altitude rose and the air did not grow thin. As we hiked my muscles never burned and my lungs never tired. From the peaks, I was able to take in the distant cityscape in its full splendor and noticed that hidden among the taller structures were countless beautiful estates as far as the eye could see. Imagine the largest subdivision you've ever seen but replace the cracker box houses shoe horned in on top of one another with sprawling, ornate mansions surrounded by lush, ample grounds stretching endlessly. Now, I wanted to see that city close up so we began our descent, me, Buddy and kitty. Surely we would find other people there.

As we continued on this adventure, my mind drifted back to the question which remained unanswered, was I in heaven or just dreaming? It was still unclear but I began to apply what logic I could summon in an earnest, thoughtful manner. I knew for certain from the Bible that our bodies and souls separate upon death and believers remain as spirits in heaven until the final judgment day when we are reunited with our risen, glorified bodies. Yet, here I was seeing, hearing, smelling, feeling and moving about, so I couldn't be in heaven, right? I must be dreaming, under the unconscious illusion that I was enjoying all of these experiences bodily. From nowhere, I was able to recall a scripture passage as though my Bible were open in front of me. It was from Matthew 24 where Jesus went to the house of a certain ruler who had implored him regarding his dead daughter ..."He said unto them, Give place: for the maid is not dead, but sleepeth." Yes, Jesus often referred to the dead as sleeping. Then another pertinent proof passage popped into my head as if I had a photographic memory of the Bible. In I Thessalonians 4:13, Jesus used this term again in directly addressing the condition of dead believers, "But I would not have you to be ignorant, brethren, concerning them which are asleep, that ye sorrow not, even as others which have no hope." I recalled what an old, visiting seminary professor said about this in a Bible class at our church before he died, "When we die and go to heaven, we will not realize we are just spirits without bodies. It will be like we are sleeping and dreaming. We will still feel as though we have bodies with our senses intact."

This didn't settle the question for me but gave me hope and confidence as I resolved to move on toward the gleaming city. There I would find the answers, I was sure. Something else dawned on me that seemed related but didn't help to settle the matter at hand. I had traversed hill and dale, meadow and field but time stood still. There were no clocks and the sun and moon were not present in the sky to help track the passage of time. Surely such a long journey must have taken days but there had been no night time, dusk or dawn. Was I in Alaska or heaven? How long would it take me to reach the city? Did it matter in the context of eternity? I reckoned not; in heaven or dreams time was immaterial. All I knew was that I was not beset with hunger, thirst or fatigue … only curiosity. That and joyous, giddy anticipation gripped me as we drew nearer to the great city. About halfway there, I marveled as it loomed ever larger, nearly beyond my grasp to comprehend.

As we neared the outskirts, the colossal skyline soared above us but our vision straight ahead was obscured by boundless groves of trees bearing every kind of delicious fruit imaginable. It was an amazing sight to behold but prevented me from searching the horizon for some sign of life, other people. This only served to instill our quest with new energy and determination as we forged onward. We were getting close to the edge of the enormous orchard when a vision emerged from out of the trees. I squinted in spite of my visual acuity because I could not believe my eyes. Could it be? If this was a dream, I never wanted to wake up and face the cruelest hoax of all. If this was really happening, I had found my destination in heaven above. I stood transfixed as they came toward me with outstretched arms. Yes, it was Syl and Devon. I cried out with a loud voice, "My God and my Savior, thank you, thank you, thank you!"

I rushed to meet them and we embraced as spirits. Then I stepped back to behold them. Syl was restored, whole and beautiful. Devon appeared as a young man in his prime but I recognized him as if we had never been apart. They were arrayed in pure, white garments that were perfect, spotless, without blemish and shined like the stars. There were no tears; only hearty laughs as we shared our joy. We sat down right there on the soft grass and talked. I started, "It's so good to be here. I've missed you both so much." It was Syl who spoke first, "I can't say we've missed you, Twain, but we've looked forward to seeing you." She paused to absorb my hurt feelings and continued, "Don't get me wrong, Twain. It's just that here we have no worries, cares or concerns, so it is not possible to miss someone or feel anxiety. There is only joy in knowing a reunion awaits all believers. We're so happy to be with you again." I smiled with understanding, "Yes, to be reunited with you my beloved wife and our dear son is truly a cause for the most joyous celebration." Syl had to gently burst my bubble again, "Now Twain, you know better. There is no marriage in heaven. Remember what we said, until death do us part? And families are different too." I nodded to the first but had to question the last, "You're right Syl but what do you mean about our family? Should we no longer call Devon our son?"

This time Devon spoke up, "I'll always remember you as my father but it's different now, better. Now we're more like brothers and mom is a sister in Christ to us." Syl elaborated, "Twain, we haven't lost our wonderful family bond, not at all. But now we're part of a blessed family that extends across heaven to include all the saints, every believer." "Syl, do you mean like our old church family and our brothers and sisters there?" "Yes, that's right Twain but in a much higher, more meaningful way. Our church family was never as close as you, me and Devon in an earthly sense. Here, we share an even closer bond than we did on earth and it extends to everyone. The love we feel for each other extends to everyone and vice versa. At the head of the family is our Heavenly Father and we are all the closest of brothers and sisters in his adopted family. We've been adopted as first born sons; every man, woman and child; believers of every race and nationality. And like first born sons of old, we receive the Father's inheritance. It's a treasure like no other; worth more than all the money, power and pleasure the world has to offer."

Syl was bubbling with exuberance as she shared the good news with me, "Our Father is perfect in every way. We can trust him completely and he never fails us. He loves us perfectly and it never changes." I was equally caught up in her enthusiasm, "Have you seen the Father?" "This is hard to explain. Our

Father is a spirit so we don't see him in the normal sense but we are able to dwell in his presence and speak with him directly. It's like prayer but there is no gulf, no intermediary. We are able to approach the Father and communicate directly." My amazing new powers of recall kicked in and I offered from I Corinthians 13:12, "For now we see through a glass, darkly; but then face to face: now I know in part; but then shall I know even as also I am known." Syl blurted, "Yes, that's it exactly!" I was hungry for more, "But how can the Father deal directly with so many believers, all the saints?" Syl was almost breathless, "It's so amazing, Twain! His knowledge, wisdom and power are infinite, incomprehensible. How do you think he keeps track of the prayers of all earthly believers and every tiny detail of all our lives down to counting the very hairs on our heads? It's the same here. He is able to address every need of every believer, all the time, perfectly. I guess I shouldn't have said all the time because here there is no time. Eternity is apart from, completely outside of time. There is no waiting or impatience, no deadlines or stress. There is only peace."

Syl went on, "I almost forgot. While the Father is a spirit, we are able to see him face to face. That is, we can behold him bodily in the person of our Lord and Savior, the God man incarnate, Jesus Christ."

"Oh Syl, please tell me that you've met Jesus!" "Of course, I have, Twain. He's so wonderful in every way! He is God, yet man and can relate to us as a man. As the only begotten Son, he is also literally our brother and best friend. I guess you could say he's our *big brother*." "What does he look like?" "It's much like you would imagine … not too different than the traditional paintings except that he's not so Anglicized. He's a handsome man with Hebrew features, long hair and a beard. You might not recognize him at first though because his body has been glorified. It's hard to explain. Think of the story of his transfiguration, if you will, but you'll just have to see for yourself. One thing you'll notice right away is that he still bears the scars on his hands, feet and in his side. It's not as ghastly as it sounds. In fact, it's beautiful because it provides a constant reminder of his infinite love and the great price he paid for our sins, to win our souls and reconcile us to God, to himself. It is so thrilling to see Jesus in his glorified body because it's the perfect harbinger of what our resurrection bodies will be like when we are reunited with them on the final day of judgment."

It was exhilarating to hear these Biblical truths brought to light in such plain, eyewitness fashion. I could barely contain myself and the more I heard the more I wanted to learn, "Do you know when judgment day is coming?" "Twain, you should know better than to ask a question like that. Only God the Father knows the day and time of the end. Not even the holy angels know the appointed time." That reminded me, "I almost forgot, Syl. Have you seen the angels?" "Why yes, of course I have, Twain. They are magnificent. We're able to see them clearly now, in all their power and glory. There are so many of them; legions of angels serving God and man faithfully." "Do they look like men?" "They're not men, they're spirits but they have the power to manifest themselves as men." She paused and then Syl showed me that a good sense of humor is still welcome in heaven, "And boy can they sing … you should hear it when they break into the Hallelujah Chorus around Christmas time!" I laughed and smiled but was still thirsty for knowledge and wanted to get back on track, "So how do you keep from going crazy not knowing when judgment day will finally come? Aren't you anxious to get your new body back? Don't you get bored waiting and waiting?" Syl was patient with me, "Of course we're all longing for that final day of triumph but there is no anxiety, impatience, worry or consternation of any kind. Remember that in eternity a thousand years are as one day and vice versa. More importantly, we're blessed with certainty. We know what is coming and have perfect assurance that God will bring history as we know it to a close at his perfect, appointed time. It is good that only God the Father knows. It's in his hands so we can rest in peace until then." Then, in regard to boredom, Syl gave me a crooked smile, the kind a loving mother might display to a young child who had just voiced something absurd but cute, "Are you serious, Twain? Do you really think heaven could be boring?" I sheepishly admitted, "Well no, I guess not." "You better believe it, buster. You're still hung up on the concept of time. Eternity is not endless time, it's outside of time. Just think of the most thrilling event you've ever experienced, for example, if our beloved Tigers won a national championship and we were at the game. That's a spit in the ocean compared to the glories of heaven. Being in the presence of God is unlike anything you've ever imagined. Seeing Christ Jesus face to face is indescribable. There is no thrill like singing along with the heavenly host, all the saints and choirs of angels in praise and thanksgiving to God. But it's not all about nonstop excitement. There is perfect peace and tranquility too. There is no sin … imagine that! There is no strife, greed, jealousy, anger, back biting or evil of any kind. There is only peace and harmony. Everyone pulls in the same direction, in accordance with God's perfect will. There is no lying or deception, no false teachers, no persecution, no dissention. Truth reigns forever, God's word stands and there is nothing but true fellowship, spiritual unity and brotherhood. "

As if that wasn't enough, Syl applied a little icing to a perfect cupcake, "There's something else you should consider. Just imagine the conversations. Would you like to meet Noah and ask him about the great flood? I have, and Peter has told me about walking on the water with Christ. I've met King David and Mary, Joseph, Elizabeth and John the Baptist to name a few." My eyes lit up, "Have you met Babe Ruth? Or how about Abraham Lincoln, have you talked to him yet?" "Twain, there are certain things I'm not at liberty to share and one of those is who's in heaven or not. That's something you'll have to find out for yourself when you enter the great city, New Jerusalem." That prompted a question that had been burning in the back of my mind, "When can we go to the city? And why is it called New Jerusalem?" Syl tackled the easier question first, "Don't be confused by the name for this city has almost nothing in common with Jerusalem or any earthly metropolis. This city is truly holy. The name is appropriate though because it is home to Israel, spiritual Israel. That doesn't

313

mean the nation of Israel, the political entity but rather God's chosen people from every race; Jew and gentile." I was learning to use my scriptural recall at will, "Romans 9:4-6 … Who are Israelites; to whom pertains the adoption, and the glory, and the covenants, and the giving of the law, and the service of God, and the promises; Whose are the fathers, and of whom as concerning the flesh Christ came, who is over all, God blessed forever. Amen. Not as though the word of God hath taken none effect. For they are not all Israel, which are of Israel."

Syl nodded approvingly and then paused as she became very serious, "The word of God has no doubt edified you with great wisdom about the Holy City. But some things are beyond our comprehension, beyond what God has revealed in his word. Even here in heaven where our dark glasses have been removed, there are things we cannot know, things reserved only for God." I sensed Syl was trying to break something to me slowly, "What are you getting at Syl?" "It's about your entry into New Jerusalem, Twain." I grew nervous which I knew should not be happening in heaven, "Is there something wrong, Syl? And why am I not robed in white like you and Devon? Is there some kind of ceremony that must take place first?" "There's nothing wrong, Twain. There's no ceremony required. It's not quite time yet for you to go into the city." "What … how can that be? I thought there was no concept of time in heaven? What's the matter Syl?" "There's nothing wrong. Twain. It's just that there's something that must be done before you enter." My heart began to race and I was about to press further when I was distracted by some movement that caught the corner of my eye.

I turned my head toward the grove to see two figures emerging. One was a man and the other was a very large animal. As they approached, I was startled to see that the animal was a huge beast of prey, an oversized tiger regaled in its gold and black stripes with striking white accents. It moved with ease and fluidity as its powerful muscles and sinews flexed under its velvety coat with each step of its massive, deadly paws. My whole being tensed as an adrenaline-like rush coursed through my veins but nothing could have prepared me for the next shock to my system. The man's face came into view and, to my horror; I was clutched by a gut wrenching pain that brought me low. I recognized my foul nemesis, the Renaissance Killer, released from the pit of hell to claim my soul for Satan. Sheer panic struck me like a thunderbolt as I realized, I wasn't in heaven but was caught in a dream, a nightmare of the worst order. I squeezed my eyes shut as tight as I could and screamed, as if afflicted with night terror, at the top of my lungs in an effort to awaken and escape this hellish phantasmagoria.

13 Another

When my screams ceased, I opened my eyes slowly to escape the darkness and regain consciousness. I fully expected to be in my own bed, soaked in a cold sweat. However, all I saw was the gentle, green grass at my feet and I raised my head bit by bit to see the same cloudless sky, crystal river, endless orchards and spectacular skyline in the distance. And there was the ominous figure of RK flanked by the menacing beast. I shivered at the thought that Cane had found a new, living instrument of torture and, like a demented Roman emperor, would have it disembowel me for his delight and entertainment. The fearsome creature now raised his head, bared his gleaming fangs and let loose a rumbling roar that seemed to shake the ground. I let out a blood curdling shriek and wondered frantically, "Why can't I wake up? This can't be happening! I've got to get out of here!" Then I noticed that Syl and Devon were gone and I was left alone with the two dreaded figments of my imagination. I spoke to myself as if imaginary RK could not hear me, "I should have known this was a dream! What is wrong with me? Why am I doing this to myself; the cruelest hoax of all? I must be sick, the worst kind of twisted, demented masochist!" Then to my utter horror and amazement, the ghostly figure interrupted my mad ranting, "Twain, settle down, relax!" I snapped to attention as if ice cold water had been poured down my bare back. I tried to regain my composure but had difficulty holding panic at bay because this was like one of those weird, claustrophobic nightmares where you think you're awake but can't move your numb, paralyzed body. I just wanted to wake up and escape. I tried to reason my way through my own dementia by confronting the spectral intruder, "I couldn't figure out if I was dreaming or in heaven but now I know the truth. If this isn't a dream, I'm most certainly not in heaven, not here with you, you denizen of hell. So, I'm just sleeping. This is all a bad dream and as soon as I wake up, you'll disintegrate like so much harmless smoke in a gale force wind."

There was just one problem, I didn't wake up and the nightmare continued. Sight lines in dreams are so strange. Sometimes you pick up on the smallest oddities. Perhaps deep in my psyche my mind was plotting to secure my rescue through the type of absurd twist that can only be manufactured in the subconscious world because I noticed a slight change that gave me a ray of hope. The tiger was just behind RK and outside his vision. A glint appeared in his eye as if he was marking some imaginary prey. To my great relief, he had turned his attention to Cane. Yes, my mind was making a devious, delicious way of escape. If only the tiger would devour Cane, the saga would end and I could awaken. My face didn't betray the conspiracy to Cane as the great cat laid back on his haunches, tensed and ready to spring. Then, in one deadly instant, fang and claw were launched like a ground to air missile at the unsuspecting Cane who collapsed under the weight of the ambush. There were no screams though, only laughter. Was my imagination slipping and going off script? Cane smiled and addressed the furry prankster who had pinned him to the ground, "Cut it out Truman … you're always clowning around." The beast licked Cane and raised up to release his captive, then circled himself several times before curling up in a big ball. He actually purred but it sounded more like an idling Harley as he lay there peacefully. Cane turned to me and offered an apologetic grin, "I couldn't help but name him Truman …you know … M-I-Z … Z-O-U. "

I was so stunned I verbalized my inner monologue without realizing it at first, "What kind of dream is this?" Cane brought me back to reality … maybe surreal would be more accurate. "You've been asking yourself the right question, Twain, but just in the wrong way. It's not an either/or proposition.

319

You see, you're sleeping **and** you're in heaven."
Even under these bizarre circumstances, I found a
way to be offended, "That's impossible, Cane. If
this is heaven, how can you be here?" Cane sat
down next to the reclining cat, crossed his legs and
patted the ground inviting me to join him, "Please,
hear me out, Twain." I dropped down, not too
close, kept a wary eye on Truman the Tiger and
smirked, "Okay, it's my nightmare so I'll humor
myself. So here we are and somehow you've been
admitted through the pearly gates along with Syl
and Devon who you brutally murdered. Yeah,
sounds just heavenly. Do I have it right, RK?" Cane
was calm, patient and considerate, "I don't mean to
sound wishy-washy but I've got to say, yes and no.
Everything you've said is true except that the
Renaissance Killer is not here, he's dead." This
exasperated me, "We're in heaven and you're here
too but you're not here? C'mon, Cane, which is it?"
"I know it sounds crazy but it's true. I'm here,
Charles Darwin Cane, but my former self, the
Renaissance Killer, is no more." I huffed, "Oh, I see
... you're a new man. Hallelujah, RK is dead, long
live Cane ... bull! Don't give me that existential
baloney, Cane; I'm not buying it! Don't forget, I
caught your act before. Fool me once, shame on
you; fool me twice, shame on me."

I shook my head, "Look at me, sitting here in my own dream having this idiotic conversation with you. I must be losing my marbles." Cane pleaded, "Twain, this is not a dream. Please give me a chance to explain." I let him proceed with a mocking wave of my hand. "Twain, I know it seems crazy that someone like me could be in heaven. By all rights, I should be burning in hellfire. People with far fewer transgressions are suffering in hell at this very moment. But here's the key ... none of us deserve to be in heaven, not a terrible sinner like me, not anyone, for all have sinned and fall short of the glory of God, his standard of sinless perfection. If entrance into heaven depended on our own merit, even just one tenth of one percent, heaven would be a lonely, empty place indeed." I was in no mood to listen, "Are you trying to say that we're all, every one of us including me, just as sinful as you?" Cane shrugged, "I know you can remember James 2:10." He was right of course and, with my newfound power, I rattled it right off the top of my head, "For whosoever shall keep the whole law, and yet offend in one point, he is guilty of all." Cane laid the puzzle pieces together for me using my own memory as the glue, "God has a different view of sin than we do ... thankfully. I bet you can recall Jesus' Sermon on the Mount, word for word, can't you?" I thought through it and it was as if I flipped a page and it came into plain view. It hit home as I pondered Christ's words. He was right. God's full judgment rested on everyone who sinned against any commandment and breaking one was as bad as transgressing the whole law. On the mountain, Christ made clear how impossible it is for anyone to keep the law and escape God's wrath by themselves. If you look at another person and a lustful thought crosses your mind, you are guilty of adultery in God's view. In God's eyes, one who entertains a malicious thought against a neighbor has violated the Fifth Commandment.

Just then, as Cane's inspired wisdom was sinking in, something else happened to put an exclamation point on how upside down this whole situation had become. Buddy and kitty wandered over toward us then past me to the lumbering giant and laid down beside him. Truman moved nary a muscle except to gather them in against his warm, soft belly like they were his own little cubs. I couldn't help but mellow a bit against my otherwise feisty temperament, "All right Cane, I'll grant you that, in God's eyes, I might be just as sinful as you. But that just means we should both be bound for hell. So, what is this charade of heaven, another one of your ruses?" Cane saw that the word of God was able to persuade me so he maintained that tact, "There's no doubt that you and I should be cast into hell but thankfully God's heart is infinitely more charitable and full of mercy than ours. He does not mete out his just punishment as would we. We couldn't begin to fathom the wonders of his grace were it not for his precious gospel. Doesn't it melt your heart in thankfulness when you hear the words of Romans 5:6-8?" A dreamy feeling washed over me as I recited them, "For when we were yet without strength, in due time Christ died for the ungodly. For scarcely for a righteous man will one die: yet peradventure for a good man some would even dare to die. But God commended his love toward us, in that, while we were yet sinners, Christ died for us." Not only my heart but my eyes melted too and I added Romans 8:1-2 without prompting, "There is therefore now no condemnation to them which are in Christ Jesus, who walk not after the flesh, but after the Spirit. For the law of the Spirit of life in Christ Jesus hath made me free from the law of sin and death."

Cane took note of the breakthrough and poured out his heart to me, "I am that man; I am the ungodly … yet Christ died for me too. Praise be to our God for his love is incomprehensible save for his mighty acts of mercy! Only God could save such a sinner as me! Only God can save any sinner." Then Cane demonstrated that he too had the power of the word as he recited Ephesians 2:1-9, "And you hath he quickened, who were dead in trespasses and sins; Wherein in time past ye walked according to the course of this world, according to the prince of the power of the air, the spirit that now works in the children of disobedience: Among whom also we all had our conversation in times past in the lusts of our flesh, fulfilling the desires of the flesh and of the mind; and were by nature the children of wrath, even as others. But God, who is rich in mercy, for his great love wherewith he loved us, Even when we were dead in sins, hath quickened us together with Christ, (by grace ye are saved;) And hath raised us up together, and made us sit together in heavenly places in Christ Jesus: That in the ages to come he might show the exceeding riches of his grace in his kindness toward us through Christ Jesus. For by grace are ye saved through faith; and that not of yourselves: it is the gift of God: Not of works, lest any man should boast."

Cane allowed precious moments for us to luxuriate in the truth of God's gracious promise fulfilled before addressing me again, "My dear brother that is what I meant when I said that the Renaissance Killer is dead. You see, before he reigned in me while I was spiritually dead to Christ. I was a slave to evil until God quickened me, brought the new man to life anothen. I had no power to accomplish this on my own. It was solely by God's power, working through his word, that I was born again, given new life from God above. Then I was like you Twain … just like your name ascribes, I was torn asunder with two persons, the old and the new, battling for supremacy inside me. You knew the power of the evil that lurked within me, the corruption of my flesh and soul. I could never have won the battle on my own. But Christ claimed me as his own and sent the Holy Spirit to wage war on my behalf. He sent my grandparents with that first Bible. God sent our brother, Reverend Floyd, to assist in my edification by the word. The battle between my two natures raged on until my execution but God lifted up the new man through his word and sacraments and drowned the old RK daily in the waters of my baptism. He declared me righteous, though I wasn't, until the day I died and then … praise God … he made me righteous and buried my old corrupt self forever. "

Then I said the words I thought would never pass my lips, "Charles, my dear brother, thank God for his mercy and praise everlasting to our Lord and Savior, Jesus Christ." I couldn't help but laugh with joy, "What's in a name? Isn't it funny how all along

I bore the truth in the name I found so embarrassing as a child? Twain Newman … from my baptism I was rent in two but God preserved my new nature unto eternity." Then the childlike enthusiasm and wide eyed wonder I had experienced earlier with Syl and Devon returned, "Charles, there's so much I want to know! I don't know where to start. Well, speaking of the war between the old man and the new, have you met him, have you talked to Paul?" Charles' smile stretched for miles, "You better believe he was one of the first souls I sought out! Oh how we marveled together at the might of God's transforming power and the way it had turned our lives completely around. The most marvelous thing happened during our discourse. We had moved beyond the recounting of our own lives and wrestled with the doctrine of original sin. I struggled a bit in the presence of one so erudite but rather than enlightening me on his own, Paul tickled my fancy in the most delightful way … he introduced me to Adam! Talk about the mother of all object lessons! Adam was able to clear up any misconceptions about the creation. Let me just say; he was not into evolution."

"What did he say about the fall?" I breathlessly inquired. "Imagine the depth of his sorrow for not only bringing condemnation down upon himself and Eve but then realizing he had corrupted all of future mankind through one simple act of disobedience. He understood corruption better than anyone who ever lived because he had experienced the perfection of God's creation and its complete goodness. Adam was able to fully gauge the infinite loss that occurred. He helped me to understand how God has no hand in the evil events that mar our fallen world. Adam explained it to me this way. He said our sinful world is like having one bad egg out of ten. If you mix one filthy, tainted, rotten egg with nine that are fresh and pure into an omelet, you would not eat it under the misconception that it is ninety percent good. He really opened my eyes when he thanked God for cursing him, Eve and all of us with death. He called it the greatest blessing that God spared us from an eternity in corruption and sin. Adam understood better than anyone that temporal death is an essential element within God's plan of salvation. As one who had dwelled in the presence of God, he understood his true, immutable nature. Adam explained that God had no choice but to punish sin and pour out his just wrath. To do otherwise would have denied himself and his holiness. Adam showed how this impossibility cast God's plan of salvation in the most glorious light. He had to punish sin but he loved us, his children, so much that he decided to punish himself in our place. He sacrificed himself in the person of his own dear, perfect, sinless, holy Son, so that we wouldn't have to pay that terrible price. God's justice was satisfied in his own perfect love. Adam helped me to see why God had to leave those Cherubim with flaming swords to guard the entrance to the Garden of Eden so that man could not return to eat of the tree of life and bring about his own eternal damnation in a perpetually sinful state."

This took me back to my earlier conversation with Syl, "Speaking of the angels, you've just answered another question. I've always wondered why God sent Jesus to redeem man but not the angels. Why wouldn't God save the evil ones that followed after Satan in rebellion? Are we less sinful than them? Are we not subject to the same laws of God? I used to rationalize that perhaps the angels were held to some higher standard or maybe they had transgressed against greater knowledge than man and somehow sinned the unpardonable sin against the Holy Ghost. But you may have solved the mystery for me. The Cherubim at the gates of Eden and all the angels in God's domain already had the gift or, in the case of the evil angels who followed Satan in his prideful plunge, the curse of eternal life.

I guess we can't say for sure but the important thing is the lesson Adam shared about God's good creation and the utter corruption that followed at the hands of man under Satan's beguiling influence. Charles, I resented God for so long by holding him wrongly accountable for your evil deeds. In so doing, I denied his powers of forgiveness, grace and salvation and, in the process, stubbornly and jealously withheld my own forgiveness from you. What a fool I was. Thank God for his patience! Please forgive me, my friend."

"Twain, that's all behind us now, as far as the east is from the west." That sparked another curious inquiry, "Charles, there's something else I don't understand. How can you recall your sins in heaven and still exist in perfect bliss and peace. It seems impossible." He hesitated a bit then did the best he could, "This is one of those things that you can't grasp fully apart from the Holy City. You just have to trust that with God, all things are possible. It is true that there is no sin, no corruption of any kind in heaven. But just as Christ still bears the scars of his crucifixion, our sins can be remembered in the context of the gospel. That is, we all realize that we were corrupted by sin but only in the context of God's forgiveness and Christ's sacrifice. There is absolutely no guilt or shame, no condemnation, malice, vengeance or unsatisfied justice of any kind in New Jerusalem." My reply was inquisitive, not accusatory, "Do Syl and Devon know that you murdered them?" "Let me put it this way, Twain. They know me as a brother in Christ, a fellow saint who reigns in heaven only by the power and grace of God. We rejoice together as fellow forgiven saints in perfect harmony with each other and God. The most important thing to remember is this. We have all been covered in the blood of Christ and robed in the white garments of his righteousness so that when God looks at us he never sees our sins. He only sees the sinless perfection that Jesus has imputed to us. Jesus Christ, our Lord and Savior; paid the full price for all our sins, once and for all, on the cross of Calvary. This was accomplished at an infinite price that all of mankind collectively could never repay at the moment Christ declared, 'It is finished.' That is the knowledge and truth in which we dwell here."

I pressed further, "Then, it's safe to assume the same is true with all of RK's victims?" Now a sly smile crept in as Charles gently admonished me, "Twain, I think Sylvia already covered this ground, didn't she? You know that I can't discuss who is in heaven other than what's already been revealed in scripture. I can tell you this though. Not all of RK's victims are in heaven." I gasped in astonishment rather than anger, "You mean to say that you're here while some of RK's victims are in hell?" Charles did not flinch for he knew I already possessed the truth, "As strange as it sounds in a worldly sense, it is unfortunately true. The wheat and chaff are not divided among victims and perpetrators for we all fall into the ranks of the latter. It's beyond anything I can grasp ... strictly a matter of trust in God ... but some died in faith like Syl and Devon while others perished in unrepentant disbelief and rejection of God's mercy and grace. None were pre-committed to hell for Christ died for all and God truly finds no pleasure in the death of the wicked. That they suffer eternal damnation is no one's fault but their own. Thankfully for all the believers in heaven, we are spared all remorse over the lost ones. That pain is removed forever and is filled only by our trust in God's holiness, divine justice, infinite mercy and love. In heaven, there is only rejoicing over the salvation of all of God's saints from before the foundation of the world."

God surely presented a puzzlement; beyond man's comprehension and completely foreign to our former lost and fallen world. My curiosity for truth was insatiable, "We may be shielded from every unpleasant memory in heaven and thankfully there is a great gulf that separates us from the affairs of the world below. But God can't spare himself. He knows of every sinful pox that blemishes mankind and our doomed planet. How does he cope? How does he shield his adopted children from this knowledge?" Then Charles befuddled me with a statement that seemed hopelessly inappropriate, "Twain, he just laughs it off." Noting my slack jawed stupor, he tried to explain, "Do you remember some of the things that would drive you crazy or consume you in anger; the sheer stupidity and audacity of earth's *wise* inhabitants? Let me refresh your memory with one of God's favorites. How about the notion that Christ is a communist and came to spread a social gospel requiring us to turn all our money over to governments to judiciously redistribute the wealth as they see fit? Never mind Christ's constant instruction that his kingdom is not of this world. God loves a government-mandated giver, cheerful or not, right? Whereas we get our knickers twisted up in anger and embroiled in political bickering over such issues, God is able to laugh it off. He likes to say that Christ was the first communist who came down from heaven for the redistribution of sin ... all of ours heaped upon him, the sinless Son."

I wasn't ready to concede, "The Psalmist tells us in 2:4 that 'He that sits in the heavens shall laugh: the Lord shall have them in derision.' That term, derision, sounds kind of spiteful and vindictive, doesn't it?" Charles was not deterred, "I know you recall when Christ drove out the money changers in the temple. I also know that you don't believe that Jesus broke the Fifth Commandment or ever sinned in any way. With God, these things are different than with men. As a perfect, sinless God-man, Christ was able to express righteous anger without sinning. Think of a glass of water with impure sediment sitting in the bottom. That dirt represents our sinfulness. With men; our anger shakes the glass and agitates the impurities polluting the water. Christ had no sin and thus could express his righteous anger without polluting the water. In the same way, God can laugh in derision without any malice. His perfect, holy love remains intact even while recognizing the folly of his foolish, impertinent children. I'm sure that Devon said and did things that made you laugh at him but you never ceased to love him. God has a great sense of humor, he really does. He can laugh these things off because he possesses the truth and knows that he will lose none of his elect to foolishness or the lies of the devil."

Charles mused, "God is a conundrum and so often serves as a paradox to our puny, finite minds. We so often chafe under the iron rod of his law not realizing that it's always intended for our good. Even the ceremonial laws served God's good intentions for us. Why did he command circumcision on the eighth day for his Old Testament believers? His people lacked the medical knowledge at that time to realize that, without outside agents, babies' blood did not acquire the clotting capability until the eighth day. Likewise, God provided standards of sanitation that eluded the heathens' body of knowledge. Israel was thus spared from accepted practices of the day such as applying boor's vomit or animal dung to *cleanse* open wounds. Instead they were instructed in the proper way to handle corpses and dispose of waste to prevent crippling diseases and death. There was a time when only God knew the dangers of inbreeding and thus offered prohibitions." I jumped on that last statement with zeal, "Wait a minute Charles. You talked to Adam. How did he explain the incest among his children? Obviously, brothers and sisters must have married and bore children together." That sly smile returned, "You're absolutely right about brothers and sisters of Adam and Eve's time. But there was no prohibition from God then. It came later. Think about it. The gene pool was vastly different then. Mankind had not yet degenerated and there was no risk of recessive flaws and mutations being passed along. Later as man's descent or devolution worsened, God changed the law for our well-being. God's moral law never changes but there are many instances where the ceremonial laws changed over time. For example, in God's good world before the fall, there was no killing and men and animals were designed to live on vegetation alone. All of the necessary proteins our bodies required were available in nature's bounty. But then the time came after the flood when climate swings became severe and degenerative agriculture combined to rob us of enough of these natural nutrients and God allowed for the killing of animals to provide meat. By the way, God gets a laugh out of some of the vegetarians. They are unwittingly following his original plan for all the wrong reasons while outright rejecting the notion of a Creator who set the plan in motion in the first place. If you need any more evidence of this truth, just keep an eye on Truman and his new pals. He has no desire for these tasty morsels and gets everything he needs from the rich grasses and potent plant life that abounds in its original, glorious diversity."

My mind was a sponge as I jumped from one topic to the next, "Charles is everyone equal before God in heaven? Is there no difference between me and the prophet Moses or the great evangelizer Paul?" "Twain this is another one of those yes or no questions. God sees us through the righteousness of Christ which covers us so, in a sense, we are all equal. Yet, somehow there are different rewards in heaven for acts done purely out of love … not self-righteous good works done in the vain hope of earning salvation, things which God abhors, but pure kindness flowing from faith in God who is the source of all love and goodness. Here's the amazing thing that could only exist here in God's heaven. No one begrudges another for these rewards. There is no greed, envy, jealousy or covetousness here in God's kingdom. Everyone here possesses an endless, priceless, immeasurable treasure. There is no want whatsoever. But within this limitless bounty there are some with diverse recognitions that can only be bestowed by the Father as he sees fit. In heaven, these glories only evoke joy and gratitude from all believers because we know they reflect God's good purposes for us all. We know that all truly good works done out of love were empowered by the Holy Ghost so these special rewards just remind us of God's goodness and reflect his glory in his broken tools that have been raised up as saints. It's truly a wonderful place, God's heaven."

I loved every moment of this thrilling, enlightening exchange with my newfound brother in Christ and felt like I could continue forever but I sensed he wanted to draw it to a close. It made me think of where I had left off with Syl and Devon, "Charles, I'm not arrayed in a garment like yours and Syl told me I could not understand some things until I reached the city ahead. She could not tell me when I would be able to enter the Holy City. I suspect it had something to do with needing to meet and reconcile with you first. Is that the case? Can you tell me if I'm ready to make my way to New Jerusalem?" Charles took my hand by the spirit as if to offer support, "Twain, I've been sent to counsel you and advise you that your time has not yet come." I needed his support as this stark revelation nearly felled me, "What do you mean, Charles? Is my fate in question? Am I somehow caught between heaven and hell? How can this be for God has declared it is appointed unto men once to die, but after this the judgment?" Charles continued to patiently explain the unexplainable, "You need not question this for your salvation is secure, forever sealed in the blood of Christ. It's just that ... that God has work for you yet to do in the world." I made a plea in earnest, "But Charles, I want to stay here; I don't want to leave … please, oh please, take me to the city!"

"Twain, you feel the same way that Peter, James and John did on the high mountain after Jesus' transfiguration. They did not want to depart from the partial glory that had been unveiled before them. However, Christ's work of redemption was not done and he had much work left for his apostles in the saving of souls and building of the kingdom. They dutifully complied with Christ's command to their eternal reward and Christ's everlasting glory. They lived on in grave hardship, persecution and even martyrdom but, as we know from hindsight, were able to mine immeasurable riches in the kingdom by God's guiding hand. You also are greatly privileged my brother. I do not know what awaits you, whether there will be trials and tribulation, but I'm sure of one thing; that God's good purposes will be served and in his due time we will be reunited again for all eternity."

It was so hard to grasp, "How can this be, Charles? It seems to extend by leaps and bounds beyond everything I learned from the scriptures from a child on up." "I know Twain; this is extraordinary to say the least. But God is not bound by the laws of his

338

creation as are men. He is only subject to his perfect, holy nature and word of truth. Think back to all of the times that God has intervened in the lives of men in a supernatural way. Elijah was transported to heaven in a chariot of fire without tasting temporal death. Moses and Elijah were transported across the great gulf between heaven and earth to appear at the transfiguration. Lazarus and many others were raised from the sleep of death to walk this earth again. The sun was made to stand still on Joshua's long day. I could go on. God has something for you to do on earth. I don't know what it could be but if he has appointed you as his servant to bring one soul to saving faith by sharing his word, then you should be overjoyed as the recipient of such a divine privilege." "Tell me, how is it that you've been chosen to deliver this message to me and why can't you tell me more?" "I'm not sure how to put this, Twain. Let's just say I've been given a special dispensation by God to reveal things that would normally be left in his providence. I too am just a servant. But, I have been granted limited knowledge and no more. The rest is not for you or me to know. We must simply trust in God."

It was time to part and Charles gave me a proper sendoff, "Twain, you have not been dead but only asleep. Your body awaits your return. What memories you have of this place will be preserved as it pleases God. The most important thing is to be faithful to your calling and carry out God's work with joy. Your power rests with God, so remember to let him feed you daily. Stay in his word and it will sustain you for whatever lies ahead." Our fond farewell was interrupted by a voice near the grove. It was Syl with Devon who called out to Charles, "Come with us now brother and rejoice." Charles left to join them but then turned back toward me when he was side by side with them, arm in arm. They called out in unison, "Go with God, dear brother." Then Syl couldn't resist one last bit of humor as we bid farewell, "We won't miss you Twain but we'll look forward to your return."

The next thing I knew, I was staring up into bright lights overhead. Once my eyes adjusted; the first thing I could see was the startled face of the ER attendant who yelled, "Hold on folks, we have a live one here! They didn't let their shock prevent them from dutifully turning their attention to administer life saving techniques. I wasn't affected by the urgency in their voices or the flurry of activity. I knew God wouldn't let anything happen to cause his plan to fall short. It seemed like no time before I was on the mend and released from the hospital to the kind and loving care of Bud and Lilly. There was one other thing that passed swiftly; something that had languished for many years. I was able to complete my book in just a matter of weeks. I think you know how it went. It was easy really. I simply told the truth. The ending was kind of sappy … something along the lines of … they lived happily ever after. As for the rest of my life, I'm not sure what God has in store for me but I can tell you I'm excited. For now, I just want to reconnect with family and old friends … and brothers and sisters in Christ. Come to think of it, I might try to make a few new friends while I'm at it … maybe even a lady friend to keep me company along the way.

AUTHOR'S NOTES

As an author who writes from a Christian perspective, it struck me as odd when I first conceived the idea of writing a Christian murder mystery. That term, in and of itself, seemed like an oxymoron. I sincerely hope I have not offended anyone with the gruesomeness of this tale, especially in the earlier chapters. Most certainly I did not want to turn away anyone in disgust. If you persevered to the end, then you know my purpose. It was not to use gratuitous violence but to depict the evil heart of man at its worst. The Renaissance Killer had to be thoroughly wicked, cruel and depraved so as to evoke no sympathy from any quarter. He had to be so vile that even the most rabid bleeding heart liberal would see the wisdom and fairness in his death sentence. The most earnest Christian would need to scoff, from an earthly perspective, at the notion of forgiveness and salvation extending to RK. That was the only way I could pay proper homage to God for his glorious mercy and unfathomable love toward all sinners including me. May this work, though just a fictional account, succeed in its mission to magnify the amazing power of God to transform lives and give new spiritual life to otherwise lost and condemned souls, whether they be newborns through the miracle of holy baptism or adults by the Holy Spirit working through the word. To anyone who may still be troubled by this book in any way, I leave you with four truths and promises from God that have uplifted countless souls including me and ... in a far off, make believe world, Charles Darwin Cane.

Jesus Christ is the light and life of the world who will guide your path here on earth and illuminate your steps in eternity. Psalm 36:9 ... "For with thee is the fountain of life: in thy light shall we see light."

We the members of God's one, invisible, Christian church have been saved from the wasteland of our own desolate souls and covered with the righteousness of Christ so that we may inhabit the promised land of heaven. Ezekiel 36:35 ... "And they shall say, this land that was desolate is become like the garden of Eden; and waste and desolate and ruined cities are become fenced, and are inhabited."

God's grace and love toward us sinners is impossible to understand. But even though we cannot comprehend the mind of God, we have sure hope in his promises thanks to our God-given faith and his edifying word. Romans 11:33 ... "O the depth of the riches both of the wisdom and knowledge of God; how unsearchable are his judgments, and his ways past finding out!"

We never have to worry whether we've been good enough or done enough to please God; an impossibility. We only need to repent and believe in Jesus Christ as Lord and Savior. Even Charles Darwin Cane could rest assured in his salvation because it was accomplished totally apart from himself, solely by God's omnipotent power in Jesus Christ's all availing sacrifice. Galatians 2:16 … "Knowing that a man is not justified by the works of the law, but by the faith of Jesus Christ, even we have believed in Jesus Christ, that we might be justified by the faith of Christ, and not by the works of the law: for by the works of the law shall no flesh be justified." Titus 3:4-5 … "But after that the kindness and love of God our Savior toward man appeared, not by works of righteousness which we have done, but according to his mercy he saved us, by the washing of regeneration, and renewing of the Holy Ghost."

Glory to God in the highest!

Proof